The Golden E

Stanley Middleton was born in Bulwell, Nottinghamshire in 1919. He published his first novel, *A Short Answer*, in 1958 and went on to publish 45 novels in a career spanning fifty years. He was joint winner of the Booker Prize in 1974 with *Holiday*. Stanley Middleton died in July 2009.

Acclaim for Stanley Middleton

'At first glance, or even at second, Stanley Middleton's world is easily recognisable... The excellence of art, for Middleton, is an exact vision of real things as they are. And because he is himself so exact an observer, his world at third glance can seem strange and disturbing or newly and brilliantly lit with colour.'

A.S. Byatt

'We need Stanley Middleton to remind us what the novel is about...One has to look at nineteenth-century writing for comparable storytelling.'

Ronald Blythe, *Sunday Times*

'Middleton writes carefully, but his touch is light and astonishingly assured. One rarely reads dialogue as good as Middleton's; it makes his characters instantly alive.'

VS Naipaul

ALSO BY STANLEY MIDDLETON

The Golden Evening

Evening

STANLEY MIDDLETON

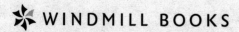
WINDMILL BOOKS

Published by Windmill Books 2014

2 4 6 8 10 9 7 5 3 1

Copyright © Stanley Middleton 1968

This edition copyright © The Estate of Stanley Middleton 1968, 2014

Stanley Middleton has asserted his right under the Copyright, Designs and
Patents Act, 1988, to be identified as the author of this work.

First published in Great Britain in 1968 by Hutchinson

Windmill Books
The Random House Group Limited
20 Vauxhall Bridge Road, London SW1V 2SA

Addresses for companies within The Random House Group Limited can be found at:
www.randomhouse.co.uk/offices.htm

The Random House Group Limited Reg. No. 954009

www.randomhouse.co.uk

A CIP catalogue record for this book
is available from the British Library

ISBN 9780099591986

The Random House Group Limited supports the Forest Stewardship
Council® (FSC®), the leading international forest-certification organisation.
Our books carrying the FSC label are printed on FSC®-certified paper. FSC is
the only forest-certification scheme supported by the leading environmental
organisations, including Greenpeace. Our paper procurement policy
can be found at: www.randomhouse.co.uk/environment

Typeset in Bembo by Anchor Press, Essex

Printed and bound by Clays Ltd, St Ives plc

1

IN A pleasant wind of early summer, the red and white flags high up on the golf-course were flapping. The afternoon blew sunny and white dabs of cloud moved quickish, flinging shadows over the road, the railway lines.

The front door banged; the family moved along the path.

'Did you make sure you've locked up, Bernard?' Aunt Jessica said. She was a blight.

'Yes.' Bernard, tall, twenty-two, carefully fingered the catch of the garden gate into place.

The party moved uphill, southwards. The father, Ernest Allsop, with his sister went first. In his hand was a bag, while she carried flowers cut that morning from the garden. Bernard, army pack on one shoulder, walked behind with his sister. They did not speak; all four listened to the sound of their footsteps. People were crossing the station railway-bridge on their way to bowls or cricket or a chase with dogs and a ball over the coarse grass. Two girls in white, swinging tennis rackets, cycled past, their pedalling naked legs mottled gold in the sun.

The Allsops turned right, over waste ground at a street's corner, and walked downhill, among terraced houses, towards the trolley route. A small boy carrying a music case smiled and spoke to Mary. She barely replied.

'Who's that?' Bernard asked.

'A boy in my Sunday-school class.'

Aunt Jessica looked back, with reproach. Casual conversation was indecorous, since they were making for the hospital, to visit their mother. She was dying. They could visit at any time, but were not to do so, Mary had heard, lest Mrs. Allsop should also understand that she was done. Mary was aware of the heat from the houses and flagstones as she walked. She peered into the windows at front-room furniture.

A man approached, with open-necked shirt and new cloth cap. He barely nodded, averted his eyes, as if he were ashamed to be out for pleasure when these were walking to see wife, mother, sister-in-law die.

'Who's that, Dad?' Bernard said. Back-glare from aunt.

'Albert Matley.' Allsop changed his bag over from left to right hand. 'Married a Walker, didn't he, Jess?'

'Doris.' The word closed the conversation.

Mary watched the rise and fall of her father's trouser-bottoms over his heels and took comfort from the clack of feet on the pavement. She was divided in herself; hated the hospital, but knew she must go. She hated her name; Mary Evangeline Allsop was ridiculous and yet her mother had chosen it, and to reject it now was to insult a woman with only a few days at her disposal. At fourteen the girl was sharp, careless, stupidly beautiful. The crack of shoes on stones distracted her sufficiently to contain her grief and the annoyance, hardly checked, that her mother was dying at so inconvenient a time. The other girls at netball or Latin knew, and Miss Sayers, her house mistress, and Eric, whom she loved, he would have heard. Tongues wagged; eyes watched. She shrugged the blue gaberdine from her shoulders. To have to wear this thing on a hot day. But Aunt Jessica had said she should.

'You wear your coat, Mary.'

'Why?'

'You never know. We might have a thunderstorm.'

'We might not.'

'What did you say?'

'Do as your aunt tells you. There's a good girl.' Her father's patient, thin voice had interrupted her revolt. She

6

saw his narrow nose, with the flat end, and was sorry. But she knew why Jessica wanted her muffled up; it hid her breasts. She'd heard her talking, and not once, about them.

'She's a woman, Ernest. Look at her chest. She's as big there as our mother ever was, and she'd had five children.' She'd not brought herself into it. She'd breasts like everybody else, hadn't she, the baggy, saggy, scraggy hag?

Mary, angered now, looked at her brother as the solemn party turned the corner. Bernard smiled, winked, and pulled a cross-eyed clown's face. He was Mother's boy. They grouped themselves round the bus-stop. Aunt Jessica led them on to the lower deck, though it was crowded, and the two young people were constantly up and down offering their seats to shopping women and harassed mothers lugging babies.

'Perfume,' Bernard said, nudging his sister, pretending to faint.

She laughed at the scenty reek of a hatchet-face girl who had pushed past them. An old man was telling the world he was off to the county cricket match, grousing before he'd seen a ball bowled. Nobody knew who the others were. Mary was a disguised duke's daughter, an international athlete, a policewoman. Somebody stepped ruthlessly on her toe, and she bit her lip, acted agony.

'Seat,' Bernard said, pointing.

'No, you.'

'Daren't.' He with a wiggle at his knees and a jerk of the head suggested he might crumble into unconsciousness, if he sat next to the scented girl. Mary laughed outright, and her father, up the bus, heard her, turned and smiled. Aunt Jessica stared forward, making much of death.

They arrived at the hospital exactly as the porter cleared the waiting-room. Flowers, bottles, grapes were rushed along the corridors, up the frightening bare staircases. The Allsops trailed in behind the aunt, to the far end of the ward, by a bow-window that overlooked slate roofs, factory glass walls, smudges of train smoke, and, nearer, the shaven lawns in the castle grounds. Jessica sat down, by the locker, moving the tubular chair. The other three stood awkwardly round, staring down.

There was no change in the mother's face. It was yellowish, tired, dazed. Her hands were flopped parallel on the sheets.

'Well, now, Ivy. How are you?' Jessica demanded.

Mrs. Allsop nodded as if speech were too much trouble, but roused herself, looked at her children and said, 'You're soon back, Ernest.' He'd been that morning.

'Well, the children were coming, so I thought I would,' he said, embarrassed. 'Will these flowers be all right here?'

'Put them on the end-table. They'll see to them, I expect.'

There was silence.

'It's a lovely day,' Jessica said. 'You have got a nice view from that window.'

The yellow eyes of Mrs. Allsop met those of Mary. The girl stepped forward. A hand was raised from the sheet to hold hers. They were worst. The face was wrinkled, dull, but the hands were emaciated, scrubbed claws.

'Are you a good girl?'

'Yes.'

'Helping your daddy?'

'Yes.'

Mary was soothed by the exchange. There were no histrionics. These were questions from the humdrum, not from eternity. Mrs. Allsop heaved herself over, sighed, grimaced.

'Are you in pain, then, Ivy?' Jessica asked.

'No.'

Now she turned to Bernard.

'Well, Mother, how are you getting on?' he said. That was the voice. Her face was momentarily animated, and she pushed a wisp of hair back behind her ear.

'Not so bad.'

'Dad's got the garden in shape for you, and we'll have your bed over by the window so you can see him slaving there.' He said this every time.

'Yes.'

'And Mary. She's quite good. You wouldn't believe it.'

'And you?'

'No, not me. I don't know a packet of seeds from a packet of fags.' They laughed, even their aunt. It was harsh to see how quickly a real smile died on Mrs. Allsop's face.

She spoke to her husband, before returning to Bernard. For the first time there was a flicker of life in her voice as she questioned him about his work at the university, where he was a research student. He knew how to hold her interest.

'Would you like an orange?' Mr. Allsop interrupted. His wife nodded, and turned back to her son. 'I'll peel it for you.' He chose with care. 'Is there a plate, Ivy?'

'End of the bed,' she whispered. 'Or in the locker.'

He got up and searched in vain.

'There isn't,' he said. His face was pale, but the skin seemed unlike hers, which was clayey.

'You'll have to ask.' The pianissimo of her voice did not disguise her annoyance at the spoiling of Bernard's anecdote. She did not apologise, did not pity her husband's trouble. Now she asked crudely, without dissimulation, for what she wanted.

'Mary can go.' Jessica.

'Run and ask the nurse. In the room at the end,' her father said.

The girl rose with hesitation. She wanted to quit this bed-side, if only for a minute or two, but not to walk the ward. Those without visitors would follow her with their eyes; some would speak. That crone with a nearly bald head and black mouth open would shudder herself awake to stare. The fat woman who asked everybody to give her a drink and then deliberately spilled it on the bedclothes. Mary walked along, eyes straight ahead. Visitors were huddled over each patient, but the room seemed uneasily silent.

She stood outside the office door, watching a nurse sort impatiently through a file of cards. The sister flicked one out and said, without turning:

'Yes?'

'Could I have a plate, please?'

'A what?'

'A plate, please.'

'Ask them next door.' The nurse poked her pen backwards over her shoulder. Mary knocked there, opened. It seemed some sort of store, with cupboards and racks. Two West Indian women were bent over a sink.

'Could I have a plate, please?'

They looked at her in incomprehension, before the younger stooped and drew a plate from a cupboard. She smiled at Mary, with large curved teeth over blue lips. Mary thanked her, and both grinned wide and nodded their heads.

Her father took the plate, and with his beautiful pearl-handled knife began to peel the orange. Bernard was telling his mother about his professor, Dr. Bryn Meredith, and imitating his Welsh accent. She had always enjoyed that performance even before her illness. Mary had heard a lecture at the Girls' High School on the medieval wall from Professor Meredith, but though you could tell he was Welsh, he never said 'look you' or 'bach' once.

' "Now look here, Bernard, boyo," he said to me, "that would do for the purveyors of the text-books but not a bit of good, look you, for us, now, is it?" '

A short smile touched the mouth of his mother as she lay, right ear down, on the pillow. She was proud that a real professor, whose books stood in paperback in the glass-fronted case at home, called her son by his christian name.

As Bernard talked, his father painstakingly tore out the segments of orange. Mrs. Allsop, very slowly, ate three or four, then shook her head. She sighed and pushed down deeper, restlessly into the pillow.

'Are you tired?' Bernard said. His face was strained, peaked. It had been difficult for him to keep the trickle of talk bubbling, and now that his mother had wearied of it, he showed his pain. Her eyes remained shut.

'Try a bit more orange, will you?' Allsop said.

'No.'

'It'll do you good.' Jessica.

'No. I enjoyed it. Let Mary have the rest.'

The plate was passed over the bed. Aunt Jessica stood up and began to pluck the bedclothes straight, pat at the pillow. Bernard was unmoving. Mr. Allsop stared at the flowers lying on the bed-table. Mary began to eat the orange, unhappily. She chewed the white pithy strings, with absorption, so that she had something to do. The aunt had now resumed her chair, and was nosing around. They did not speak. Sometimes, not often, Mrs. Allsop let out a shuddering breath, as if she had fallen asleep, but she opened her eyes.

'Are you all right?' Allsop said.

She nodded.

'Comfortable?'

Five minutes later she would ask a question, and the three older people would jangle sentences at her. 'Has Mrs. Pearson been up at all?' she asked once. Later she asked to see the flowers, but by the time they had been fetched from the end of the bed she'd lost interest.

'Very nice.'

'They're from the garden,' Jessica said.

'Did you grow them, Mary?'

'No.'

'I know Bernard didn't.'

They laughed, but the exchange had flattened her. At the bell she spoke to each, but lackadaisically. When she thanked them for coming, there was a whine, a nasal whimper in her voice. But she was polite, formally so.

'Now, hurry up and get better, Mother,' Bernard said. 'So you can enjoy this garden we're doing for you.'

They came up, one by one, and kissed her. Her mouth smelt of orange, Mary thought. Allsop held her hand, and she squeezed his. As they looked back from the door, her head was flat on the pillow, and she did not acknowledge their waving.

Outside it was hot still.

'She's weaker,' Jessica said, for the fourth time.

They trudged down the hospital hill where the light-suited

crowd was thick. On the bus they did not speak. Jessica got off one stop before the rest.

At home, Mary busied herself with the tea.

'How long, did they say?' Bernard was asking his father, out of the way, in a corner. The girl clashed her spoons, and listened.

'They wouldn't commit themselves.' Mr. Allsop had spent five minutes with the nurse.

'Is she in pain?'

'They said not.' Mr. Allsop sighed, unaware that he was making any noise. 'Bernard. It might be any time.' The son sucked air through his teeth. 'It's a bad job.'

2

AFTER TEA, Bernard changed his suit.

The conversation played itself through accustomed grooves.

'Well, I think I'll go out now.'

'Where?' Mr. Allsop asked, looking up from the evening paper.

'Dunno. Might visit some friends.'

Both knew exactly where he was going, but neither would speak openly. He was going to the house of Jacqueline Ridell, Mrs. Ridell, a widow. In a thoughtless vacuum of embarrassment, the relationship of Bernard and Jacqueline was never rationally considered between the two men. More-over, here was a dying mother. She knew about this, had not expressed an opinion to her son, and this was rightly taken, by her family, as disapproval. Bernard had not finished at the university yet. He oughtn't to spoil his chances. Not one of them had seen Mrs. Ridell, and certainly no hint of scandal about her had reached them. He was too young. She is not good enough for my son.

Bernard lounged his way upstairs for final preparations.

'Are you going out?' Mr. Allsop asked Mary. She nodded. 'Have you finished your homework off?' Nod again. They were all workers, neglecting nothing. Mary leafed through her library book, as her father toiled his way out to the bright garden, to grub there with his grief.

Ten minutes later his son was waving from the back gate.

The old man hoeing again. Push, push, and stroke the face. Bernard's shoes shone as he stepped away; his suit was elegant. It would take nearly half an hour to reach Mrs. Ridell's.

She lived in what had been, sixty years ago, the next village, but now industrial building, terraced streets, bus routes made no differentiation between one place and the next. The name remained and the high street, narrow, bending like an elbow, was vaguely rustic as it swerved off from the railway. The shop-fronts on the old stone houses might be chromium-faced, neon-outlined, or Edwardian-fancy still; three cottages with gardens stood back from the street, thick with apple trees and marigolds. About half-way along an eight feet stone wall curved back in an arc from the pavement, and in its centre, topped by an arch, hung a heavy wooden door of discoloured green. A brass plate, polished nearly to illegibility, but tarnished now, spelt out Ridell.

Bernard pushed through, and was immediately in a rising garden on a flagged path lined with currant bushes. He walked gently up the hill as the walled garden swept wider on both sides; vegetables, trees and soft fruits gave way to flowers and an oval lawn, and above that, sixty yards from the street, the back door of the house.

He knocked.

The door and two of the three windows were covered with a projecting slate roof supported by white, circular pillars. The covered area, perhaps five feet out from the wall, was cluttered with pot plants, faded deck-chairs, a pair of gardening gloves, trowel, secateurs and a pile of wooden planks, sawn, split, splintered, thrown down anyhow.

Jacqueline Ridell appeared, patting her hair.

'Won't you ever walk in?' she said.

A small chandelier glistened in the hall, where the wooden door faced east and the fanlight and side-slits were of stained glass. There was brass, white paint, on the stairs, three white chairs in a row, and a bristling dark carpet.

'Come on,' she said. 'Tom's here.'

He grimaced and she touched his arm. Briefly she inquired about his mother and was quiet after his reply. She led him to the study library where in the half-light her brother was sprawling, eating an apple, eyeing beer, handling a book. He nodded at Bernard, and his thick-sided glasses flashed. An inch-wide beard traced the outline of his face, of the same dark spikiness as his crew-cut hair. His legs were stretched out, his fawn trousers tight in the crutch.

'What's the form?' Tom Butler asked.

Bernard raised a hand, saying nothing. He disliked Jacqueline's brother, as did she. Butler was a commercial artist, and said to be successful. In the lace market somewhere he rented an office up a flight of filthy stairs and he slaved there, all day, thrashing drawing-board or phone, until at five-thirty he donned his student-type duffel-coat, hitched his jeans and whistled off to fetch his Jaguar, parked in a pub yard. He was quick with a pencil, faster with words, but would prefer to be thought a pornographer rather than a ratepayer. He had not married, and at forty-one lived in a private hotel. Visits to his sister were rare.

Now he raised the glass of beer.

'To you, lover-boy,' he said.

Jacqueline sat down, without offering to get Bernard a drink. She handled, then put on, her glasses before returning to a cushion cover she was embroidering. Smiling, she looked at them primly over the top of her spectacles. Tom downed his ale.

'Well,' he said, 'if nobody's going to talk to me, I'll move.

Nobody answered.

'Perhaps you can interest our young friend.' Butler slapped his knees. 'We could do with some intellect. Pure intellect,' he repeated.

Bernard looked across the porch, the front lawn, the rough grass with its silver birches. On the other side of the high wall was a back street with a long terrace of brick houses, and corner shops, plastered still with pre-war metal adverts. From this room one heard nothing, but a few dozen steps up the path would fetch the sounds of street games in, the raucous calls from front-door steps. Sometimes a ball would fly over or an urchin climb the wall and peer under the barbed wire, over the daggers of bottle-glass. No one came down.

Butler was on his feet, stroking his groin.

'Well, don't forget then. You. Me. Him. 'Er. All.' He zipped up his light waterproof jacket over his unbuttoned shirt-front and walked out. They heard the door slam.

Neither spoke for some time; both in the end looked up and smiled.

'He's had a good idea,' she said.

'Such as?'

'This place is without culture.' She sorted amongst her silks, fetching up each card to examine it on the flat of her hand. 'This town.'

'Oh.'

'Get yourself a drink, Bernard. And I'll have one. Orange, please.'

When he returned with the glasses she had dropped her embroidery and was sitting with hands and spectacles in her lap.

'Has he been worrying you?' he asked.

'No. Trying his ideas out.'

'Good? Rotten?'

'I didn't listen. They'd be goodish, I expect. He's clever.'

'I didn't say he . . .'

'There, there. Diddums.' Her voice was cold. As she sat there, pale hair in a plait round her head, she seemed strong. She was, in fact, rather small and white-faced, with blue eyes

15

and a delicate nose. Her movements were rapid if close, as for instance breaking off a thread, or selecting a needle, but her walk was slow as if she were always listening. To look at her, the pallor of face and hair, the whiteness of the skin round the faint purple of veins, the smoothness, one thought of fragility, the ephemeral, musical notes. When she spoke there was quick frigidity, a kind of authority.

At twenty-five, nearly three years older than Bernard, she had been a widow for twelve months now. Her husband, a carton manufacturer, a television trader, an engineer, a successful money-lender, a man on the make, had been killed in a road accident. They had been married since she was almost twenty and he thirty-four.

'Tom said something about asking you to join in,' she said, relenting.

'Kind of him.'

'It won't do you any harm, Bernie.'

'No, no, no.'

She threw the embroidery into another chair, tucked her spectacles into a case, and stood.

'What about your mother?' she said.

'I didn't say . . . I didn't say anything.'

'As usual. One of these days you'll grow up.'

'One of these days somebody'll swipe you,' he said.

'Yes.' She touched her face. 'I want to see your mother.'

'She's dying. I don't want her bothered.'

'Look, we're either getting married or we're not.'

'We are,' he said, standing, moving towards her. She stepped to him, kissed him, leaned on him and poked his waistcoat.

'You think your mother wouldn't like me?'

'I've no evidence,' he said, offended, one hand on her breast. 'Nor will it make any difference. We shall still get married.'

'Against your mother's dying wish?'

'If that's so, yes. She is dying. She just lies there, half drugged, rotten-yellow.'

'I want to see her.'

'Then you'll go on wanting,' he said. 'I'm not having her disturbed. She's not getting any better.'

'Very well.'

She stood cold-still, in his embrace, but her mouth was wide, laughing, forgetting.

'I'm serious, Jacqueline,' he said.

'So am I.' She sighed. 'One of these days this'll come up. "My mother didn't want me to marry you!" It's no use fooling. I've been married. I've quarrelled. Everybody does. And I don't want that one, thanks.'

'I see.'

'So?' She was laughing still, very attractive.

'Nothing. You're not going.'

'Right, Mummy's boy,' she said, moved from him, sat down. He made no move to stay her but slouched over to the window.

He did not understand her attitude. They had known each other for five months, and been determined on marriage for three. Soon after this his mother had gone into hospital for the second time. Jacqueline, diffidently, had asked if he'd like her to visit with him. He'd said 'no', but was pleased she'd raised the matter. As soon as the hospital authorities had pronounced Mrs. Allsop incurable, Jacqueline had demanded to be taken there. He'd regarded this as kindness to him, support, but expected her to be relieved when he refused. Instead, she'd become almost quarrelsome at once, urging that he'd regret not having his mother's approval of the marriage. She was so vehement, shortly, and so off-hand that he thought she was deliberately trying to break off her engagement with him, perhaps because she resented the secrecy he'd imposed. Though he was afraid, both of her sudden harshness and of losing her, he spoke his mind plainly. At this, she was touched to tears, but as inexorable in her demand. She must see Mrs. Allsop; she must gain admission there. Now he was almost won over, but could see no advantage.

At times like this he feared her. It was as if her former marriage had set her right apart from him, giving her experience or knowledge that could never be his. When they'd met at a party, he'd been attracted by her small body, the fair head, the miniature beauty, but she seemed older, not wiser, rather armoured, trenched against him. That he was attracted to her was not surprising; almost any girl of the right class or intelligence or comeliness could momentarily catch his interest, but it came as a shock when she first held his hand, a smack of delight. She had been married, had rolled naked in bed, had abandoned the poise, the delicacy, the pale beauty in a flurrying ecstasy of sexual surrender. He was a virgin. And now when she placed the smooth hand in his, like any girl, he was physically shattered. She'd smiled up at him, mouth wide, teeth perfect, as if she had not the faintest inkling of what he felt.

He'd no idea how to treat her, could hardly bring himself to believe that she had interest. When he'd invited her to a dance, she accepted but had taken command. They'd gone in her car; she delivered him back home; she'd refused to let him buy her drinks. He moved proudly with her in his arms, scared of his pride. She was a widow, had money. He had nothing much. But to wheel her about the floor, to hear her laugh, to feel her hang breathless on him at the end of a violent dance was exhilarating. In her way she was shy, or rather uncommunicative. There was no attempt to stampede him. She waited for him to talk of loving. She loved him, she said, when he had confessed, but there was a realism about her as if his declared feeling was play-acting, childish nonsense.

This puzzled him.

He was overwhelmed that she loved him, but amazed that it literally seemed to stop there. Not for a minute was he allowed to idealise her; it was as if she were on the watch, to knock his imaginings on the head with some sarcasm or deflating phrase.

'I'm lucky,' he said one evening, arms round her, 'to have you.'

'Why?'

'You're marvellous. Fabulous. In its proper sense.'

'I'm very ordinary,' she said. 'Because I've been married you think I've got something your other girls haven't. Forget it.'

'That's not it,' he said. 'I'm twice the man when I think about you. That's the truth.'

'Kiss,' she said, 'and don't talk so much.'

He had, in fact, once seen her husband, and remembered him. A broad man, hirsute, with a big face and a cleft chin. Bernard had seen him step into his Mercedes, and poke a heavy finger out at some crony on the pavement. He could remember that black-hairy back of the hand under the cuff and the fine links, the good, untidy suit, the fancy alpine hat. Ike Ridell had been powerful, ruthless, a fierce worker, mad for money, and Bernard recalled him, scraped clean, heavy with after-shave lotion, attractive, loathsome, significant. Now he was dead. And Ike's Jackie loved him, the schoolboy who'd gaped at her husband.

Now as they sat opposite, she dropped her hand on his to show the argument had momentarily ceased. He pulled back.

'I'll tell my father,' he said, 'that you want to go with us.'

'Thank you.'

'I don't know what he'll say.' He clasped his own hands together. 'He might even refuse to let you . . .'

'I know. It's hard,' she said. 'You're embarrassed. Might do you good.'

'I like that.'

'You're a mother's boy,' she said. There was no malice in the voice; she spoke the truth, it appeared, as she saw it. 'That's perhaps why you like me. But it's about time you did a bit for yourself, don't you think?'

They kissed and as her mouth flushed his and her hand raked his hair back from his forehead, he flinched at the accusation. The two Jacquelines did not match. As he walked home, half an hour later, dismissed so that he should catch his father before he went to bed, he was fighting angry with himself. He had never made an impression, initiated nothing. For example, a month ago, she'd refused to be his mistress, and on the fumbling approaches had told him to keep his hands to himself. As always, after a rebuff, she was extraordinarily kind, but he was reminded of the few occasions when his father had given him, as a lad, a thrashing and then had treated him with an indulgent courtesy as if to make certain that he realised the fault was expiated. He'd hated his father; he loved her. Both surprised him.

He walked quickly for that stilled his discomfort.

His father sat in front of the fire, with an empty pipe in his mouth. In the west window there was still some light, but this was dimmed by the blue blaze of the television screen from which Mr. Allsop half turned. The satirical team were in session; round their crescent of tables they postured and laughed at each other's jokes and slips of tongue. The camera caught wrinkled fingers, like sausages, patting a bald head; teeth were devilishly blackened.

Mr. Allsop smiled, nodding his head.

'I want to talk to you,' Bernard said.

'Turn that thing off, then.'

'Isn't it any good?'

'I haven't been listening.' As Bernard switched off he saw the blankness of his father's face, and wondered what he had been thinking about. His wife? The separation? Some happiness? Fifty-two years old, and decent. A good-living man. And his wife was to die. The fear he read into the blank face was puzzlement, perhaps, utter bewilderment. Or fatigue? Lethargy? That thin nose, skin nearly transparent, those lips round the pipe-stem, the well-pared fingernails were all exhibits to him, like a death mask in a museum, a plaster-cast of a hand, set out for him to peer down at, and bamboozle himself as to the bed where they were made, the thoughts that existed contemporaneously, and the craftsman, himself dead, who'd done this service for prying posterity.

'You know where I've been?' Bernard said. He sat, proud of the manner in which he banged these words into the room.

'Eh?' His father took out the pipe, and rubbed the stem dry on his ragged cuff. His face was smooth still, without curiosity, blank. Bernard repeated his question, more slowly.

'To this, er, woman's, girl's,' his father answered.

'She's got a name.'

The face was lifted in the half-darkness away from the lamp. The eyebrows were clamped together.

'Ay. I suppose she has. Like all of us. Mrs. Ridell. That's it, isn't it?'

'That's it.'

Bernard felt the flush on his cheeks; his face burnt. His father was looking down now, bending forward, polishing his pipe-bowl awkwardly on the carpet. The boy wished he could bounce up, wrench the tie from his neck, strip it with fierce wrist-play to tatters. If he could leap and hammer a gong, smash-clash the fire-irons, kick the glass of the china cabinet in, he could have quieted himself. He sat, blushing, hunched.

'I want to talk to you about her.'

'Go on, then.'

'I'm serious about her, Dad. I shall marry her.'

'You've found Miss Right, have you?' There was a kind of giggle in the voice. Bernard bit his lip. Was that bloody idiocy all his father could manage? In death's presence? Where was dignity about that? He looked across to the stem which was now exploring the outline of the chin.

'Yes,' he said. His voice was metallic, he thought, a clang. 'And there's something. She says, well, er, something. She wants . . . She says . . . She wants to go up with us to see my mother. What do you think?'

Mr. Allsop's thin fingers came down to fondle his bony knee.

'Well, yes,' he said. 'Yes. I can't see much wrong in that.'

'Has she, my mother, ever said anything to you about Jacqueline?' he asked.

His father nodded, and rubbed, like a clockwork man. He cleared his throat.

'Well,' he said. 'Yes, she did. In a way.'

Bernard waited.

'I don't want,' his father began, 'to spoil anything. She wasn't pleased. No, now. That's putting it too strongly. She thought you ought to finish at the university before you had anybody. That's about the short and long of it.'

'Nothing about Jacqueline's being married?'

'Married? She did mention it, bring it up. But you see, Bern, she was ill, very ill, and worried with it. She thought she'd got . . . what she had got. And that makes a difference.'

'And you. What do you think?'

'I'm old-fashioned. Not that that's anything to go by. I don't know. I haven't seen her, have I? If you're satisfied, that's what counts, isn't it? But your mother didn't want you to spoil your chances, up there.'

'Yes.'

'She didn't like your going about with that Blankley girl, just before you took your degree. That's more important than anything else, she said, many's the time.' Ernest Allsop sighed, leaned forward. 'You must please yourself.'

'Are we going tomorrow?' Bernard asked.

'I am.'

'Anybody else?' Shake of head. 'Aunt Jess?' Denial. 'Can I, can she come then?'

'I haven't thought about it. Well, I can't see much harm. I suppose it ought to be broken to her.'

'Broken?'

'Told. That she's coming, she's there. But I could do that, couldn't I? Go in first.'

Allsop took the pipe out of his mouth. 'Yes. You tell her she can come.'

3

BERNARD RUSHED to the telephone, but Jacqueline heard his news soberly, said she'd take them in her car.

Next day, soon after two, the Allsops were ready. They had washed up, though there was still a smell of roast beef round the house. Bernard had put in three hours' hard work at his thesis, while his father had prepared the meal and his sister had been out teaching the infants in her Sunday School. The men sat, in their best suits, as Mary read a novel at the dinner table now covered with a heavy plush cloth. At ten minutes past the hour Jacqueline rang the bell. She wore a white coat Bernard had never seen before; it was light, and half-military, with a blue stripe in the collar. Her face was unsmiling as she stepped into the house to be introduced. Mr. Allsop and she shook hands; both claimed to be pleased. Mary looked up, the only one with a grin, to say hello. Mr. Allsop then fussed about to make sure that everything had been packed before he issued final, useless instructions to his daughter, who nodded solemnly, and returned to her book. She got up, however, to come to the gate to see them off in a car.

The journey was dumbly made.

They had nothing, for the moment, in common. Bernard sat at the front with Jacqueline. Once, she apologised for suddenly braking and once made some remarks to Mr. Allsop about a block of flats that she claimed were luxurious. His fumbled answer discouraged her, and she gave up. When they had parked the car, Bernard shook his embarrassment off and said to his father: 'You'd better go in first. To tell her we're coming.'

Allsop glanced at Jacqueline like a begging dog but moved off, the paper carrier, H. R. Wilkinson, High Class Fruiterer, in his left hand.

'It's sensible that he should go in,' Bernard said, gruffly. She looked at him very carefully, as if she was about to de-

23

molish that with a sarcasm before she smiled and settled the lapels of her coat. They stood in the sunshine, by a high brick pillar and wrought-iron gates with a freshly painted city coat of arms.

At the end of five minutes' fidgeting he said, 'We'll go in now.'

'Are you sure?' she asked, but put a hand on his coat-sleeve.

They sauntered indoors, into the smell of healing and dying. Here and there green blinds were drawn; elsewhere great splashes of naked sunlight patterned the terrazzo corridors, creamed the buff walls.

Bernard scrutinised his mother from the far end of the ward. She was propped up, wearing a bed-jacket. She had been doing her hair, but as soon as she saw her son at the door she handed the comb and brush to her husband. The two young people advanced to the bed. Mr. Allsop stood up.

'Mother,' Bernard said, 'this is Jacqueline.'

The claw-like hand, flesh eaten from the bones, was advanced. Mrs. Allsop's cheeks had grown faintly red. Her eyes were bright with a yellow ugliness.

'Good afternoon,' Mrs. Allsop said.

Jacqueline took the outstretched hand, held it. She was smiling.

'Sit down this side,' Mrs. Allsop said. 'Here's a chair.'

The small rearrangement seemed welcome. Mr. Allsop advanced the chair for Jacqueline; Bernard held his mother's hand.

'How are you today?' he whispered.

'I'm a bit better, I think.'

'No pain?'

'No.' There the two were closeted together, very still, like lovers.

It was a little while before Mrs. Allsop turned her eyes from her son.

'I've heard a lot about you,' she said to Jacqueline.

'Yes.'

'It's very nice of you to come and see me.'

'I'm glad I can.'

'You've brought them in your car. That's very convenient. Dad wouldn't have one.' Mrs. Allsop's voice was fainter, but she smiled, shaping the gibe against the men. 'Perhaps he will, now, when I come out, to take me for a ride round.'

'Yes.' Jacqueline leant forward, fingers on her left lapel which stuck outwards like a fin.

'I'd like that. When I lie here I sometimes think to myself, "I wish I was up park." That's what the children used to say. "I'm going *up* park." I stopped them. I thought it was a common expression, but that's the way I think about it now. "I wish I was up park." Funny, isn't it?' At the end of the speech she seemed distressed, as after violent exertion.

'We'll take you,' Allsop said.

'When you're fed up sitting in the garden,' Bernard said. 'That's like Buckingham Palace now.'

'You and your garden,' his mother answered. But suddenly, it appeared, she was in pain.

'Are you all right?' Allsop asked. Bernard put a hand in the crook of her elbow. For a minute she was dumb, struggling with some agony, until she shrugged this off to ask her son to rearrange the propping pillows and her husband to hand her a tablet from the locker and a drink of water. They completed their tasks so that now she sat, as earlier, gulping but without discomfort. Immediately she turned to Jacqueline.

'There's one place, there, in the park, you know, that I like very much. Just in front of where the old hall used to be. And you're in a sort of circle of grass and the woods are just above you up the hill. And away to your right you can see, through a gap, it must be a mile or more off, a factory chimney on the horizon over all this green. I like that very much.'

'As soon as you're out I'll take you there,' Jacqueline said.

'Near the bandstand,' Bernard said.

'You can't remember that,' his mother answered.

What he could remember were his mother's stories. They

all included these little sentences of natural description, based on places she knew, he guessed. Mrs. Allsop had been an infant teacher and had perhaps padded her make-believe with these 'to the rights', 'just beyond the end of the fence', to convince herself that she convinced her audience. Her fairy lore was set in real fields, on known plough land, this side of mapped hills.

'They built it after the First War,' she added.

They had never known her talk so much for weeks. She had always been ready to listen, to add a confirmatory phrase, to show them that her mind was still lively. Today she seemed to have struggled out from the vague comfort of sedation, to lead the conversation. It did not take long to exhaust her, and she asked that the pillows be moved from behind her shoulders, the bed-jacket removed. This time Jacqueline assisted the men.

When all were settled again it was Jacqueline who began to speak. She described a headland near St. Bees where she had spent an almost tropical fortnight as a girl. Her descriptions were accurate, in that shrill voice that had nothing childish about it. The warm sea, the sheltered purple shadows, the black-and-green pools. There was something of the mother's method in it, except that Mrs. Allsop's seemed deliberate, the topographical exactitude introducing the dragon, dwarf, mermaid. Jacqueline talked on and they heard about the scar, with stitch-marks, on the leg on the boy she played with, and her father's fall, the hotel's buttered girdle-cakes. About this there was nothing fantastic, for she openly announced that she'd be disappointed if ever she went back.

Mrs. Allsop's eyes were closed so that they'd no idea whether or not she was listening to the recital. The father was captivated, nodding at each point, but watching his wife's face, perhaps for a sign of approval there. In the end the men asked Jacqueline a few questions; the three of them laughed quietly, guiltily at the answers, and once Mrs. Allsop smiled and took Bernard's hand. They waited for her to speak, but she said nothing.

Conversation became desultory; gaps long.

Allsop tried news of the neighbourhood. This failed. Bernard raked up a story about 'Aunt' Betty Stocks, the eccentric woman next door. He did his best without much encouragement, though his mother opened her eyes once or twice. Jacqueline took the cue, and told them about her uncle, a Mr. Holywell, dead now, who was for months on end under the impression that burglars accompanied by murderous ravening dogs were upstairs in his house. His wife dared hardly move upstairs because of the useless string traps he constructed which would certainly have caught neither thieves nor hounds, but might easily leg an old lady down. Bernard had heard nothing of this before and found the insistent small voice uniquely fascinating. Holywell's delusions used to whirl to a climax then he became suddenly sane again, to sit in his garden, reading and smoking.

Mrs. Allsop's eyes were closed.

At one point of the story she asked for an orange. They all rose and searched. She sucked loudly. When she had been herself she had always eaten fastidiously, without noise, lips clamped, veiling serviette handy. Now she licked like an old woman, and juice wetted her chin. However, today she finished the fruit.

'Give me a handkerchief, Ernest,' she ordered.

He took and unfolded one from his pocket. She wiped fingers and mouth, said:

'I meant from the locker.'

'You can have that.'

'I don't want it.'

They were all silent. Bernard was tired out. He could not help making the comparison between Jacqueline's high-pitched lively voice and his mother's whisper, between the rounded tinted eye-socket of the one and the gouged, wrinkled hole of the other. He saw both straight; Jacqueline without lust, his mother without love. That did not last; he was himself again, involved, comparing the two to the detriment of one. Mrs. Allsop was now down flat, her mouth

27

almost covered by the sheets and her hands below the bed-clothes.

'Are you all right, Mother?' Allsop asked.

'Yes. I'm very tired. Don't talk.'

Time moved sluggishly. Each fidgeted unobtrusively. Allsop compromising, fingered the hair gently from his wife's forehead.

'Is there anything you want?' he asked.

'No.' The breathy, guilty monosyllable seemed to hover. She might be dead, Bernard thought, from her face. And lack of manners. His mother used to be stupendously polite. Even when she turned tramps and hawkers from her back door, as she invariably did, she treated them to a courteous dismissal. She was sorry that their time had been wasted. The absolute standard of decorum would be applied whether she were welcoming a visitor in or quelling the back-door ebullience of a roundsman.

'Ten pounds eight and threepence,' the Co-operative bread-boy would bawl. He wore tight jeans under his smock, and his hair slopped over his sideburns. 'I'll let you off the ten quid, madam. It's me birthday.'

'That's very kind of you.' There was no irony.

'Gentleman Jim, that's me. And the number?'

'51264. Thank you very much.' She collected her change, counted it, and thanked the man again. He snatched up his wicker basket and fled the door. She thanked him, wishing him good morning, from a distance, meaning it, neither overtly condemning his familiarity nor encouraging him, merely expressing with great clarity what she felt, thanks that he was doing what he was paid for.

In the same way she would observe the niceties if her children did her a favour she could have done without. She thanked them first, then told them to take the gift elsewhere or clear up the mess. She insisted on an equal punctilio from them.

Now she said what she meant, as she had always done, but unsoftened by social words. Nothing, not the wrecked hands, the breath, the yellow eyeballs, exhibited her illness like this bareness. She was somebody else; at the beginning of a visit she would be the self they knew, polite, not effusive but looking out for the chance to speak gratitude, but within twenty minutes pain or drugs or weariness had stripped off civilisation and they were back with plain 'yes' or 'no' of barbarism, the slum, the crisis, the deathbed.

In the silence which hardly seemed affected by talking in the ward and the whirr of traffic outside, Bernard found himself observing Jacqueline. She was twisting her wedding-ring. Suddenly she became aware of his attention, and instantly stared back at him steadily. It was a trick of hers, this what-the-hell scrutiny, suggesting that his college-trained intelligence, his academic patient awareness were wasted here, that the hard world of rebuffs, rudeness, insult, malice, violence, madness were in wait for him. He realised this was all his own gloss; she had caught him staring, and in defence had stared back. A child might do it. All the reference to experience, to the harsh dilemmas outside the student's libraries, came from him, not from her. He begrudged her wedded life. That was the top and bottom. Both suddenly noticed that Mrs. Allsop's eyes were open, fixed on the fingers picking at the ring. Jacqueline very slowly blushed; her pale face was touched to pink, and she puckered in her lips.

'Now then, Mother,' Bernard started.

Mrs. Allsop shook her head. The father opened her cupboard to see what she needed at the next visit. He groped about, asking unanswered questions, before he walked along the ward to consult the sister. Once he had gone, Mrs. Allsop took a hand from the sheets and laid it as near to Jacqueline as she could.

'It's very nice of you to come.'

Jacqueline took the hand. The white plump skin encircled the ugly bone.

'He's a very good boy.'

The girl nodded.

'He was always clever. His father's a good man.' She

29

gestured in the direction her husband had taken. 'I'm glad to have met you.' The voice was all but inaudible. Jacqueline, serious-faced, mouthed a reply, said she'd come again, that she'd look forward to their car-ride together in the park.

'I hope we can.' Mrs. Allsop's voice was louder, with a sort of desperation.

'It won't be long now, either,' Bernard said. 'You're a good bit stronger than this time last week.'

His mother looked at him hopelessly, as if the lie had taken her quite aback. Deliberately after a time, she nodded, mumbled. A spasm of irritation raked the boy so that, un-thinking, he nursed an anger at his mother's incapacity, her ugliness, her approaching death.

After they had left the hospital Bernard permitted himself to wonder at the life going on, the courting couples, the families parking their cars alongside the Castle, all in Sunday best. It was warm yet, and the trees were heavily green, over-hanging high stone walls. Bernard opened the car windows and all sat quite still.

'Shall I drive back now?' Jacqueline asked Allsop.

'Please,' he said, after hesitation.

Again they were silent until, within a hundred yards of the Allsop's house, the father spotted Mary, walking along with a boy.

'That's our Mary,' he said. 'Who's she with?' No answer. As the car drew up outside he asked again, 'Who's that our Mary's with?'

'Eric Parkes.'

'The greengrocery people?'

'No. That's an uncle. His father's in the offices of the Coal Board.'

'Local?'

'Burnside Avenue.'

Once this conversation was complete, Allsop returned to Jacqueline.

'You'll come to tea, I hope, Mrs. Ridell,' he said.

'Well, if it's not . . .'

'We'll be glad to have you. When we come out of that place we're at a loose end for a bit. You'll understand.'

'Yes. Yes.'

They stared at each other, stonily, on the sun-drenched road, as if the one were trying to convey some inkling of sympathy to the other. The three walking the front path gave the semblance of a rout. In the front room it was cooler; Jacqueline put herself in a corner with her back to the windows.

'Is it too early for tea yet?' Mr. Allsop asked. He paced about the house as if he'd little idea of what he was about. The others did not answer. Jacqueline studied a silver-framed photograph of the mother, hanging on the far wall. It was large and fairly recent. Mrs. Allsop was sitting on a rustic garden seat, her hands clasped in her lap, an expression of surprise on her face. It was as if, browsing there, she had just caught sight of someone she liked but had not expected.

The back door was banged open. They heard Mary in the kitchen.

'We're in here,' Allsop shouted. The child came through. 'We passed you,' her father said.

She blushed.

'On Bannerman Road?' she asked.

'Yes,' Bernard said. 'You were just doing a bit of courting.'

'I wasn't.' The words burst from her.

'I beg your pardon. You were walking up the street with a young man.'

'Well?'

'What's a well without a bucket?' Bernard answered with the childish cliché, to close the conversation. Mary sat down on the edge of a chair.

Ten minutes later brother and sister were laying the table together. Clinking and slopping spoons, Mary said:

'Is my dad mad with me?'

'No. Why?'

'Nothing. Because of Eric? Walking up with him?'

'It's a free country.'

'I know. I thought he might be mad,' she said. 'He helps run the Sunday School, you know.' She advanced on a cupboard. 'Is he clever?' This over her shoulder.

'Don't ask me.'

'He's at the university, isn't he? He said he sometimes cycles up there with you.'

'Yes, love. But I don't test his intelligence.'

He tapped her face very delicately, and she laughed.

4

ALLSOP REPORTED to his son that his wife had approved of Jacqueline Ridell.

'She really was taken with her,' he said, returning from his Tuesday visit.

'How was she?'

'The woman in the next bed said she has been very poorly, but she seemed better to me, livelier.'

'And the doctors?' Bernard asked.

'I didn't see anybody tonight. The sister was busy.'

'How long?' The question was flung down like a challenge.

'They said last time I asked perhaps, you know, a month or two. They couldn't tell me exactly.' He coughed, eyes watery. 'Perhaps less, very much less.'

Each time his father visited the mother on his own, Bernard demanded to be told how long she would last. The boy could not help himself; he asked as if some authority at the hospital had the exact date of her death, and control of that time so that a carelessly given answer needed to be honoured and the life therefore prolonged. Allsop did not resent the reiteration, or did not notice. He answered politely, drily and, it seemed, went out of his way to inquire when he would have preferred not to do so.

'She really liked Jacqueline,' he said.

'What did she say?'

'One thing. How young she looked. And how well she spoke. She wants to see her again. Do you think she'd go?'

Mary came downstairs.

'Finished your homework, love?' her father asked. 'What was it tonight?'

'English, Bio, Latin.'

'Balbus still building that wall?' Bernard asked.

'Accusative and infinitive, clever-dick. I'm going for a little walk.'

'It's ten to nine,' her father said.

'Well, it's light, and I shan't be long.'

'Where are you going?'

'Just a little walk round. Up on the common.'

She went out, hating them. There was no excuse for their prying. It was warm, and she needed fresh air. She looked back where her father stood, with dejected shoulders, speaking to Bernard, the big man, who had an arm stretched along the mantelpiece. As she rounded the wall of the outside lavatory she stopped, performed a short shuffled dance of joy, and laughed. The sky was duck-egg green and pink, like nougat-fluff.

She crossed the road, walked the short hill, turned on to the bridge by the station, to the 'stumps', wooden posts which prevented motorists from driving on to the sand, grass and gorse of the common. There a group of boys lounged, a transistor set screaming. They whistled, called out. One staggered, clutched his genitals, groaned with assumed sexual ecstasy. Mary felt herself blush, walked straight. She heard one of the boys say coarsely what he could do to her.

She moved out of the rain-runnels in the sand, and up on to the short grass. A girl, light raincoat over tennis dress, cycled past her, waved a racket. Nancy Parkes, Eric's sister. Mary flushed again, but did not turn at the whoop as Nancy shot through the 'stumps'. Queerly, in spite of the girl's brief shorts, long legs, shouting was directed towards class-division, not bedwards. 'Any more for tennis? Rather, ol' chep.'

There were few people about. Away in the dip, in the half-dozen silver birches, a man was signalling to his dog. Some assorted couples sauntered. The odd golfer left the clubhouse and clambered into his car. Mary looked about her. A touch of wind cuffed the thin blades of grass. Now, by an iron fence, rough and cool under her touch, she stopped, and stared down the long lumpy hill to the first green and the sandy streak of a path. Everything was still. The country was laid out like a smudged map, the viaduct, the massed plume of woods, the raw-cut fields dug for new houses, the clock-tower and the winding gear at the colliery. She looked out in the luminous green of the sky to the church spire, tiny as a toy, on the northern horizon. On her left, over the railway lines, she could see the dark windows of her own home. Nobody was sitting in the front room.

Her face was hot; an anger burnt in her head. She had no control over her world. At this moment she wanted to see Eric Parkes. If he came she'd blush flame-red to her navel, and wriggle her pointed shoes in embarrassment. He might hardly speak; she would not know what to answer. She wanted him, here. He was not about. Again she stared northwards, to the

> Hills of Annesley, bleak and barren,
> Where my thoughtless childhood strayed.

He'd said that. Eric. To a crowd of them, when he was showing off in front of Deirdre Fenton. As if she'd notice poetry. She went round with men who had cars, though she was only seventeen and still at school. Eric Parkes. Sometimes he brought his dog up here in the evening. When he saw her he'd stroll across, and stop, with his eyes bright as if everything he said were a joke. But he wasn't here. Not here.

She looked right, where the sky was darkening. About that ugly finger of a works chimney there was poignancy; some secret of life was poised there, unknown to any but her. The girl rested her left hand flat on the point of one of the spikes of the fence, pressing gently. The faint pain ground pleasurably, as she searched the low hills behind the embankment. Below, straight ahead, black figures walked the path; a courting pair, locked closely so that they staggered, came behind her quietly and she gasped, startled. The two leaned into a kiss, disregarding the child, laughing as they broke, then bent again.

Mary blew a fierce sigh.

Now she was petulant. Not that she minded anything, she told herself. Thoughts of her mother's illness clawed in her. She could bear that; only when she compared her mother in health, dominating her by love, with the stick of a woman who'd yelped out loud at home, like a puppy, and was dying, did she feel pity. She could switch the feelings on and off, set these stimuli or those, find herself dry-eyed or crying at her own command. Her breasts were hard against the cross-bar of the railings. The wind touched the hair round her forehead as she moved away.

She hurried down the hill, in the sand, crossed the railway lines and passed the Irishman's puzzle-gate. She moved more slowly up the hill. As she entered the back door Bernard came out.

'Did you see him?' he asked.

'Who?' Red face.

'Parky-boy.'

'No. Should I?'

She banged into the kitchen. Her brother stood irresolutely at the front gate. Mr. and Mrs. Simpson passed, middle-aged, arm-in-arm, both straight-backed, both smoking cigarettes. They muttered a greeting. Bernard was undecided whether to ring Jacqueline or stroll out for half an hour. Though he made no attempt to solve the dilemma, did not think of it, merely drummed the stone pillar with his fingers, his uncertainty annoyed him. With a clang he slammed the gate back, walked to the phone box.

It was almost a habit now, to be breathless as he waited.

As soon as he heard Jacqueline's high voice, he reported

that his mother wanted to see her again. Coolly she told him to fix the time. He could hear the piano, asked about it. Tom had come up with William Riley, to tell her more about his attempt to inject culture into the place, and the two were now hammering 'The Arrival of the Queen of Sheba' all over the district. She seemed unwilling to talk, announced that the Handel was her favourite music and now she'd have to ask them to start it all over again. Bernard was dashed.

'You don't want to talk to me, then,' he said.

'No, darling. Not really.'

'Right, then. I'll ring off.'

'Yes. 'Bye, sweet. Look after yourself.'

He heard her replace the phone, scowled at his face in the mirror, glowered at the cluster of pimples at the corner of his mouth. He'd not yet got used to Jacqueline's independence. If she was busy, she said so. He would drop anything to entertain her. Not that this was likely; she never interfered when she thought he was occupied or considered any problem of her own worth any of his valuable time. She'd be sitting there, with her glasses on, she wore them, the bitch, for effect, smiling at bashing Tom and scurfy-head, fancy-fingers Riley whacking all the sense out of Handel. No. Wrong. They could both play well. Tom with the panache; Riley like a professional, clear, accurate, powerful and at the end he'd poke his finger into his nostril and say, 'Be improved with a D sharp there, Tom old bird, just there,' and the nail would skedaddle from the nose and rap the copy, one, two, three, four. Two know-alls. Bernard stumbled out of the kiosk.

The Simpsons marched up the hill again. They swung along at light-infantry pace, arm-in-arm. Both were under five feet six. This time they stopped, briefly, to inquire about Mrs. Allsop, nodded solemnly, marched off, the man smartly changing step. Bernard watched their ridiculous progress and slouched off towards the Common.

Back at home, Allsop was writing painfully to his wife's sister in Canada. He'd put this off for weeks, and found himself unable to concentrate. 'Ivy doesn't seem, now, to be in any pain, but the doctors don't give her much longer to live; only a month or two at the most. This will be a great shock to you, Elsie, as it was to us. We all thought, as Ivy did herself, that this last operation would clear the whole thing up, but it wasn't to be. It seems hard, and I can hardly grasp yet what it means to me.'

He grasped only too well. The house was exactly as dirty when he came home as it was when he left it. There were meals to prepare, and though the children helped, he was on his knees by bedtime. There were visits, four, five times a week, and the uncomfortable hour with her drowsiness, or depression, or complaints. He was faintly optimistic, even now, had not quite decided that she'd be better dead. He hoped, squinted, for the miracle.

Blowing on the top of his pen he recalled his wife's youngest sister. Elsie Caunt had been a fly-by-night, with a peroxide head, who'd married a Canadian captain at the end of the war. Now both were hard-faced, well-to-do, fat-necked, flew back to England, threw their weight, advice and money about. And she, with her plunging neckline and her perfect legs, would read this, and think that if Ivy had caught it, so might she. She'd eye the glassy shoes and polished furniture and smell her husband's whisky and wonder when, how she'd die, and she'd hate Allsop.

The Caunts were brassy, but decent. Perhaps she'd come over, with a straight face, and she'd set about his house, and cook rich meals, and hector them with that crackling accent she'd acquired in her first year out there. She'd sit by Ivy's bed, and the tears would wet her cheeks.

'There's no hope, but Ivy's very brave. I don't know whether she knows or not. They told me not to go too often in case she suspects something. But I think she must. You really can't hide it from them. The way she looks at me, sometimes, I'm quite sure she knows. Of course, she has a lot of drugs, and this means she's drowsy. But her memory's un-impaired. She suddenly said to me the other night, "Do you remember our Elsie telling us about that minister?" I didn't get it at first, but she meant the man who went round in a truck with a harmonium and a cornet. You told us about him, and his family.'

That his wife remembered so well grieved him. Otherwise he could let that bag of bones die. But she'd recall, suddenly, unexpectedly, like a living person, something trivial or important. Like a living person. He put his pen down on the writing-ped, squared it with the edge.

Bernard came quietly in.

'Hello,' Allsop said. 'What's the time? Um? I'd better go up and see if Mary's got the light out. She'll read all night, if you let her.'

'I'll go.'

'No. Don't bother.' Allsop stood wearily, creaked up the stairs. His daughter was asleep, her book open on the bedside table. He was too tired to bend and kiss her, but turned and closed the door.

'I've been writing to your Aunt Elsie,' he said. 'I'll finish it tomorrow. I'm off to bed now, I think. What are you doing?'

'I'll put an hour in,' Bernard said.

'At your books?'

'Yep. Yep.'

'Lock up, then, will you?'

He shuffled towards the stairs again. These two had nothing to say now. Both were tired.

'Good night, Bernard.'

'Good night, Dad.'

5

THE RECORD PLAYER thrashed the noisy air.

At the youth club five girls stood within a couple of yards' radius of the machine, eyeing moving shoes, swishing skirt-ends. Faces showed a sullen lack of all interest, but now and again, in the racket, some remark would be exchanged, and expressions would brighten; one might realise these were young teenagers. Further down the room two boys practised ostentatious table-tennis, smashes, low chops from ten feet back, flicks, and at the end of each rally panted 'Too much top on that' or 'Remind me to get my specs changed'. At the far end, on a quarter-size table, two long-haired youths in shirt-sleeves played billiards, slowly, mostly standing like statues with cues at an angle swapping sad observations that were lost in the fog of record-din. In two smaller rooms, a few shuffled or fewer wove baskets. Tonight the club was badly attended, but this was expected since a popular group was performing at the monthly dance in the church institute half a mile away. The leader kept his doors open for the un-enterprising.

Mary Allsop jigged with the rest.

She liked this weekly jaunt. There was one other grammar school girl here tonight; the rest attended the local bilateral. They'd spend another hour round this player, and then drift into the kitchen for coffee, where the boys might talk to them. Bob Flyte, one of the table-tennis pair, would boast how he'd taken a county player to 21-9 or some such at the Athletic Club Rooms in town. The girls would ignore this, even Maureen Taylor, who was sweet on him. But if Harry Walters turned up, not often, they'd be laughing round him, and touching his hair, and he'd have one of them on his knee and put his hand on her belly. He was nearly twenty with stringy side-burns and a black-shaven chin, but he made them scream with his hoarse whispers and screwed-up eyes. But nobody trusted him; the boys said he used to go in to a married woman in Taplow Street; every girl in the place knew how free he was with his hands.

Mary was pleased here. Nobody asked questions; some-times one would spit out some secret, about another girl, or a boy, or oneself. And if somebody broke the rules and pried, no one need answer. Cock the nose, set the face and jig on. The adults were busy. Mr. Morrow, the leader, was dashing here and there in his shirt-sleeves, cleaning up messes, arranging for rallies or rambles, checking the subs, placating the committee, thinking up excuses to give the trustees of the chapel where the club met because somebody had cracked a chair-back or poked a ball through a window. He hadn't time to ask after Mrs. Allsop; and his deputy couldn't think. He, the assistant, sat on a seat in the basket-weaving room, sweating like a pig, strumming his guitar as he grunted songs of prison and disaster. He was useless with the members, but first thing on Saturday morning he'd be in at seven-thirty and by eleven the rooms would be spick and shining again; he'd lift the instrument down and try some other notes of slavery or incarceration. They called him 'Mad Len', because when the boys teased beyond endurance, he'd set about somebody, half-maim him. He never asked Mary how her mother was.

The last of the pile of records had dropped into place, had screeched its length as the needle scored through its ravaged groove, and there was silence.

'Going in?' Lynne said, nodding at the coffee-room.

'Want any more, Bob?' Maureen called, pouting at the machine.

'What?' A handsomely executed backhand flick.

'I ask you.'

They moved out. In the kitchen the big iron kettle was steaming as Mad Len's sister filled the cracked cups. The girls made a circle round a coke fire. Eric Parkes appeared, stood in the doorway, showed his university scarf.

'Is Mr. Morrow about?' he asked.

'In the big room,' Maureen answered.

'Lah-di-dah,' Lynne said, when he'd gone. 'Posh Peter.'

Mary blushed, lifted the scalding coffee to her lips.

'He's nice looking, though,' Susan said. 'Ooooh.'

'I could tell you something about him.' Maureen.

'Don't be bashful.'

'But I'm not going to. I'd make his ears burn for him. And somebody else's.'

'Don't you like him, then, Maur?'

'I do not. Since he's gone to the college he's as stuck-up . . . Our Denise says his brother was just the same.'

'You've been talking about him, then.'

'Go an' tittle,' Maureen said, and put her cup by the mirror so that she could adjust the lacquered lump on top of her head.

The boys trooped in from dominoes, all four, chaffed the girls. Ten minutes later the leader, Mad Len and Eric Parkes returned, made a solemn committee, at which Mr. Morrow scratched his upper lip with the tip of his forefinger, and Len clumped his right fist into his left palm, but did not speak. The trio went out, reappeared immediately with coffee. Eric walked straight over to Mary.

'Hello, ladies,' he said. 'Any secrets?'

'Not for you.' Maureen.

'Why not?'

'You're too young.'

'Ask me when you're twenty-one,' Lynne said, while the others cackled with laughter.

'Hello, Mary,' he said. 'Let's see the fire.'

'It's not cold,' she answered. In this room with its windows high in the thick grey wall, it was always chilly. He stood side by side with her, leaning on the steel fire-guard. Their hips were touching; they were aware of it. The boy called a question over to the other side of the room where the table-tennis players were flat out in chairs, tipped back on to two legs, mopping boiling heads. Conversation was slung across, loud, boastful, dull, but Mary could feel Eric close and his arm, moving to raise his cup, rested now on hers.

Lynne, the oldest of the girls, was teasing him about a green corduroy jacket he'd been wearing at tennis the night before. Mary was jealous, without reservation, at once, that she had not been there to see him, but the warm body, the elbow, were restitution. She pressed her leg on his.

'I said to our Ray,' Lynne told them, ' "Who's that? Robin Hood in his Lincoln green?" ' The girls gurgled laughter.

'Wrong colour,' Eric said.

41

'And his shorts, and all.'

'Has he got hairy legs?' Pat demanded.

'Did he win, though?' Sue asked.

'He didn't even take it off. Sat there all night in a deck-chair with this silk how-de-doo round his neck and his velvet jacket.'

'Truth,' Eric laughed. 'You'll get pimples on your tongue.'

'Never took his racket out of his press.'

Eric patted Mary's thigh as if it were his own in mock exasperation.

'Who beat Ray and Mandy Farr?'

'Can't you take a joke?' Lynne sounded waspish, suddenly.

'Who were you playing with?' Maureen asked.

'Oh. Deirdre Fenton.'

Mary was struck miserable, edged away from him. He moved off to put his cup on the tray, came back.

'Yo' want to watch it, youth,' Mad Len shouted at one of the table-tennis boys.

'Aw, taters.'

'Ah'll smash you.'

There was silence; the girls huddled, looked away.

'Len,' Mr. Morrow called from the door, 'give us a hand here a minute.' The assistant did not move, crouched threateningly, then said:

'Yo' just watch it. Ah'm tellin' yer.'

He slouched away; the girls shifted arms and legs again. The tennis boy's face was bleached blank. Chatter broke out; some shifted away to wash the cups. Soon afterwards Morrow announced the end of the session. Eric did not speak to Mary, but went off to fetch his coat. She, with the other girls, took her time, chattering, peering into the mirror.

Outside in the street he was leaning on the low wall. He saw her, waved goodbye to his friends, did not even wait but walked slowly enough for her to catch him before they reached the corner.

'Hello,' he said.

'Hello.' They went along the main street, not speaking, in

42

no hurry, paying attention to nobody. When they crossed the zebra near the market-place he took her hand awkwardly but let it go as soon as they mounted the pavement.

'It's quite light still,' he said. The face of the church clock was faintly illuminated from behind in the green-yellow evening. 'Not many there tonight.'

'No. St. John's dance,' she said. They turned down Church Lane.

'That,' he said.

'Why didn't you go?'

'Too crowded. Always is.'

His face was momentarily sulky, as he thought of Deirdre Fenton, who might be there, if she weren't racketing round with the Watson boy in his white car. He snatched Mary's hand, forced his fingers roughly between hers.

'That hurt.'

'I'm sorry.' It took him some seconds to recall what he'd done. 'I'm sorry.' He put his arm round her waist, loosely, then suddenly cupped her right breast with his hand. They walked together unspeaking. As his fingers caressed her, she felt with a shamed pleasure her nipple stand hard. He would know; his finger-ends were at it, urgently.

'Where are you going tomorrow?' he said, stroking, voice restrained.

'Might watch the cricket. I might have to go up to the hospital.'

'Yes.' His hand fell away; he put a yard between them. 'Is your mother going on,' he hesitated, 'well?'

'She's very ill.'

Both translated this. He looked at the brown bushy hair, the wave deeply indented. Her face was undisturbed, her lips colourless in the dregs of daylight. Now the soft exploration of her breast was sacrilege because she had pronounced words that meant her mother was dying. It had killed his excitement. She was a little girl even if her body swelled like a woman's. Thirteen? Fourteen. Deirdre was an adult, with the wiles and caprice, the acquired female accessories. Mary was

43

a child, with rounder breasts and buttocks than the elder girl, rich with innocent sexuality.

'I saw Bernard this morning,' he said.

'Where?'

'At the university. In the refectory.'

They emerged at a new road, with white kerb-stones. Eric snorted like a conductor demanding a powerful entry of the brass. She looked up at him, but his eyes were straight ahead. He began to recite:

> 'Oh, the pearl seas are yonder,
> The amber-sanded shore,
> Shires where the girls are fonder,
> Towns where the pots hold more.'

'William Shakespeare,' she said, fruitily. His nostrils twitched.

'Housman. A. E. Housman,' he corrected.

'Who's he when he's at home?' she asked, willing to rile him.

'Do you mean to say you've never heard of A. E. Housman?'

'No.'

'What do they teach you at the Lady Manners Grammar School?'

'For girls,' she said, laughing at herself as well as at his prissy voice.

'Housman was the Professor of Latin at Cambridge. The Kennedy Professor. He edited Manilius. And wrote "The Shropshire Lad". You've heard of that, surely.'

'No. I haven't.'

'God.' He now appeared annoyed, Olympian, arrogantly superior, beyond her. She became afraid, uncertain, careful, utterly humble.

'Was that "The Shropshire Lad"? That amber-sanded thing?'

'No, it wasn't.'

44

At the snubbing tone she gritted with anger. He'd no right. She couldn't know everything, could she? And just because he was studying English. Her eyes flashed tears, but she turned her head away from him, slapping the triangular top rail of the wooden garden fence they were passing. A needle of pain jabbed her finger.

'Splinter,' she said, hand to mouth.

'Let me look.' He examined it, seriously. 'It's too dark. If you bathe it when you get back, you'll be able to get it out.'

'It hurts,' she said.

'What do you expect?' He lifted it to his mouth, kissed it.

'You.' She snatched it away. He laughed, was not annoyed; for the rest of the way he described to her the latest record he'd bought. Schubert's Fifth Symphony. In B flat. D485. He was solemn-faced when he announced, 'He wasn't much older than I am when he wrote that. And it's a masterpiece.' He hummed a bar or two of the slow movement. 'Tar-rah-rah-rah-raah, tar-raaah-tiddy-tarra-tah, tar-rah-rah-tah-rah . . . ' There was nothing he liked better than to impart information. How long the composition had taken, the instruments used in the scoring, the keys of the movements, the relationship to Mozart's Symphony in G Minor, No. 40, K550. It poured out until they reached the place where she'd know whether or not he'd decided to walk the whole way home with her.

'Will you be all right?' he said, nervously.

'Yes.'

'Sure?' They were standing dumb. A few seconds earlier the Schubert symphonies had been receiving encyclopaedic treatment.

'Yes.'

' 'Bye, then.' He put his hand out, blandly, and laid it flat on her breast. She stepped back in surprise so that he was left leaning forward. With a flick of his fingers he shaped a comic salute and turned away, smiling, under the yellow pool of street lamp.

Her father was sitting at the table, writing.

'Been to your club?' he asked. 'You're a bit late.'

'Yes.'

'Do you want anything?'

'No, thanks.'

'Get yourself a drink of lemonade before you go to bed.'

She kissed her father, formally, and he stared vaguely across at her. He was always writing now. Hundreds of letters to break the news.

6

BERNARD BARGED up the back garden path of Jacqueline's house.

No one about. He stamped into the hall, bawled her name, waited. She shouted down that she wouldn't be long. He settled on one of the hall chairs, something he'd never done before, and pulled faces at the pitted, bright brass warming-pan hanging opposite.

She stood on the landing, one hand on the white balustrade, the large window behind her bright in the evening.

'What are you doing there?' she said.

'Waiting for you.'

'Oh.' She flounced up to him, presented her cheek, ordered, 'Kiss.' He pecked. 'Passion,' she said, and moved into the study. He sat down in the hall again, and allowed two minutes to pass before he followed her.

'Take your time,' she said as he entered. She was lifting down glasses from the cabinet, polishing each, examining it.

'Company?' he said.

'Yes. You don't mind, do you?' She knew he did.

'I'll go then.'

'You won't do anything so silly,' she said.

There was silence while he reached for a book of poems. This meant opening a heavy glass bookcase. Difficult, but he kept his eyes downwards, working, working. He flicked the pages, found something he knew, 'Au Cabaret-Vert', that old Piddle-duck had made them translate into English verse:

> Et ce fut adorable
> Quand la fille aux tétons énormes, aux yeux vifs,
> —Celle-là, ce n'est pas un baiser qui l'épeure!—
> Rieuse, m'apporta des tartines de beurre,
> Du jambon tiède, dans un plat colorié . . .

Jacqueline was setting out the bottles, taking no notice of him.

'Now then,' she said at length. 'What's wrong?'

'Nothing.'

'You don't seem very pleased.'

'You weren't very pleased yourself, were you?' He was determined to quarrel.

'When?'

'When I rang up. Last Tuesday.'

'I was busy. I had those two louts thrashing the piano. I didn't have a minute to spare,' she said. She appeared doubtful herself.

'That's not how it sounded to me,' he announced. 'You wanted to be off listening to that Queen of Sheba thing. You said so. You didn't want to talk. "No, darling, not really." ' His mimicry was hopelessly out.

'Yes,' she said, and sucked her thumb-end, thinking of something else. 'I was a bit throng. They were so noisy. But it's nothing to quarrel about. I like Bill Riley very much, but not in the way you think, so there's no need to be jealous.'

He looked at the carpet.

'Take your glum face off,' she said. 'I want you to look specially beautiful tonight.'

'Who's coming? The Queen?'

'My mother and father.'

He had never met the older Butlers. They didn't go about much, but prodded round in the half-acre of garden behind a big modern house out in Ruddington. Frederick was a retired engineer, had served out East, where, in Ajmer-Merwara, Jacqueline had been born. What little she had said about her father had given Bernard the impression that she feared him, even now, though he could not for the life of him guess why this should be so. 'Daddy makes his mind up, and sticks to it,' she'd said, and that with approval.

'Can I help?' he asked.

'No. It's all done. They're coming to inspect you.'

'You don't scare me with that.'

All thought of quarrelling had been brushed away; he was braced, on his best behaviour.

'No,' she said. 'They won't eat you.' 'They.' She'd never spoken about her mother before. 'It's a great honour when Daddy turns out.' She laughed at him over her shoulder so that he began to suspect she was nervous. He clapped his book shut and dust flew.

'And those huge breasts, and her come-hither eyes,' he said.

'Don't be filthy.'

'Rimbaud,' he said, patting the cover. 'In my translation.'

They said no more. She trotted from the room, still laughing as if some practical joke were to be played. Very shortly, before she had returned to the room, the door-bell rang and a cultivated voice called:

'Can I leave my car out there in that damn' back-street o' yours?'

'Run it into the garage drive.'

'Right. I will.'

'Hello, Mummy. How are you both?'

'We're very well, really, very well.' The voice was high, a whispering high parody of Jacqueline's own, but posher.

Mrs. Butler walked into the study in front of her daughter. Bernard stood, awkwardly, half supporting himself on the arm of his chair. The elder woman looked at him, quickly away, critically at the room before she held her hand out. After the briefest shake, she sat down and said:

'I like these curtains. Don't you, Mr. Allsop? I always have

48

liked them. They suit this room.' The sentences were delivered steadily, in a friendly quiet manner, so that Bernard was immediately relieved. The voice had the high pitch of her daughter's, but lacked the dryness, the off-hand quality.

'This is an interesting room,' Bernard said. Certainly it was not four-square, and the wall by the window was cottage-thick.

'When the sun's out, it's really quite rustic. I don't know why the Ridells kept this house. Do you, Jacqueline?'

'Couldn't sell it, perhaps.'

'You can sell anything made of bricks and mortar. The grandfather built it, didn't he? The elder Henry?'

Jacqueline vaguely outlined the house's ninety years of history.

'The railway would be here, then,' Bernard said, 'when they put it up.'

'I suppose it would.'

'Um. I'd always thought of it as out in the fields. I wonder how much building there was. Some of those stone shops the other end of Duke Street must be older. And they probably pulled a fair amount of old stuff down to get those terraces up at the back.'

'This is the sort of history you're interested in, Mr. Allsop?' Mrs. Butler asked.

'Well, no. Not really. I'm a paper man, if the truth were known.'

Mr. Butler clattered into the hall, stood in the doorway breathing heavily, his face darkly red. His hair was thick, but shortish, and rose in tight white-grey waves above his smooth forehead. He wore a dark green suit of tweed, highly polished brown shoes, and he was very broad across the shoulders. After he had sat down in a rush, he crossed his legs and folded heavily veined, purplish hands across his pot-belly.

'Hello, Bernard,' he said, and almost immediately stood up again to shake the younger man's hand. He sat slowly the second time, coughed his face redder, and told his daughter that the drive gates needed oiling.

'Give this young fellow the oil-can,' he ordered, hacking still.

Bernard shot up. 'Where do you keep it? I'll go and get that little job done for you.'

'Not tonight you won't,' Jacqueline said. 'What'll you drink, Daddy?'

Her father chose whisky. He was a formidable man, rather like his son in the heavy aggressive slant of the shoulders, the boxer's trick of tucking his chin into the collar and squinting upwards through the eyebrows.

'We were just saying,' Jacqueline put the glass into his hand, 'that the railway would be built before this house.'

'Of course it would,' he answered. 'They came through here in the fifties, and what's this place, sixty-nine, seventy-six? You showed me the deeds.'

'Mr. Allsop had visions of the place out in the open fields.' Mrs. Butler.

'You don't stick a house in the middle of nowhere. This would belong to, oh, I don't know, one of the small dye works or hosiery chaps along the river. Not much of—well, not a palace. I expect he'd move into the Park if he prospered or build his own mansion, and that would be out in the fields somewhere. Carriage-drive, grey slate and trees. Eighteeneighties—nineties.'

'Isn't it a bit late starting?' Bernard asked. 'In the seventies.'

'May well be. Don't know. All sorts of little concerns got under way, did well or fizzled out. I don't know. You're the historian, aren't you?'

They both knew, then, something about him.

'We wanted to meet you,' Mrs. Butler said, once they were engaged with drinks. 'Jacqueline has talked a lot about you.'

'On the phone,' Butler said. 'She never comes out to see us.'

'Daddy. That's not true.'

'My husband loves to get people arguing,' Mrs. Butler claimed. 'He enjoys quarrels. I think it's with living in India. It's something to do with the liver.'

'And all those chota pegs and bara pegs.' Jacqueline.

'Women, women.' Butler coughed again. Bernard had the impression that the old chap liked playing a demented colonel. 'Still, we thought we might as well have a squint at you.' He laughed, choking. 'Nothing like an inspection.'

The last remark led to an anecdote about some friend on tour in the Central Provinces investigating a snake who had bitten a woman, repented, sucked out the venom which it had then squirted into a bowl of milk. This was delivered in perfect innocence, as if he believed every word, but the background was carefully realistic, and flurries of Hindustani, translated at Bernard, spiced the telling. Butler talked well, listened to the frequent interruptions of his women-folk, turned them to his advantage by introducing some further anecdote or remembered phrase, smell, cameo. The younger man enjoyed the half-hour.

When the two women went out to prepare supper, the father stood, poured himself more whisky, and eased himself puffing back into the chair.

'Jacqueline tells me you're thinking of getting married. Is that so?' Before Bernard had the chance to reply he was off again. 'Don't mind my talking like this to you. I don't bother myself much about preliminary negotiations. Now in the Far East . . .' There followed, however, two sentences only of illustrative material, and he was back to his topic. The winding narrative, with a welcome for every opportunity to digress, of the earlier evening was out. 'We were a bit surprised, y'know. I'll be blunt. When Jacqueline got married before (you don't mind mention o' that, do you?), we hardly thought Ike Ridell was her type. Her mother was, in fact, quite upset. But he was, oh, y'know, forceful, getting there, and that's what the girl had always liked.'

'Yes.'

'Not that I'm saying it was perfect. Ike worked too hard. Jacqueline's self-reliant, but she likes some attention. They all do. He'd not always got the time. On holiday, of course, he did her well. A fortnight's high-powered pleasure. Still, that's neither here nor there. Let's get on to you. You're something at the university, aren't you?'

'A research student.'

'That means you're not earning anything. When you've finished, qualified yourself, what will you do?'

'Teach, probably. If I can't get a university job, then it'll be in a school.'

'When?'

'I'll have it tied up in just over a year's time, I hope,' Bernard said.

'Will you get married before that?'

'Well . . .'

'Ah. You're hesitating. I see. Looks bad, doesn't it? Let's say it plainly, shall we? You'll be living on Jacqueline's money. Now, now, steady. Don't bite my head off. Do you like the idea?' He laughed.

'Well,' Bernard said. 'I don't know.'

'In what way?' Mr. Butler was slopping the dregs round his glass, his head cocked to one side. His expression was benevolent, inquiring. Bernard liked the idea of marriage, and the sooner the better, but couldn't say just that. That she had money was, he supposed, part of the attraction; he had not sorted it out in such detail.

'Anything I say will pretty well damn me,' he answered.

Butler looked up.

'Not at all. Most men would marry money if the other things were right. You seem a bit diffident, quiet.'

'In what way?' As soon as Bernard had spoken the words they seemed an ironic echo of Butler's earlier question, but he noticed nothing.

'You're very non-committal. You don't say much for yourself. You're presentable, and presumably clever in your own line, but . . . You see what I mean. You couldn't sit in a room with Ike Ridell for half an hour without learning something about him. Frankly, I don't care too much for what I did learn, but I'm old-fashioned, and when I see the damn-fool way my own son, who's getting on for forty, no, over, capers round, I've nothing to boast about, I suppose, but there you are, there you are.'

'You mean, you can't think why Jacqueline's attracted to me?' Bernard brought the words out carefully. His listener didn't know, but it was a fair imitation of Professor Bryn Meredith in a tutorial, sorting out the exact question that a few pages of fuzzy verbiage had failed to pose or answer.

'Yes. That's about the strength of it.'

'Surely it would be sensible to ask her.'

Butler looked at him very hard, before dropping his arms over the sides of the windsor chair he was in.

'Do you think it's reaction to the tycoon type?' Bernard asked, smiling. He was angry. The old man had exceeded his licence. He was not having it all his own way.

'Likely,' Butler said, yawning, putting his glass down. 'Might be.'

'I take it,' Bernard said, 'that your impression of me is not altogether favourable?'

'Come, now. She's older than you, isn't she? Big enough to know her own mind? Uh. I can sit here and ask awkward questions all night, and I'll tell you, now, that they won't alter her decisions by one iota. But that doesn't mean I shan't ask them. Parents might have abdicated from their responsibilities nowadays. Let their sons and daughters clear off and marry in their teens to unsuitable partners. Well, there it is. But I'm doing my useless bit here clearing my mind and yours for you.'

'Yes.'

'What's your father say?'

'He hasn't said anything, really.'

'He knows?' Mr. Butler's voice was sharp.

'Yes.'

'You think you're going to be happy with Jacqueline?' Bernard did not answer. 'Will you live here? In this house?'

'I haven't thought about it.'

'Don't you think it about time you had, then? I don't want to be rude, Bernard, but you seem unprepared. You can't get

53

married as you go to the theatre or on a half-day trip to the seaside.'

They sat together, very still. Bernard felt the blood drumming in his head. Butler was saying, in fact, what he had often set about putting to himself. His questions were better organised than the old man's, more concise, more wounding. It was true that he'd often thought the relationship with Jacqueline was unreal. She was sexually attractive, she was older, more experienced, wedded; she had money, a car, a wider circle of friends. He ought to have disliked such a person, out of envy, and so he would if she had not said she loved him. That altered it. But when he grew older, maturer, more experienced, when his superior intelligence, stricter training, greater opportunities were given moving space, what would the relationship be then? She had tried at nineteen what he was about to test now. That gave her the advantage for the present. Present? But this claim of his to a sharper intelligence? What was that but a defence against his present, admitted disabilities?

Over the other side of the room Butler was breathing heavily and patting his Kaiser's hair with closed fingers.

'We haven't made much progress, you and I, have we?' he said.

'Oh, I don't know.'

'No. I don't deceive myself. I've had a fair experience of dealing with men. An engineer's job isn't only stresses and strains on metal and concrete. It's on men.' To Bernard that sounded pretentious, though it was delivered distantly, breathily enough. "Not crowns and thrones, but men." 'More often than not I had to convince some petty official that heaven wouldn't devastate the place with plague if I threw a bridge over the local river in a sacred spot.' 'Threw.' What was his line now? The expansive man? The old clod was off again. His head rested horizontally on the back of his chair so that his words rose straight up, like smoke on a windless day, were difficult to catch. 'And India is not the only place of taboos. Though I remember one occasion; it was in the

Bombay province . . .' There followed an anecdote telling how he had been stoned by children out of a ramshackle village. 'Had to pick up m'theodolite and run for it. Not more than a dozen or fifteen. Damn' nasty. Couldn't tell a word they were saying. Must have been Marathi; supposed to be somewhat like Hindustani, but I couldn't . . . Turned out there'd been some soldiers round the place, after the women. Of course, I don't know. Never could tell out there.'

The ladies returned with trays.

'*Thik hai, sahib?*' Jacqueline said, saluting, laughing.

'*Baghal meri chhuri, munh men Rām Rām.*'

'What's that mean?' Bernard asked, when Jacqueline and her mother went out.

'A polite greeting in the mouth, on the lips, y'know, and a dagger under the armpit.' He was launched on a digression about methods of greeting. Again his head was right back; his neck bulged purple, but words rose delicately. The trays of eatables were set in the middle of the room; coffee was poured.

'Has Daddy given you some good advice?' Jacqueline asked, when all were seated.

'Well, er, yes. I suppose he has, in a way.'

'You don't seem very certain.'

'If you listen to my husband, Mr. Allsop, you'll find a certain substratum of sense in what he's saying.'

'But it needs some digging out,' Butler said.

'You said that, Fred, now. I didn't.'

'We all thought it.' Jacqueline.

They laughed politely, and ate the savoury bits Jacqueline had put round. Butler did not eat much, although he made large gestures, achieved facial athletics. His forehead was only lightly lined, but the wrinkles round his eyes were scored deeply. He did not look his age, sixty-six; there was, however, about him some appearance of ruin, as if he were the handsome wreckage of his younger, powerful self. He sat well back into his chair, twisted, as though waiting for a violent spasm of indigestion. His hands dwarfed his coffee-cup.

'We don't know your parents, do we, Mr. Allsop?' Mrs. Butler said.

'Call him Bernard, Mother.' She sounded cross.

'If he doesn't mind. Do you?'

'No.'

'Your parents,' she insisted. There was something hard about this woman. Bernard nodded, but that was unsatisfactory. 'We won't have met them, will we?'

'I don't suppose so.'

There was a pause. Butler fumbled for another dry biscuit. Bernard picked his cup from the table, timidly.

'My mother wants to know where you live, your father's occupation, and,' she turned, rather maliciously to her mother, 'was there anything else?'

'324, Forest Side,' he said. 'Chief clerk at Smallwood's.'

'Chief clerk?' Mrs. Butler said, with the air of lip-licking satisfaction. 'Yes. Yes. And your mother? Is she pleased about the engagement?'

'She's very ill.' Suddenly he was sickened; she hadn't bothered to mention that to her parents.

'Nothing serious, I hope.' Sweet as the coffee.

'Cancer.'

That stopped her. Trickle your treacle round that.

'I'm sorry, Bernard,' she said, and put a hand out, on to his arm. She was still wearing gloves. 'Incurable?'

'Yes.'

Butler was looking at him like a curious child, and loudly scratching his cheek with the nail of his forefinger. He hadn't shaved.

'Incurable.' At the word Bernard was stabbed with fright. Mrs. Butler had been shocked into this question which should not have been asked, or perhaps was pandering to an acquired social gaucherie, and now presumably her husband would begin the expected rescue, mumble about miracles, marvellous what they could do, never give up hope, and the rest. Bernard looked about him. Suddenly all was flat; nothing mattered; he did not care. This should have been the moment of the serious television playwright, when all's malicious, even normality. It was not so. Four people had sat in a room making unsatisfactory conversation.

In fact, there was a longish silence before Butler hitched his trousers high up his legs and said, sipping:

'If you put salt in coffee, can you taste it?'

Jacqueline exploded into laughter, clapped her hand on his shoulder. Both women shrieked in with information about taste-buds, mildish invective, sarcastic queries, but they were all relieved, delighted. Before the evening was done, they had discussed the exact date of the wedding, its form, grants, whether Jacqueline should take a job, the upbringing of children, religion, festivals, gods. In the end Butler shook Bernard's hand, said:

'I've enjoyed meeting you. Don't let her boss you about, Bernard. That's the mistake I made.' He smirked.

'He's done what he liked all his life,' Mrs. Butler said, 'without reference to me or anybody else.'

'I've disguised my virtues.'

'Very successfully,' Jacqueline said.

'I hope you're never inflicted with a daughter like this.'

'You spoil her,' Mrs. Butler said.

'She didn't need much help.'

'Heredity,' Jacqueline said. 'Outside. You'll ruin his character as well.'

Bernard went to the back door where he stood to watch the three walking together to the car. They were arm-in-arm, in a bunch all talking, the man's bass rumbling under the shrill women's voices. Close, united, knit.

When Jacqueline came back she threw herself into a chair, blew out breath, and said, 'Not so bad, eh?'

'They seemed . . .'

'Come and give us a kiss.' The plural marred the command, made a game of what was intimately serious, but he knelt by her, laid his head on her belly.

'Did you like them?' she asked.

'Yes.' Muffled.

'They'll go home and talk about us for two or three days. That's what they always do. Daddy'll spout most; then Mummy will make her mind up, and that'll be that.'

'She wears the trousers?'

'I wouldn't say that,' she said, apparently hardly aware of his hand stroking her flank, moving to cover her breast. 'If it were a case for a new car, or TV, he'd decide. I suppose he thinks this is her prerogative.' She pulled his head up by his hair, urgently, kissed him hard. His head was thrust back so that the pain in his neck was unbearable. 'Oh, you brute, you.'

'You've broken my neck.'

She slipped to the floor with him, and they lay on the carpet, pressed together, straining.

'Nice,' she said, dragging her mouth free, sharp elbow into his chest. 'Wait till we're married, you big boy. I'll tear you apart.'

'Start now,' he said, 'darling.'

'You'll wait,' she said, collapsing across him, fingers in his hair.

7

A LIGHT shone in Mary's bedroom when Bernard arrived back home.

He sat down, pulled his shoes off, rummaged in the corner by the bureau for his slippers. He was not too pleased; he could have shaped better with the Butlers, impressed them. Jacqueline, in his arms, had made him forget his anxiety, forced him to her view that her parents were, for practical purposes, interested strangers, that what was important was between the two, not the four. Now he lacked that ephemeral conviction; the Butlers had not overwhelmed him, but he could have been both more incisive and less self-revelatory, brilliant and reticent. He thought up these phrases on the way home; he often picked round among words for his historical writing as he pushed along the streets. But here they referred to little. Incisive? Cutting? Trenchant? Why must he hanker after exactly what he was not?

The door was pushed open.

His sister stood on the threshold, as she used to when she was small and had come down for a drink, peering. Her hair was tousled.

'Hello,' he said.

'I thought perhaps it was Dad back.'

'Back? Isn't he in bed?'

'No.'

'Where is he then?'

'He's gone to the hospital. He was waiting for me when I came in. He said: "I've got to go to the hospital, Mary. Mother's worse." He'd stayed till I came back.'

'What time was this?' Bernard asked.

'Just before nine. I'd only come in for an apple, really. We were up on the Common.'

'You didn't go out again?' he asked.

She shook her head. Her dressing-gown was short, and shabby, pulled in tight at the waist by a frayed silk cord.

'How did he know?' Bernard began.

'I don't know. I suppose Mrs. Grainger brought a phone message. They've got her number for emergencies.'

'I wonder when that would be. You say he waited until you came?'

'Yes.'

He was frightened, and heavy. For long enough he'd been preparing himself for this, but the news shattered him. Mary still stood in the doorway.

'Shall I make us a cup of cocoa?' he said.

'No.' Her face brightened. She tugged the cord. 'I'll do it.'

He opened his jacket, stroked his chin, tried to prevent the leaden trembling of his lower lip as he stared at the clock on the wall, the picture of a cottage garden in high summer, the biscuit-barrel with its silver bands and shield. With surprise, he noticed the harsh sound of his breathing. He stopped the noise so as not to frighten Mary, who was clattering in the kitchen. Perhaps his father had left a note. With both children out, the poor man wouldn't know where to turn. He could have rung Jacqueline's. Or Mrs. Grainger would have come in to wait for the girl's return, would have been glad to, decent, inquisitive woman. Bernard wasn't sure that he shouldn't, even now, get his bike and go to the hospital. Or ring. Mary came back with the drinks.

'I wonder how Dad'll get home,' she said.

'He might be there all night.' Calm. The child was frightened. He felt slightly sick, and tender, as if each pore of his body was a point of incipient pain. His eyes, his finger-nails were touched with an ache. He was cold.

'I hope Mum's all right,' Mary said in the end, finishing her drink.

'She won't be in any pain.'

Another pause until he put his cup down.

'Shall I wash these?' she asked, standing.

'No. You get back to bed.'

'Will you ring?'

'Yes. I'll do that.'

As she went out and upstairs, he stood. Shivers creased his back; his face and throat were tight, as if cased in a thin clay mask. He sat down again to savour his own indecision, to compare it with his father's. Upstairs Mary was still stumbling about. The old man found it hard to make his mind up. Should he run down to the hospital? Would a note in an empty house frighten Mary? Was she near death? Or some hours off? What would it be like, this death he had been imagining for weeks? He would, Bernard knew, have groped about the place, leaning on this chair, touching that talisman, letting his mouth hang open. And all the time the physical pangs of fright, the movement of bowels, the sickness, the cold in the limbs, had plagued him.

Bernard, afflicted, lacerating himself as a prophylactic against new grief, got up again, called upstairs.

'Are you in bed yet?'

'Yes.'

'I'm going to phone.' No answer. 'Shall I lock the doors?'

'No.'

'You'll be all right?'

'Don't be long.' Her voice was stronger as if she'd sat up. He put on his light mac, smoothed his hair by the hallstand mirror, and grasped the bottom wooden pillar of the banisters, pressing his face to the smooth coolness. He jerked himself upright.

' 'Bye, then,' he shouted upstairs, opened the front door. There he stopped again to make sure he had the change before he hitched his collar and started.

There was one street to cross at the top of the hill before he reached the phone-box. It was, not long ago, he remembered, cobbled, but now had been covered with some sort of tarry composition. On the corner he stopped, rubbed his right shoe on the back of the left trouser leg. His father approached him, walking slowly, almost waddling, not taking the short cut over the waste ground, keeping to the pavement although it was clear he had not seen his son. For a moment it looked as if he were about to turn past Bernard without speaking, but at the last moment, comically even, he lifted his head, moved his cloth cap slightly higher on his skull. Without a greeting, Bernard swung round and together, in step, they walked the sixty yards downhill.

'How was she?' the son asked.

'Oh, oh. Not, not so bad.'

'No worse?'

'Oh, no. No.'

The son straightened his back with relief, held the gate open. When they were in the hall, which the two seemed awkwardly to crowd, Bernard, the new man, stalked upstairs to tell Mary. She was fast asleep. He'd been out less than five minutes and she was down, under the sheet, the crown of her head barely showing. He spoke, softly; she did not move.

Allsop was sitting by the grate, hands clasped between his knees. Bernard made, brought in a cup of cocoa.

'Teaspoonful of brandy in it?' he said. Father nodded. There followed the clambering to the cupboard's top for the half-flask, the rattle in the cutlery drawer for the 'medicine' spoon; the measuring.

Allsop sipped, staring at the pegged rug.

'How was she then?'

'All right. All right.' The words were whispered. Bernard, tense still, sensed an eddy of affection for his father, who, knocked about by the call and what he'd found, quietly re-assured his son. Perhaps she'd gone off to sleep. That was odd, unbelievable. The authorities didn't send phone calls out for nothing. If they'd summoned his father, it was because his mother was dying. Perhaps a mistake had been made, some inexperienced house-surgeon had lost his judgement momentarily. Would his father know that? They'd cover up at the hospital. He looked downwards at his father, who was warming hands round the cup, gingerly lowering his lips.

'Did you let Aunt Jessie know?' he asked.

'No. I didn't.'

She'd be furious. If there was to be death, she must witness it.

'I wondered. I thought if you'd sent them a message I'd nip down and tell them that everything was, er, was . . .'

'At this time of night?' his father asked.

'They'd be waiting up, wouldn't they?' And he thought of Mary, asleep. 'Who let you know? Did they ring Mrs. Grainger?'

Allsop looked up, stricken, drank eagerly.

'Eh?' He shook his head, as if recovering from a blow.

Bernard could not think why he persisted with this useless inquiry. His father was dog-tired, could barely understand English just now. The old man had been temporarily molli-fied; there would be no crisis this day. But. Perhaps she'd died. And the father was shielding them, giving them one more clear night's sleep while he took the worst of the battering. His stomach contracted. He gripped the table hard so that his arms shook in ague. Dead. His mother. Cold.

'Did they phone Mrs. Grainger?'

The damn-fool question again. Asked.

His father made a little noise, a kind of moaning grunt, then gulped. Bernard reached for his cup. Allsop's hands were trembling, thin as his wife's deadened white.

'They . . . There . . .'

He stopped, made a pass in the air with his right hand, opened his mouth. Silence and pain crowded the place. Both men breathed, crudely loud.

'There wasn't a phone call,' Allsop said.

Bernard stared, blank as a saucepan, stupid-faced.

'How did you know then?' he asked.

His father looked away, towards the empty grate, and straightening himself opened his eyes wide.

'There wasn't any message.' The words were loudly enunciated, the first strong sounds by either since the return. They cracked mildly violent.

'Not from the hospital?'

'Not from anybody.'

'But you told Mary . . . ?'

'I know I did.'

Bernard stood up, backed away from his father, carried the cup into the kitchen where he lowered it, like a relic, into the sink.

'You might have frightened her to death,' he said, standing in the doorway.

'I don't know.'

'Think of that child, on her own, here, imagining all sorts of things.'

His father shrugged, giving up, then turned away.

The movements appalled Bernard. Allsop, who'd patiently watched and endured his wife's dying, who'd seen to it that his children were not inconvenienced, disturbed from routine, had now tumbled to this idiocy. Anger was replaced, quickly. Mary may have been frightened, but what about a decent, selfless, peaceable man and this fantasy? He'd waited so long, so hard, alone, for the message that in the end his thrashed and

63

lacerated nerves had delivered it for him. That was barely believable. Not here; not this person. Allsop stood by the mantelpiece, one hand out, begging, bent.

Bernard went across, took his father's elbow, jogged it and said: 'We'd better get upstairs. It's late.'

'Yes.'

'Would you like a hot water-bottle?'

'It isn't cold.' The voice was normal. 'I don't know why I did it, Bernie.' His mother often used the diminutive; his father never. 'When Mary came in, I just said it. I knew what I was doing.' Eyes solemnly lifted. 'I deliberately said it, quite deliberately said it.'

'Did you think,' Bernard asked, puzzled, very slow, 'it, it was true?'

His father pushed hands into his trousers' pockets, a movement for which he often used to check his son. His stance was jaunty, raffish.

'I didn't think it was true. In fact, I knew it wasn't. I couldn't resist the temptation to, to say those words out, aloud, to somebody. If it had been you, I don't think I would. Mary doesn't ask any questions.'

'Well. Yes. Come on to bed.'

Allsop stood, looked round in his helpless way before he began a methodical search of the catches on windows, the locks on doors.

'I'll see to that, Dad. You go to bed. You look whacked.'

Bernard went up first, switched the light on, drew his father's curtains. He'd never done that before, and the room, its double bed still with two sets of pillows, smelt cold and stale.

'You'll be all right?' he asked.

Allsop was surprised at that, sounded indignant, so that the boy shut the door quickly and started downstairs.

'Bernard.' His father's voice fetched him back at the run. 'Don't forget to lock up properly.'

Deeply disappointed, he went down, stopping on each step, tugging at the banister until it creaked, fighting it out. His father did not look exceptionally weary, nor moved; his voice was indecisive, colourless as usual. He was not different and yet he had done something that could only be described as lunacy.

Bernard threw himself into a chair, twisted his features, pulled his fingers, wrapped a leg round the other, contorting himself to make sense of the senseless. His father had perhaps pleased himself. All these years this vague, polite, loving man had never once, in public at least, pandered to himself and now he'd taken advantage of Mary's weakness and credulity, had eased himself by harming her. But the action was too crude; it was against the nature of the man to do anything without blurring the edges, misting the effect, smoking the glass.

That way madness lies.

He was away, drawing fine words round the affair, dressing it for a first paragraph. It was history now. The treaties and intrigues, the clashes and deaths, organised by some scores and marring or making the lives of some thousands, millions of human beings which he treated so slickly in twenty pages with thirty-nine learned footnotes were perhaps as, no, were certainly as complex as this. And he had twenty years' experience of his father by which to judge this evening's aberration. Those Luddites of his, meeting in the dark; those employers, magistrates, officers; about those he had some scanty reminiscence or, inaccurate, biassed, contemporary note, some street-corner scurrility, some judicial rotundity that robbed the protagonists of their human kind. If he went to Professor Meredith and gave him an account of this evening's performance, what would that man of learning do but hum and stroke his chin and speak like any chapel-deacon about understanding and strain and charity? And yet both of them would generalise or argue or pontificate about some unfortunate workman who nearly a century and a half ago had gone with his mates to smash a machine.

Bernard amazed himself.

It was remarkable that he could sit here, getting hot under

the collar about the truth of history, while his father went mad. That was too strong. Just as he had found comfort in condemning historical judgements, so his father had eased his distress with this lie. His own thoughts were harmless, beneficial, largely indulged in. 'All history consists of intense simplification,' Meredith said in his inaugural lecture, 'and to that extent is wrong, fictitious. But this is a necessity if the subject is to exist at all. We must choose one fact, or a few, out of a thousand at our disposal, because it is salient, typical, significant, makes the most sense when compared with our knowledge of the real world of our experience and the fainter world of literature, of other historians' writing.'

Ernest Allsop's behaviour was inexcusable.

The son stood up, stared at himself in the mirror, found he was observing nothing. A mild dizziness almost drove him back to his chair, but by the time he had reached the kitchen his head was clear. He locked the door, bolted it, undid his work and walked the garden path. It was warmer out than indoors and as he stood, one hand on the rough concrete of a clothes-post, biting his lip at the Great Bear over the black terrace of houses on the horizon, he shivered. His wits wandered. Without hurry, he looked round the garden, listened to footsteps in the street beyond, admired the halo of light from a distant gas-lamp, stepped inside again and locked up. Slowly he went to his father's bedroom.

'Are you asleep, Dad?'

No answer. He moved over, stood beside the bed, spoke a second time, was left unanswered. Carefully, meticulously, he moved the sheets up to his father's chin and touched his hair. Protective. Elder brother. Child, father to man.

'Good night, Dad,' he whispered, histrionically.

As he reached the door a voice said:

'Good night, Bernard.'

His father was not asleep. That tissue-paper-thin voice shocked. All the time he had fiddled with the sheets, posturing, posing, the old man had been lying there awake, taking it in. Dark, dark. He'd enough to afflict himself with without his son's poses.

'Are you all right?' he said, back into the room.

His father turned, snuffled, did not reply. As the son stood in the corridor that movement on the right side of the bed acted as a salve. A person who could turn over in bed to find a more comfortable position was sane. As soon as this flush of feeling was turned into words, and he made the translation immediately, he laughed at its simplicity. At this moment in every lunatic asylum in England, hopeless cases were turning, twisting over. He could not dispel the momentary relief to himself. Tomorrow his father would act as he always did.

Bernard was awake early, and, contrary to custom, went downstairs and prepared an elaborate breakfast. He enjoyed this, taking care to put out a clean cloth, set the covers, use the best silver coffee-pot, in contrast to the usual haphazard buttering and swallowing of burnt toast, the slopping of tepid or boiling coffee into mugs. He carried tea upstairs and announced that breakfast was in fifteen minutes.

Allsop got up immediately, shaved and talked to Mary. The pair came down together. Both were clearly surprised at the care Bernard had taken, and all three enjoyed the almost leisurely meal. The son watched his father's fulsome attention to the daughter. He pressed the child to second helpings she did not want, chose the most delicious pieces for her, chatted to her, or rather sought information about a notorious pop-group. Mary did not understand the reason for this sudden interest, was embarrassed by it, but answered without malice, though once or twice she pulled faces at the brother over the ineptitude of the questions. She, for her part, did not inquire about her mother.

When Allsop left for work, Bernard, stacking dishes away, said:

'Mother wasn't any worse.'

'Oh. Good.' She said this like some old schoolma'am, hearing that the pencils and rubbers had already been collected in.

'Did Dad say anything?'

'No.'

'Not this morning? I heard him talking to you.'

'No,' Mary said. 'He came in while I was making my bed, and asked me if I was all right. I told him I was and then he just said, "We've got to look after you" and went on about the value of health and not overdoing it and this was a very hard time for me. I didn't know what to say.'

'Why not?'

'It wasn't like him, really.'

'Who was it like, then?' he said, laughing at her. She scratched her head.

'I don't know. He's got it on him sometimes, hasn't he? I thought he just wanted to say something to me, and came in and spouted that lot.'

'Why?'

'I don't know, do I?' she said. 'Perhaps because you took him a cup of tea and got the breakfast. He was chuff then. All that about the Lady-killers. How many children had Frank got? and all that. He doesn't want to know, now, does he?' She tightened the belt of the yellow cotton frock, summer uniform. Suddenly, he saw her objectively. She might be eighteen, grown up, sexually mature. 'Are you going to the university today?'

'I am.'

'Fancy doing History all day.'

'Not fancy, reality,' he said.

'What are you doing?' she asked.

'I'm trying to sort out just what happened to some machine-breakers hereabouts in 1811.'

'Don't they know? They're Luddites, aren't they? We did them the other day. Captain Ned Ludd.'

'The Leicester idiot?' he said. Appropriate maniac faces.

'How do you find out?' she said.

'First of all, you see what the books say, the printed books.'

'You can have mine,' she said, laughing, 'and about thirty others from our class.'

'And then,' he went on, seriously, 'you look at contemporary documents. Newspapers, for instance.'

'Did they have them?'

He shook a magisterial finger at her.

'And city records, parliamentary reports, Byron's famous effort, and correspondence, diaries, if they exist.'

'Do they?'

'Yes. I'm lucky. An old chap called Lackberry, he died in 1913, was very interested. He'd got some idea his grandfather was implicated and he started getting stuff together about, oh, about 1880, when he'd made a bit of money, and by the time he snuffed it he'd picked up reams of papers. He was always advertising for more here, and in Derby and Leicester. When he died somebody just bundled the lot together into a trunk and forgot about it. A great-granddaughter found it all a few years ago, and presented it to the 'varsity and Professor Meredith set me on to sort it out.'

'The Lackberry Archives,' she shouted, with a flourish of television trumpets.

'He was a funny old bird. He collected meticulously, in all the right places. He borrowed documents and copied them out in beautiful copper-plate. No typist then. He was looking, I suppose, for this ancestor of his. And every book that was published, if it had only one sentence about the Luddites, Lackberry bought it.'

'And what had his ancestor done?' Mary asked. 'Got himself hanged?'

'As far as I know, there's absolutely no mention of him at all.'

'He didn't exist.'

'I'm not saying that. There must have been no end of people who took part in machine-breaking and got away with it. Only the notorious, the leaders, and the caught are named. But a curious thing happened. Old Lackybody was born in 1840, and he started collecting seriously, I should say, in the 1880's. About 1895, when he was convinced that he wasn't going to find his man, he started inventing him for himself. There was a quite thick wad of papers. I thought they were copies of something or other. But it was a diary he'd fabricated, "The Journal of Thomas Lackberry, alias Colonel Ned Ludd". He made out that this man was a sort of director-general, that he planned this outburst here, or that riot. He'd got his work cut out, sometimes, I can tell you, to square this account with the facts, because the jobs he mentioned are nearly all authentic.'

'Why did he do that?'

'Write it? He started off in a modest way, really. Something like a short story, but it obsessed him by the time he'd done.'

'Is it very interesting?'

'It is. It's a bit wooden, literary, you know. He had his grandfather living up Castlegate. He was a cobbler and a lay-preacher. People picked messages up in his shop, but nobody suspected he was the writer. He never spoke about such things, and when questioned said he didn't want to know anything. There's some wonderful detail. One night they took a boy with them and he fell out of an upstairs window where he was keeping watch and broke his neck. A man called Jack Robinson carried the body back to Basford from somewhere up near St. Mary's. Just imagine staggering back with a corpse in his arms to the mother.'

'How did old Blackberry know about this, then?'

'He had accomplices who knew who he was.'

'What happened about the boy?'

'The mother,' Bernard said, 'thought they'd killed him and wanted to go to the magistrates, but her husband was frightened, didn't let her. They gave it out that the lad was sleep-walking or something of the kind. It's quite exciting, these whisperings and arguments and the boy there stiff in the position he'd been carried.'

'I wish you took us for History,' she said.

He laughed. 'Who takes you this year?'

'Miss Bagguley.'

'Old Betty Baggy-Knickers.' He pinched his face in and

began to dictate in the mistress's manner. 'There are some points of outstanding interest that should be noted. Full stop. One, colon; Lackberry was himself a factory owner so that his interest in the destruction of machinery was, comma, to say the least, comma, curious. Full stop. Two, colon: Lackberry was a strict, evangelical Anglican. Full stop. He depicted his ancestor as a hypocritical nonconformist who was, comma, in reality, comma, little more than a blatant agnostic. Full stop.'

They sniffed together in the Bagguley style.

'Three, colon.'

8

THE TWENTY-FIFTH of Brahms's variations on a theme of Handel clanged through the high barn-like room. William Riley, hands flailing into ectoplasm, crashed his way across the great dancing chords but checked himself before the fugue and turned on his leather piano-stool. Silence swamped the place like a thunderstorm.

Riley flicked the top off a beer-bottle, poured fizz, drank with a grimace. The young woman who'd been leaning over the top of the upright piano during the last shattering minutes walked round and stood by him like a guard. He raised the beer to her; she lifted it from his hands, took a swig. Tom Butler came across, put his arm round her waist, smacked her belly under mustard slacks, said to Riley:

'Time somebody spoke.'

'Go on then.'

'What about you?'

'Age before honour.'

'Right,' Butler said, 'and bugger you, then, Jackie-boy. Give us a chord.' Riley smacked down, rolled an octave of the lowest A with his left and smashed into plain Es, E flats, in octaves with his right. Chatter was insignificantly diminished.

Butler pulled a chair towards himself, stood on it. The woman in the slacks perched face-up below him, an urchin at a kerb-side meeting. Butler took a playfully ineffective swipe at her head. A few lined themselves.

'Ladies and gentlemen,' he said. Noise dropped, apart from a violence of giggles from a group in a far corner. 'Ladies and gentlemen,' he bawled. The errant party turned about. Not a glass clinked. Faces composed themselves into seriousness. 'First I must thank you for coming here. In the dark, as it were. Just as we thank Bill Riley and the kind people who organised this studio for us and the beer.' Butler blew his nose. 'You may wonder why you've come. I hope you do, and I hope you're putting two and two together. Oh, don't worry. You can keep your cheque-books buttoned away and the moths cooped up in your handbags. The only thing we want you to do tonight is to circulate, drink the ale and get to know one another.' He crossed one leg over the other, pointing the toe. 'There are some of us who think that this town is culturally dead. Where can you hear any music written after 1930, or even 1895? Modern poetry? Paintings that matter to you? Sculpture that'll keep you awake? And I don't mean cliques! Meet me at the Theatre Bar or the Tuesday Music Club or the Little Thespians for a cup of Camp Coffee and a polish for your glass eye. What good's that?'

Bernard Allsop, standing by a window, watched the performance. Six paces away from him Jacqueline had parked herself, ridiculous and beautiful in navy and white, her face held as if she were listening to a saint.

'So what happened was this. An unofficial culture-committee, a few interested, biassed bigots, zealots, maniacs, call us what you like, got our heads together and wrote out a list of people who might be expected to raise a finger to help the arts. We clubbed together for the ale, and sent the invitations out. You've come. You've picked yourselves. The culture commandos.'

Bernard was displeased.

He'd received no invitation. What he had wanted was to

talk to Jacqueline about his father. It was likely that she would have listened carelessly, offered no advice, no comment, but his act of confession would have eased him, and bound the pair of them closer. Instead, when he arrived, he'd found her fretting at the door with a hat on, dressed to kill, out of temper as he was ten minutes late, ready to rush him into the car and out to Railton, seven miles away, to this party.

'I don't know what you think,' Butler continued, 'but we say it's about time this place woke up, culturally speaking. And, what we're trying to do for a start, is to get a centre, where we can meet, hear, see, talk. ("Meet, drink and be merry," said a bystander, louder.) You may have some suggestions. I hope so, but if you haven't, we have.'

The expected ribaldry was absent.

Jacqueline, angry, had been magnificent.

The delicate nose-end was white, and she sniffed frequently, but her face was set into a kind of perfection of stillness, as if she had frozen her features into stony attraction. When she spoke her voice was lower in pitch, softer in sound, as if suggesting that she meant to be reasonable. She answered only when absolutely necessary. Sometimes, not often, but with high deliberation, she turned to stare, as if she could barely believe what she had heard and needed other visual evidence. Her hands took up formal poses, crossed on lap, straight downwards, as she sat, on her hips with elbows pointed, or clasped across the knees as if indicating her everyday approach to the ridiculous situation in which she found herself. Bernard had no idea how to deal with her; he sulked.

'We've got a festival going in the autumn from the 17th of October. Not a full-fig affair, but something happening twice a week for about a month, some exhibitions permanently open. There'll be music, some small-scale drama, poetry, some pictures worth seeing and one hell of a lot of talk. You can pull faces about that, but we want you to talk this business up; tell everybody, interested or not. There are something like forty bodies here tonight; if you really set yourself about it, we'd have the town seething in no time. And the other thing's this. We've got this skeleton programme out, but if you can add to it, in some way, with something striking, we'll be glad. The more the better. But we haven't got much time, and a fair part of that you'll spend baking yourselves black on the Costa Brava. You'll see cyclostyled copies of the outline programme. Take it. Learn it. Spread it. That's all from me. Get to know one another. Tell us where we've gone wrong, if you like. Bill Riley'll talk to you in a bit.'

The only person to move was Bernard.

He joined the group in front of him, a very tall man with a thin neck and a double-chin, a young man with curly hair, and three women in their late thirties with thick legs and devil-rimmed spectacles. They paid no attention to him, continuing to listen to one of the females.

'Of course, it isn't a blind bit of good talking to him.' The voice was sour Midland.

'He's not so bad, Vera. Give him his due. I'm not saying that he's perfect, mind, but he's not such a bad sort, when you get to know him.'

'Get to know,' the third voice said. 'You ask Madge Tallifer. And it was a case of theft, there, just pilfering.'

'She's one to talk,' said the second. 'She's hardly . . .'

Bernard shoved on past the men who did not speak, clutched their empty glasses, failed to smile. He reached the corner group, younger people, tights, long hair, thick-sided specs, faint lipstick, deep eye-shadow.

'They make twenty to twenty-five a night,' a youth was saying, 'and they'll get five engagements a week. That's money. Two of 'em.'

'Not at this time of the year.'

'At this time of the year. I'll tell you something, now, mate. You think because they're not at the Troc or the Astoria or Percy Plonker's every night they're not anywhere. You don't know how many private parties are on.'

'At twenty quid a knock?'

'At twenty quid. And more. There must be a hundred factories round here and all they've got to do is shift the

74

tables out of the canteen and they're off. And that's just here. They go to Brum, Stoke, Derby, Leicester, Lincoln. Last week they were in Bradford three nights and then Workington. They aren't amateurs.'

'Ed. Speckley's not been to work for eighteen months, now.'

Bernard got round.

Three men were discussing some architectural project; in another group, half women, a smoking-room story was rehearsed. Two quiet girls, early twenties, were holding tumblers of beer like bombs.

'Hello,' Bernard said. They seemed pleased with the greeting. 'Do you know anybody?'

'One or two,' the elder girl said, poking hair from her eyes with the left hand. She was married. Her hair hung in troughy waves, like a tennis star of the thirties.

'We know most of these,' the younger said. She wore a wedding ring.

'And wished you didn't,' he said.

'Oh, I don't know.' The younger again. 'We've come with my father.'

'Are you sisters, then?'

'No. Everybody says that. But we don't look alike, or talk alike or anything.'

'No,' said Bernard, dashed.

'Who's that over there? That very tall man, chatting Mary Ramples up?' The elder seemed excited. 'Very blond hair.'

'Oh, it's what's-his-name, the—er—furniture-fellow. Father owns the chain stores.'

'Not—er—the Elsie-Thingammy's?'

'Yes, that's right. He looks a pain in the neck.'

'I don't know.'

Both laughed, and noticed Bernard's incomprehension, and laughed again. Neither offered an explanation. William Riley erupted from the group round the piano and leapt on the chair. The young woman in the yellow slacks, holding Butler's arm, banged her behind down on the keyboard. The effect was inconsiderable so that Butler had to thump the lid and bawl for attention.

'Bill Riley,' he shouted. 'The founder of the feast.'

'He loathes everybody,' the elder girl said.

'Except himself. Look at Myra Greene, there.' This must have referred to Mustard-slacks who had an arm round Butler's neck and appeared to be trying to climb him. 'Like a monkey.'

'Who's she?' Bernard said.

'Albert Greene's wife. The drama king.'

'Is he here?' Bernard.

'I doubt it. Haven't seen him. Have you, Jean?'

There was time for this unhurried exchange because Riley had bent down and was, still perched on the chair, tying his shoe-lace. He was a small, delicately boned man, with a tiny rat-face and a bush of blond hair, almost silver in its fairness. He jerked upright again, stood puffing.

'I don't want to say much,' he began. 'I want to ask you to talk this Festival up. Tell everybody. Make a nuisance of yourselves.' He spluttered out like a candle, but still stood on the chair.

The tall man, the furniture fellow, put up a hairy-backed hand to attract attention.

'May I ask you a question, Dr. Riley?' His voice was deep, cultured, ponderously slow.

'Yes.' Ungracious.

'There will be some music at this Festival, I take it?'

'Yes.'

'And may I inquire of what sort this music will be?'

'Modern.' Modest, staccato.

' "Modern" is a word that, er, er, cloaks a multitude of meanings. Do you include Sibelius or Elgar, for instance?' His voice purred like a powerful engine.

'No. Not for my choice.'

'But, Dr. Riley, is it your choice? Will it be all Boulez and Stockhausen or even William Riley?'

'Very likely.' Standing on his chair, the musician looked

pale, delicate, like a battered miniature narcissus. He bit his lip, poked a finger into his ear. 'Have you any objection?'

'They're off now,' Jean, the elder girl, said. Bernard noticed a warm hand on his arm.

'Not particularly,' the furniture-fellow answered. 'But what's the use of arranging concerts which everybody will avoid?'

'If by everybody you mean yourself then there's plenty. There's opportunity elsewhere for you to soak up Sir A. Sullivan.'

'Who's he?' Bernard asked Jean, but her companion answered for her.

'Wharton Starkey. His father owned the chain stores.'

'What's he do?'

'I think he's a barrister if he does anything. He's rolling in it.'

'Is the cross-examination over?' Riley was asking from his chair. Starkey shrugged and smiled, thin-lipped, extending his fingers to enjoy the oval nails and visible half-moons. His opponent toppled down, stood hunched by the piano as if he were cold. Myra Greene put an arm on his shoulder as Butler offered a drink. On the ground he looked smaller, wispier, and his khaki tweed coat hung shapelessly shabby. Over at the other side of the room, stiff-back ostentatious, Starkey stood ramrod slim, his sleek hair four inches clear of any other man's.

There had been silence during the exchanges, but now everyone was livelier, circulation began. People laughed out loud.

'Who are you?' the younger girl asked. 'I'm Bettina Clay.'

'Bernard Allsop.'

'How do you get in the act?'

'I'm engaged to Tom Butler's sister.'

'Not Jacqueline Ridell?' A still small voice.

They both stared, rudely. Jean's fingers which had been brushing his coat-sleeve jabbed him hard as if to line him up for inspection.

77

'Do you know her?'

'Oh, sort of,' Jean said. 'She was at school with me. As a matter of fact my brother used to be sweet on her. She was often up at our house. You ask her. Jean Pinkett. That's not my name now.'

'You're at the university, aren't you?' Bettina asked. 'You know all about Bill Riley, then.'

'I know of him,' Bernard said. 'The music department's a good way out. I don't often see him in my part of the library. You're not allowed to make noise there.'

'You've never heard his life-story, then?' Jean asked.

'Should I?' Laughing. He had, in fact.

'He tells it when he's boozed. He was a child prodigy. Parents were mad keen amateurs, and spent no end on lessons with this notable and that. Nadia Boulanger and Britten and Maxwell Davies. Everybody. He says that by fifteen he was fed-up with music, and only took his doctorate to please his father. "My old man's a church organist and to him a D.Mus is just like God Almighty." ' Both girls laughed. 'I tell him that if you can write a twiddling fugue and a string quartet that sounds like Brahms copied out by Delius and a bloody great snorting symphony no bastard with one ear and half a brain would think of playing, they throw degrees at you, ten for twopence. Doctor of Meretricious Music of this univer- sity.' She had something of Riley's breathless, diffident aggression.

'Is he popular up there?' Bettina asked.

'No idea.'

'He's been sacked, or moved on at least twice,' Jean said. 'But somebody always takes him. The B.B.C. does quite a lot of his serious things, and he writes telly scores. They're marvellous. I don't think he's any good at teaching. He turns up and talks, and demonstrates things, but all off the syllabus. The prof. here likes him. Says he's good for the bright students. And he works.'

'A cousin of mine, a girl,' said Bettina, 'finished in the department, last year, said he composes every afternoon for three hours, you can see him at it, and in the holidays he's up half the night. The prof. never arranges committees and lectures for him in his composing sessions.'

'I know Frank Armstrong a bit,' Bernard said.

'The prof? My cousin said he wasn't a bad sort, had music organised. Composing by numbers. Cut and dried, drilled. She couldn't make out why he thought so much of Riley. He used to say, at socials, "That young man could set a grocery bill and make it music." '

'Tell him about "Nearer, My God",' Jean said.

They laughed, clasped arms, hugged, until Bernard thought they would kiss.

'Armstrong's so methodical, in exactly on the hour, out of the lecture-room on the stroke even if he's half-way through a bar, and has got it so tied up and taped that the students try to side-track him. They don't succeed. He frowns and bristles his moustache and says, "That's the third foolish question today. And the last. The next person will be dismissed." And he means it.'

'Come on, Bet,' Jean said. 'You'll take all night.'

'They think no end of themselves if they get him to answer one of these irrelevancies. And one girl, she was a favourite, tailored her fugues just right to the pattern . . . isn't she on the staff now, Jean? What was her name? Wendy something. . . . Do you know her?'

'There is a young woman,' Bernard said. 'A blonde girl. Married to a parson.'

'That'd be the one. Well, she asked old Frankie-boy if a text couldn't be spoiled for setting. She got on about the sinking of the *Titanic*, and all the old ham-and-closet versions of "Nearer, My God" until he got chocka and stopped her and bit his major's whiskers, and said: "Something in what you say. I've no literary flair to talk about. But Britten could do it. And Dr. Riley." Of course they all rushed off to tell Billy and he said, "The rotten bastard." '

'But he set it,' Jean said.

'And my cousin said it was marvellous. It made your hair

stand on end. He had two basses, two cellos, a viola, a violin, two bassoons, clarinet, oboe and piccolo. They made the most weird sounds. You should have heard her rave. Fab. And a contralto voice. He trained somebody and did it at a concert up there. Did you hear it?'

'No. Never heard anybody say anything, either.'

'Shows. She said it turned you over. You didn't want to listen any more. Just creep off.

> "Out of my stony griefs
> Bethel I'll raise."

That's what she remembered. Prehistoric, as if life was just starting.'

'And what did Professor Armstrong say?' Bernard asked.

'This girl, Wendy, asked him, and he muttered, "That's religious music" and she asked, "Do you mean it's a hymn?" and he poked his moustache and said, "It says something about God." '

'That's a compliment from him,' Bernard said. He felt suddenly envious of Riley who could think out these shattering sonorities.

'They've done it once, at least, since, on the Third,' Bettina said.

Bernard looked over at Riley who stood with an arm round the waist of the woman in slacks, smiling, slightly cross-eyed through his glasses, small, very thin.

'I didn't know he was thick with Tom Butler,' Jean said. 'Shouldn't have thought they'd get on.'

She stopped, set her face straight. Jacqueline had walked across. As she stood in front of them, small, poised, beautiful, the other two girls seemed suddenly coarse, harsh, rough-cut.

'Hello,' she said, friendly enough. To Bernard, 'I think it's pretty well over now. Are you ready for going?'

'When you are.'

'I'll tell Jack I've seen you,' Jean said. Jacqueline blushed, swept her hand an inch or so through the air by her hips. She was stiff.

'Is he . . . keeping . . . well?' Slowly, unemphasised.

'Oh, yes. He's in London now.'

'What's he doing?'

'Lecturer at a Polytechnic.'

'Good.'

Bernard suddenly became aware of himself as an observer. He wished he had recorded this snatch on tape so that he could re-play and listen hard. As he stood here, nearer to Jean, facing his fiancée, he thought he sensed hostility, even hate between the women. But he was unsure. Perhaps the conflict was inside himself, erupting at the casual remark, 'My brother used to be sweet on her'. It must have been some time ago. Their voices were polite and while Bettina was being formally introduced, there was hand-shaking, smiles broke, comment on the weather. He shrank away, into his suspicions, while Jacqueline queened it, attracted others across, started an argument about Whiting's "The Devils" that some cigar-smoking man was proposing to produce. He stood still, in the tumble of talk, gave nothing of himself away.

The group was large now, noisy, interested. Wharton Starkey, the barrister, was engaged on a near-formal speech, a kind of proposition about theatrical ventures.

'I'm only asking,' he brayed. 'What we must attempt is avant-garde, but popular, in a small sense. Who makes such sense? Brecht? Ionesco? Beckett? This last Osborne?'

'May I ask what experience of the theatre you have?' The voice was posh, plummy, from a Roedean Clara Butt. Mustard-slacks.

'None whatsoever, in a technical capacity. I'm exploring. That's all.' He smiled, a beautiful, slow dimpling. 'Am I talking rubbish, then, Mrs. Greene?'

'You're talking,' she said. Everybody laughed, Starkey included.

'But . . .' He broke off, nodding. 'We've got to make our

minds up whether or not we cover costs. And if we don't who does?'

Myra drifted off.

'Come and play us that Bartók thing,' she urged Riley.

'Not again.'

'It's gorgeous. Does things to me the way you do it.'

The circle had begun to break. Wharton Starkey was shortly surrounded by good grey suits like his own, broad shoulders, an expensive dress or two. Riley was carted towards the piano where he began on some sewing-machine violence. Bernard was alone. The nearest person was no more than a yard away, but he belonged, he knew suddenly, nowhere, to nobody. Jacqueline was in conversation with Butler and a grey-haired, iron-corset woman who was new to the place. Jean Thompson was holding hands with a pale, rabbit-toothed man, presumably her husband.

Under the talk, leaping under it, clawing out, Riley's piano assaulted, whipped the ear. It was not volume, clangour-blast, not the hubbub of hammers on taut strings; rather the rhythm, the blatant violence of repetition which tossed one, flung one up in the racket, resisting, fighting to release the nerves from punched rhythm, the piano's aching artillery.

As the sounds clashed, Bernard stood lonelier.

Suddenly, with a pang, as if Riley had snapped a string, Bernard remembered his mother. While this was happening here, and Bartók, with his drumming, climbing energy, represented life, Mrs. Allsop in that warm, antiseptic ward was dying. The thought sliced him, was unendurable. Here were plenty of people, pretentious, dull, gossipy, talented, covetous, debtors, adulterers, dyspeptics, all living, all loathing or enjoying or putting up with what was happening and there seven miles away a body was being, almost ravenously, destroyed. To feel this, unexpectedly, was like a great lead sword thrust down his gullet. As his gorge heaved he lost humanity, trembled, froze.

Bartók ended. Riley's adherents applauded. Wharton Starkey raised himself on his tiptoes, said, clapping widely:

'Could we have some William Riley, now, if you please?'

Riley stared, bit his lip.

'We'll have some, boy,' My Greene said. 'We'll have some. "A Nativity".'

Bernard leaned on the wall, dizzy. Mother. Father.

Riley tapped out a scrap of a tune, three fragments, keyless, with notes repeated, a kind of humble, back-broken carol, ending high. He paused and his left hand jangled a crumple of chords, repeated it, toppled from it; above the tune scratched on, in jerky snatches. Only rarely were the hands playing together, and then as if by chance, gently percussive below, eloquent in a foreign phraseology above; mostly the mild chordal accompaniment, with its minute variations and the disjointed recitative were kept separate. Though the volume was small, from pianissimo to mezzo-piano, each note or cluster was stabbed out, almost gravely. The upper melody staggered through its wide tessitura; the blocks below remained about the middle, moving in small rumbles, threatening in miniature, clashing coldly.

Bernard noticed his breathing, with relief. A shadow of discomfort hung on him, but bearable. He listened, heard notes, beautifully from a large piano, but at random. For the moment he wondered if his hearing was defective. Riley's curious tune ended, unrhythmical, in five high repeated notes, then two, then three.

'Good Lord,' the man next to Bernard said. Starkey was clapping hard, as if for a double century. 'Is he pulling our leg?'

'That was good, wasn't it?' Jean was speaking, was next to him, still holding her husband's hand. 'It really was.' The husband smiled, tugged at a strand of hair by her parting. Bernard hated him, felt sick again. The couple were moving off, swinging clasped hands. Over by the piano he could see Jacqueline, standing very still, frowning, listening.

'Can't make head or tail of it,' the man said. 'He played that Brahms and Bartók like a world-beater, and then he does that. I don't know. Is there something there, in it? Must be. If you can play as he can, you wouldn't just sit down and poke at the piano like a pig hobbling on it, would you? Or would you? Beats me, that does.' The man wiped his forehead, his face troubled. Suddenly Bernard's anxiety tumbled out into words he tried not to say.

'She's dying,' he said. The man stared, bird-eyed.

'Who is?' He was too startled for polite evasions or questions.

'Nobody. Nobody you know.'

The man swallowed, hugely, in the skinny throat.

'Bloody funny music, that was. Well, you could say it wasn't music at all, couldn't you?'

Bettina appeared, unescorted.

'Wasn't that marvellous?' she said. 'Really . . . really . . .' She waved her hands in search of a word.

'We're deciding here we don't make head or tail of it,' Bernard said.

'Baffles me,' the man whispered.

'Ah, I've just been getting the background,' Bettina said, 'from Myra Greene. That piece he played tonight was called "A Nativity". He wrote it when his daughter, Deirdre, was born. That'd be about eighteen months ago.'

'Poor little kid.' The man.

'He doesn't play it to the child,' Bettina snapped.

' "A Nativity"?' Bernard asked. ' "A Nativity"? That just means "a birth", doesn't it? You can't just say . . .'

'Ah,' Bettina said, ignoring him, looking grave. 'He just played the little beginning, the germ, tonight. But that caught him, in some way, and he started a set of variations, fugues, complex movements on it. He hasn't finished yet, but Lamar Crowson's going to play the work so far, next month, I think it is. And it takes half an hour, now. "Variations on a Nativity." '

'I don't think I shall listen,' Bernard said.

'Greenio says it's wonderful. Like a new world.'

'Whatever else Riley can do, he can certainly get the women praising him.' Bernard.

'Jealous. Jealous.' Her fingers fondled his chin.

'Did I understand you to say somebody was dying?' The man spoke, suddenly, flustered, back from the wall.

'Me?' Bettina asked.

'No. This gentleman. I thought I heard, at least, that's what, I, er . . .'

Bernard turned away, in discomfort again. He fumbled in his hair, dazed, sickish, veins beating. Mother. Father.

'It's all right,' he said.

'I thought,' the man continued, as if drunk, 'that you said . . . I wasn't sure I hadn't mistaken you for the moment. It's a . . . it's . . .'

Jacqueline walked over, stood a diminutive drill-sergeant.

'Like that?' she said, briskly to Bettina. 'It's time we went, Bernard. I've no end to do.' She smiled. 'You've got to hand it to Riley, haven't you? Can I give you a lift?'

Bettina agreed and refused. Bernard followed his fiancée out. She marched smartly, not stopping to wish or signal goodbye, but looked straight at the door towards which she was moving. In the car nothing was said as she sat jingling the ignition key in front of her face. Her preoccupation lasted until they were on the main city road.

'Enjoy yourself?' she asked.

'So, so.'

'What was wrong then?'

'Wrong? Nothing wrong.'

'It's all very tricky,' she said. 'The sprat to catch the mackerels. There'll be a follow-up in tomorrow evening's newspaper and in the *Chronicle* and the *Town Crier* next month. By that time Tom and Fred Clunes and one or two more will have the whole thing buttoned up. We've hardly any time, and that's the idea. In the fortnight they've chosen the Playhouse opens with *Lear*, the Music Club's got the Amadeus; Johnny Dankworth's at the Viceroy . . .'

'That's nothing to do with . . . ?'

'Tom knows what he's about. There'll be a bonanza at the university. And a lot of private shows. In the big houses.'

'I thought this was supposed to bring culture to the masses?' he said. She did not bother to answer that.

Back home, Jacqueline threw herself down into an arm-chair in her study.

'I'm tired,' she announced.

'So am I.' He knelt by her, and kissed her cheek.

'I said I was tired,' she said, yawned. He pulled her towards him, but she kissed him, full on the lips, drily, and slithered away. 'I'm too fagged, darling,' she said.

'I'm not.'

'Oh, you're not human.'

'What's that mean?' he said.

'Nothing, nothing.' She closed her eyes. 'Shall I make a drink?'

'Not for me.' Mother. Father.

'Now you're cross, aren't you?' She smiled, sat straighter. 'Come and sit on Mamma's knee,' she said, tapping her lap. He slumped down elsewhere. She watched him, desisted from her banter, put her head back on a cushion and shut her eyes. 'Go and make us a cup of tea, pet, will you?' she said.

'Why should I?'

'I've asked you, darling.'

He did as he was told. There was no mention of his father that night.

9

MARY ALLSOP flung her pen down, then snatched it up as quickly to examine it for damage. She looked out of her bedroom window from the table where she had just completed her Latin sentences. Clumps of fluffy green on the trees almost hid the raw brick of the back of the houses fifty yards away. Through the open window she heard a lawn-mower, men's voices, a shriek from children, the chatter of the birds.

She was invariably pleased to finish her homework, especially when as this evening she had included revision for her examinations. Often she drove herself to extra effort merely for the pleasure of its completion. Time was then her own; she could chase out or idle in. She consulted the alarm-clock; too late for the public library. She enjoyed visits there, in the long spick-and-span room, with the wax polish of the wood floor, and the shelves of coloured dust-covers, even when she didn't want to change her book, when she hadn't leisure for reading. But you met friends there, who'd smile and exchange a hushed word, or you dodged blushing behind a bookcase out of the way of Mrs. Warsop who'd corner you and blast questions at you about your mother so that the whole library could hear her screech. It was hopeless talking to adults; they asked questions that embarrassed, and instead of waiting for your answer rattled the window-panes with what they thought. Mrs. Marshall, today, had stopped her on the street, on the way home from school.

'Mary Allsop, isn't it?'

'Yes.'

' 'Ent seen yo' for long enough. I didn't know yer in yer uniform. Nice, like, in't it? Our Freda went there. 'Er as is married. How's yer mother, duck?'

'She's still in hospital.'

'Yes, well, she would be, wouldn't she? Wi' that? She would be. My sister, the eldest one, not th'one as went to America, our Edie, she was in months. Incurable. They sent her home in the end. She begged 'em. She just wanted to see her own bricks an' mortar again, she said. They cou'n't keep her there though. Well, you can't, can yer? She was a big woman to lug about; it used t'take two on 'em, an' her husband's no shrimp. Big chap he is. Wo'ks at Stanton, iron place, y'know. Still does.'

Mary had fidgeted one foot to the other, but the woman had clacked on, talking to herself, not looking at you, spitting mouthfuls of facts, stopping only to stare like a pig at passers-by. And the comfort she ladled out was worst. Sickly as senna.

'Well, she'll soon be home, duck, wain't she? They do miracles, they do. Your dad'll be pleased to see 'er, I'll back. Yo' will, I expect. I've known yer dad a long time. An' yer mam. You ask yer dad. Tell 'im you seen Mrs. Marshall, Edna Allan as was; he'll know. Ay, it'll be a blessing when she can come 'ome. There's two on yer, in't there? Ay. What's your brother's name? Herbert? Always a pale lad, wan't he, not very strong? He'll be at work now, wain't he?'

The woman never listened, slapped questions out like a shorthand test, trundled up information about her own affairs. And all loud. Even the lowered voice as a passer-by approached was powerful. Worst was the lack of consideration; she never let it enter her thick head that a child might feel a fool to be in receipt of these flat confidences, even to be seen talking to such a frump.

Now, in her bedroom, watching the gently moving green landscape and the pink shell of the sky, Mary luxuriated in her freedom. She looked round the bedroom, white-clean, with silver stripes and large amply spaced tea-roses on the wallpaper, the white cupboard, wardrobe, book-shelves, the glass ornaments, small gleaming lions, on the white, metal mantelpiece. Here she was alone, able to make her mind up. She borrowed *Wuthering Heights* from the front room book-case downstairs because the English mistress had read them the first page or two and made it interesting. She'd a throbbing voice, full of sex, Cecily Watts said, and she should know. And that reminded Mary; Cec had lent her a battered James Bond paperback; they all read those, or said they did. She could start that.

It looked inviting outside; voices were flying round the gardens, bursts of laughter from the women opposite, the sound of transistor radios, a shout of angry command. Her father was bent over his hoe, examining some plant, in his shirt-sleeves with a trouser-button off or undone. One leather end of the braces stuck out vertically from his back. Mary went down, stood by him.

'I don't know what that's doing here,' he said.

'What is it?'

'A little holly bush. A bird must have dropped a seed. Do you want it in your garden?'

'All right.'

He handed it over happily. In theory, he was ruthless, pronouncing any plant that was out of place a weed, but in practice he hated knocking the head off a daisy. She made a show of thinking where to put it, asked his advice, fetched compost and water; he brought out the bone-meal. They consulted again, made a ceremony of putting the couple of leaves in, stood wiseacre-fashion admiring their work.

She slipped a woollen jacket round her shoulders and went out by the back gate. Joy. Not forty yards away Eric Parkes sauntered up the street in tight jeans and an emerald-green shirt; these were brand-new, improved him, she thought. He looked like everybody else, but handsomer. Jolts of delight probed her stomach. Her legs trembled to the thighs; she blushed. Deliberately she put one hand on the wooden surround of the gate as she stood on the stone steps where she waited. He came across, hands in pockets, Cuban heels clicking at the swagger. His hair had been shampooed.

'Well, there,' he said, laughed, made his mouth a thin line.

'Well.'

'Going anywhere?'

'No,' she said, trembling. Breath was suddenly short. Had she answered right? She made sure there was no one else in the street. 'I like your shirt.'

'Yes.' He fingered it by the open collar. 'Not bad.'

'I like that,' she said. 'Bright.' She flushed hot-red. At least he'd come across the road to her. She looked at the dark line of shaven skin by his ear; he was adult, a man. There were traces of talcum powder.

'I'm going up on the Common,' he said.

'Oh, yes.'

'For a walk.' He nodded his head at her and that was enough. She joined him in a street that was hot still with the day's sunshine. A yard stretched between them. They barely spoke except that once he complained how rotten lilac blossom looked once it had turned brown. At the stumps on the Common's edge a group of roughs about Mary's age were kicking stones, shuffling dust and chasing, punching each other. They waited until the two were past before comment began.

'Look at 'er. Wibble-wobble, wibble-wobble.'

'Baby-snatchin'. Where's your pram?'

'Ooh, our Mary, went to the dairy; he showed her his little canary.'

She, shamed, reddened, but he looked down at her and wrinkling his eyes said:

'The peasants are enjoying life.'

That made it easier, and as they rounded the iron-spiked fence he jumped high, twisting, over a gorse-bush.

'Let's go across to the tennis-courts,' he said.

'All right.'

He grabbed her hand, pulled her at him so that she nearly tumbled. Both laughed. Mary knew what he was about; he was using her as a cover, to give the planned walk an occasional character. What he wanted was to find out if Deirdre Fenton was here. It wasn't likely. She and her escorts usually went off by car to the Park Club, but sometimes they started late, sat too long over her father's gin and had to slum it locally. Over in the distance the white girls flitted about in their tall wire cage.

'Is Deirdre playing here tonight?' she asked.

'Don't think so.' He looked guilty.

They stood together on the asphalt path surrounding the courts. A small boy, lurching on the pedals of his sister's bike, slooshed past across the 'No Cycling' notice. An elderly couple paused solemnly to watch their dog wet a bench-post.

There was no Deirdre.

'Who's that girl?' he asked. The one he pointed to was heavy, with red scorched legs, and straggly hair. Mary had no idea. For a few minutes they watched, before they moved towards the pavilion. The grass, the walks were littered with ice-cream wrappers, lolly-sticks, dogs' mess. As they walked finally away, by the thin silver-birches, the sky swirled pink and green; houses over the hill-top were purplish dark.

They crossed the road at the low point of the dip, wandered under the railway bridge.

'It's quiet here,' she said. He hummed to himself. They passed the wagon factory, by the short terrace of Victorian street housing, used now as offices, that stood ungainly out here in the fields. The dirt road was dusty, sand-dry, and the high hedges closed them in. 'It might be the country.'

Eric, rather slowly, began to describe the lanes in Devon where his family stayed every year in August. Mary paid little attention; she enjoyed being with him, hearing the sound of his voice, but could disregard his geographical lecture. For his part, he liked nothing better than interminable explanations. They swung past a farm, where a car and three lorries stood smart in the yard; somebody was talking heatedly and an electric light bulb was suddenly switched on.

Now they were mounting a hill, and he picked a smooth stone, like a grey potato, from the path. He held it in his hand and began a further lesson about the last ice-age and the glaciers grinding south, the moving and honing of pebbles, and their depositing here, on these shaped hills, ten thousand years ago.

'And they've been here ever since,' he said. 'Isn't that marvellous?'

'Marvellous?' she asked. 'I don't know. Things have been everywhere for donkey's years.'

'But to think back,' he said, 'ten thousand years. Before the biblical patriarchs, Abraham and Isaac, these stones were here. It's frightening.'

'It doesn't frighten me,' she said.

'This stone,' he said, tapping it with his fingers. He looked at her, sighed, let it thud to the ground.

'Well, what?' she said, laughing. 'I thought you were going to tell me something.'

He twisted away from her, then took her hands, lifted them to waist level.

'It makes sense to you, does it?'

'What?'

'That the sun there is the same disc, seen by everybody, every single body in history. The caveman, Sappho, Attila, Columbus, St. Thomas, Newton, Shakespeare, Clerk-Maxwell.' Its rim lay, egg-red, to their left, behind the trees of a second farm. 'Do you realise that? Wherever they lived, or when?'

'I suppose so,' she said flatly.

'That sun shone, these stones lay here on the day Jesus was crucified.'

He'd turned her towards the sun, so that she stood with her back to him, and cupped her breasts with his hands. She leaned on him, stiff, excited.

'If you think about it like that,' she said. 'It might have been raining.'

His hands were moving; his cheek was laid on her hair.

' "Today the Roman and his trouble. Are ashes under Uricon",' he said. His arms went tight round her, roughly, knocking the breath from her.

'That hurt,' she said, passive.

'I'm sorry.' He spoke in a different voice. He turned her towards him, kissed her on the mouth. Their lips met awkwardly, unopened, pushing, stick-dry.

'No,' she said. While his fingers played with her breasts she could disregard the movements, acknowledge them to herself as chance, shiver with the pleasure and discount the origin. A kiss was deliberate, known by both as such, to be verbally discouraged. 'There's somebody coming.'

Eric stood back. A man in a raincoat and cloth cap kicked along the path below them. He paused to light a cigarette. They saw the flame jump once, clear and lively, before he turned in their direction, stared, looked as if he was going to shout up at them, blew a cloud of smoke and flicked the match away from him.

'Who's that?' Mary asked.

'I don't know. He's not a friend of mine.'

'Do you think he's a poacher?'

'At this time of night? Out here? It's not very likely.'

'What would he be doing then?' she asked, stubbornly.

'Going for a walk. Like us.'

'He doesn't look the sort to go for a walk for nothing,' she said.

'What sort does?' he asked.

'You,' she answered. 'Me.'

She moved slowly down the path, disappointed, uneasy after the exchange.

'Where are you off to?' Eric asked.

'It's getting late.'

'I thought you were chasing the poacher.' He laughed.

'He'll hear you.'

He joined her, in sauntering, and put an arm round her waist. Still she would not lean on him, was disagreeable, uneasy, squinting into a frown, pouting. The poacher, hurrying, turned down into the farmyard, banged with a flat hand on the lorry door as he passed.

'He must live there,' Eric said. 'What about your suspicions now?'

'I haven't got any,' she grumbled.

Just past the farm, which lay below in a valley, the path dipped steeply for a few yards, a vertical sandbank on one side, a hedge on the other. Another sheltered lane crossed it at right-angles before their own widened to an orange-smooth sandhill. At the intersection stood an oak tree, peeling, with roots exposed, both dead and living, powerful, dwarfing, sick. Eric sat down on the thickest root, his heels dug into the tawny earth, still littered in the niches with last year's crumpled leaves. He laughed up at Mary, who stood above him.

'Come and sit down,' he said.

'Why should I?'

'Because I asked you to.' He spread his knees, and patted

the ground in front of him. Obediently she squatted there, but upright, inches close but not touching. He had a finger at her hair, curling it, corkscrewing it, letting it jump loose. Now, palm at her cheek, he forced her back, leaning on him.

'That's better,' he said. She seemed to feel his voice inside him, inside her, in the backbone, part of both. A root dug harshly into her buttocks. 'We can sit here and listen to the country sounds.' A diesel engine beyond the common blew its two-note call; they laughed. He kissed her along her parting, suddenly stopped, his chin uncomfortably pushing the top of her head.

'What's that?' she said.

'What?' he lifted his head.

They listened. The wind, a distant car, bird-noises, cat-screech, a cough. The pair were ineffably still. Again he put his arms round her, hugged, squeezing her breasts together. This time she said nothing, sat crushed, her knees up to his arms. Without warning he released her, spread his arms wildly like wings, flapped them in, grabbed her coarsely under the crook of her knees, pulling her into him. The movement was slow, warm, uncouth, so strong that she began to slip, very slightly. He tightened the grip; she felt one hand exploring the tendon, then pause on the thigh, held there, chilling, hateful, choice, lovely, to be rejected. She was afraid, remembering the shaven dark face; he was a man, grown-up, no boy, a dangerous force. A shiver convulsed her momentarily. The hand was quite still, calm, holding, a support, without menace. She remembered school-yard talk, and a curious warning her mother had given when her periods had begun. Her mother was ill, but there was a kind of hate, a blistering in the obliquely threatening words. 'The men will be after you now. Keep yourself clear from them or they'll never respect you. They start with their hands.' The embarrassed dropped sentences from the stricken woman had been suddenly issued, like a branding, a day or two after some clear, flat remarks about menstruation; but she knew about that, since they'd explained at school. Cec Watts had worn towels for over two years now, from the first forms. This was perhaps such a beginning. With the hands. His was warm, now, quiet, settled.

She felt pleasure in the contact, and fear, as if his nails were about to rip the flesh raw. Above was the scuffling whisper of leaves; away to their back the clatter of a train. With surprise she was nestling close to him, on the new shirt, hiding from him within himself, finding harbour with the pursuer. Her legs melted with shreddings of weakness; her breasts burst; the cheeks of her buttocks locked. Still he did not move; the whole world seemed frozen into this marble of ambivalence.

Like a lead weight, swung to kill pleasure or apprehension, a thought dropped. She spoke it.

'Don't you wish you'd got Deirdre Fenton here?' she said.

'Uuhh?' The sound sagged between questioning and animal joy.

'Instead of me?'

He paused. There was not observable physical difference; she leaned on his chest; his hand was unmoving on the thigh. He seemed to be staring away, making his mind up, adding to his self-respect, picturing himself as caught by a problem that would not prove insoluble.

'No, I don't,' he said at last.

She was satisfied, for the moment, but a different girl. She had asked the wrong, awkward question, out of self-protection, perhaps even in percipience. She was not convinced by the reply. She knew better. If he had been more skilful, more experienced, less innocent, he could have talked, lured doubt into conviction, but he knew nothing, with her body against his, dizzy with heat and flesh.

'Eric,' she said. 'Do you know what love is?'

He could not believe that she had asked the question. This child, whose womanly frame belied the wooden kisses, the slightly sour breath as if her teeth needed cleaning, was demanding metaphysical explanations. She should sit still.

'I don't know.'

Now he shifted his hand so that it rested on the cloth of her knickers. She allowed this for a moment, then tore at his fingers with her own, saying in a little, firm voice:

'No.'

He moved his hand. She had fallen forward on to her knees so that he could put both arms round her, resting his head on her back.

'No,' she said.

From the farmyard, hidden somewhere in front and below, a door slammed, and a self-starter griped vainly through its metallic scale of agony. Again. This time the engine took, boomed, throbbed so that they could feel its power in the ground.

'See yer, then,' a voice called.

'Ah. Don't come too early, though.'

The vehicle crashed away like a tank. It was the lorry, rattling as if its load were metal sheets, dustbins, milk-churns. It lurched past the end of the transverse lane, down towards the bridge, in the ruts, the driver's elbow loosely projecting from the cab door.

Mary was standing, dabbing at her hair. Eric scrambled up, beating the sand from his clothes, looking everywhere but at the girl.

'Time we went,' she said, steadily.

They made tracks down the sandhill. Ahead the lorry still clanked. Lights sparkled on the farm up the hill.

'What time is it?' she said.

'Five to ten.'

'I'll have to hurry,' she said.

'Let's run.'

He took her hand and they began, moderately at first, trotting, boy-girl running. Energetically, she tried to forge ahead of him, but he would not be beaten. The jerk on her arm pulled it from its socket, she thought, and now he was dragging her, so that her footsteps beat, leapt, wild-capered the path, avoiding the grass hump in the centre, the tyre-marks, the churned ash-and-oily sand.

This was excitement which washed clear the dread, the shivering of a few moments back. There was danger here, as arms rammed, and feet hit the path, staggering, and he rushed her on beyond her pace, but this was known fear. With breath pumping she kept up with him, met his jerking, declared herself his equal. Eric would not have it, lurched forward faster. A slide opened, her hair gushed, flopped bouncing as the slide dangled loose tapping on her face. He was going hard now, making blood beat, sight dizzy, ears hum. Outside the intensity of physical action she knew nothing, feared not at all. Bound into a ball of furious energy, the pair hammered, reeled forward, wildly, unrealistically magnificent. The slide clawed into her face and dropped.

'Stop,' she shrieked. Her heels went into the ground and for five feet he dragged her, until wheeling he'd met her, swamped her into his arms. She broke loose, the evening hedges red about her, the noise of heart a fierce drum. 'I've dropped my slide,' she said.

She found it without difficulty a yard or two back from the skid-marks. Still thumped with her exertion, she re-clipped her hair, arranging it easily by habit. Eric came up, laughing, took her to him, handled her breasts.

'No,' she said, breaking away. She found it difficult to speak. Her whole being seemed concentrated somewhere in her forehead, midway between the eyes and until it spread again, along the limbs, she wanted nothing but a sober walk in silence. It was not a rejection of his advance, merely a statement of her own momentary inhumanity. 'No,' she said, and began to walk.

She did not notice that he put some distance between them, was abashed. Now she recollected the heaving of his chest, his rough breath as he'd caught her after the running, but she could not know that he found her collected, unruffled, stand-offish, self-sufficient. He walked without speaking until they reached the bridge. The sky seemed especially bright through the arch, like a sun-polished lake.

'Mary,' he said. 'Will you kiss me?'

She put her mouth up to his, enjoying the fitting of his body to hers; it seemed harmless and right. They were breathless.

'Everybody'll see us,' she said.

'I don't care.'

'Well, I do.'

They crossed the road, his arm loosely round her waist. Men walking their dogs, other lovers disregarded them.

'Don't dawdle,' she said.

'Why not?'

'My dad'll wonder where I've got to.'

She wondered as she said this whether it was true. There was no way of judging her father; one day he'd be absent-minded, the next loving, thoughtful to a degree, the third raving-mad about nothing. As they approached the stumps she noticed that Eric removed his arm, but she was relieved. It wouldn't do to be seen tangled like that. Even walking along the street was embarrassing.

She used the back-garden gate, not loitering although there was no one about. Bernard was sitting in the dining-room, radiogram full blast, shaking his mane at Tchaikovsky's First Piano Concerto.

'Hello,' he said. 'Where've you been?'

'For a walk.'

'My dad's been looking for you.'

'Where is he now?' she asked, guilty, scared to the bowels.

'He's just gone down to the Fletchers'. Something about plants. Do you want anything?'

'No, thanks. I'll get a drink myself, and go to bed.'

'I should.' He looked grim, turned Tchaikovsky down. 'Go for a walk with young Parkes?' Casually, corner-of-mouth.

'Yes. Why?'

'I saw you coming over the Common bridge. I was upstairs.'

'Looking out for me?'

'Yes,' he said. 'If you must know. Dad had been chuntering.'

'Uh.' She went to the kitchen, drew a drink of water,

returned, stood by the door with the glass in front of her, stiff. 'There's nothing wrong with it, is there?'

'With what?' He affected suddenly to have heard.

'Going for a walk? With . . .'

'That's up to you, not me,' he said, sourly, offhand.

She stared, said, 'I thought you didn't like Tchaikovsky.'

From his expression she might have uttered some obscenity he'd not quite grasped, that he'd have to ravel out. His face cleared, and he laughed, twisting the knob until the room rocked with Horowitz's magnificent hands and the composer's sliding soul.

'Get off to bed.'

Mary whistled to herself, but the moment the door of her room was closed she was cut about with cold fright. There had been, she felt, an initiation, with Eric Parkes; that in itself was not frightening now, but she was guilty in her own eyes, though of what she would have been troubled to say. Her father might have been angry, have struck her; his grief might have been scoured deeper on her thoughtless account. She was just lucky he had been out. She braced herself against herself. What did it matter what he said? She'd done nothing wrong. She kissed him, but that was what you did in Christmas games. He'd, he'd tampered with her, let his hands feel her, her nakedness. That wasn't true, in literal fact. But the word 'naked', spoken, thought, in this bedroom, exactly matched what he had done and she had allowed. Again she stood obstinate. She had not been naked; she was intact, clothed. Her body trembled and burnt round her thinking. Eric and she, in nudity, on some hot beach. It was hard to visualise him, though not long ago she had come across Bernard strutting about thus in his bedroom. Reluctantly, scowling at herself she began to undress, so that she could stare at herself in the spotted mirror.

The garden gate clacked.

She lifted a corner of the curtain. Her father was coming up the path, still in shirt-sleeves, carrying a box of plants; it was too dark to make out what they were. He walked slowly, as if he were pushing through a resistant sea, neck-high in small, greasy waves, choking, lifting, hindering his progress. Half-way along the path he stared up at her bedroom with such fixity that she thought he must be able to see her peering out from the chink. Obviously he could not, and after he had gaped there for some seconds he turned round, slunk back to his greenhouse, where he deposited his box and then emerged, smartly, beating his hands clear of earth. Tears mustered. She forgot the shamed, secret delight in her body at the thought of her father, the near-bereaved man, the scarecrow. Downstairs his voice cracked clear.

'Mary back yet, Bernard?' Stern.

Her brother must have reassured him. The sound of his voice brushed her compunction aside. If she'd not come up quickly she'd be getting the length of his ugly tongue. Or worse. There was nothing wrong in what she'd done. She touched her leg in the place where Eric had been. Nothing. Antiseptic. On the edge of the bed she drew her knees up, took up the position she had in the fields, replaced her hand, moved it. A small tingle. She remembered his fingers. Jerking, she straightened her legs, undressed quickly, bundled into bed.

Downstairs Bernard and her father were talking, and on the gramophone Pamina and Papageno, archly sweet, sang together:

> 'Mann and Weib, und Weib und Mann
> Reichen an die Gottheit an.'

10

IN JACQUELINE RIDELL'S study, she and Bernard were listening to Dr. Riley. He perched on the edge of a windsor chair, wriggled and waved his glass about as if to spatter the room with beer.

Bernard, arriving for his usual Monday evening visit, had been set on by Jacqueline to help her address envelopes. It had taken an hour to get this complete, and they had no sooner done than Riley had trotted in, looking, he described it, in a vague way for Tom Butler. He'd been very interested in the piles of envelopes, fingered them, knocking one down, frowning over the names, sighing.

'He's good, our Butler,' Riley said, when he'd got hands round a drink. 'There'll be at least a dozen personable young women employed like you tonight. And by the end of the week every nob, culture-vulture, egg-head, Sunday School teacher, pederast and magistrate in three counties'll know what we're about.' Riley was the sort to laugh, comb-and-tissue paper, at his own jokes. 'You should have seen him rake the Lord Mayor in.'

'Wasn't it short notice?' Bernard said.

'Exiguous. That doesn't stop our Thomas. He's organised his nibs into two of the affairs, and the Sheriff, and the Duke of Annesley.'

'Is he interested?'

'Annesley?' Shouldn't think so. Wife's said to be, and one of the daughters. Pestering me for lessons. They're opening the long gallery or whatever its name is at Westwood for a chamber concert. It's to their advantage. Bill or Clarrie Byrne'll get contractors in who'll spring-clean the place for them, and that'll save 'em a bob or two this year. And we shall cover our expenses. You'll be surprised how many people will be falling over themselves to pay two, three, five guineas to be seen there. Oh, the festival's catching on. The agents are pushing now to get their performers in.'

'And what are you doing in the great war, Dr. Riley?' Jacqueline asked.

'Getting in the way. Making sure that the two university concerts are, er, capable, and finishing off a song-cycle that Todd Wyvill's going to murder.'

'Do you mean that?'

Riley looked up, startled, a puppet.

'No. He's quick, and he's seen five of the seven songs.'

'He's got a beautiful voice,' she said.

'I hope he puts it on the right notes.'

'Doesn't he usually?'

'Well, yes. He's not bad.'

Riley, Bernard guessed, seemed unsettled in Jacqueline's presence, wanting to impress, uncertain, suspicious.

'Is your wife interested in music, Dr. Riley?' she asked.

'Wife?' He repeated the word, stumbling on it, winded by the switch of subject. 'She is, in fact, but we've got four kids. That takes all her time.'

'How old are they?'

'The eldest's six, the baby three months.' He laughed. 'When we troop out you can hear people saying, "Catholics".'

'And are you?'

'That's not a joke.' He spoke with a stern, furious stutter as if she should have known the areas where levity was permitted. Bernard was angry, wanted to butt in, support Jacqueline.

'Is this festival going to do any good?' he said, aggressive.

Riley frowned, spectacularly.

'I know what you mean,' he replied, heavily. 'We shall get several thousand in to listen to music. Ninety per cent we can write off. They're in at the accepted place; they're good for a bit of free publicity later. I'm not saying they don't like music, that they're just there boring themselves stiff keeping up with the Joneses. But if one work were played instead of another, it wouldn't make a ha'porth of difference to them.'

'It wouldn't to me.' Bernard. 'As long as both were masterpieces.'

'What are agreed to be masterpieces. That's different.' Riley waved his fingers as if in water and did not go on, pursing his lips. Probably he thought he had made some significant distinction.

'What do you consider a masterpiece?'

'You mustn't expect much sense from me. I don't talk the

language. Suppose I agree that the last movement of, oh, *Eine kleine nachtmusik*, or the Jupiter, or the E Flat piano, is great. I can explain why it's technically superior to my students, or you, if you've some training or interest, but as to its emotional content, well, now. You'd think I'd be attitudinising, wouldn't you, if I said I could stand hearing those works once in six months. But that's about right.'

'Why?' Bernard was interested now.

'I'm a composer. Oh, I know I earn my money explaining classical, tonal music to students, but it's not what I'm about.'

'What's that, then?'

'Working my music out. And don't ask me what that means.' He laughed. 'Certain combinations of sounds and rhythms I find satisfying.'

'That's no sort of criterion. Any fool can claim that about any sort of noise he cares to make.'

'Any fool can claim anything,' Riley said. His voice was mild, a little push or two of air. 'You don't have to tell me. That's one of the horrors. The average citizen, brought up on Beethoven and Tchaikovsky and Bartók, can't tell the difference between the new sonorities a genuine composer makes and those of some blatant charlatan. You don't need to tell me that.'

'That's never been the case before, has it?'

'No. It hasn't. I know the old brigade said they found Beethoven and Wagner mere row, but they didn't mean it in the sense they do now. That's true.'

'Why's that?'

'I don't know. You're a historian. Ask your prof, old Dai Jones, Meredith, Chapel Choir, he's got a bibble-babble to label everything. Blame what you like. The break-up of European consciousness, deaths in the Great War, the i/c engine, Schönberg, the bomb, psycho-analysis, international Jewry, general lunacy, the decline of intelligence, I don't know. I'd blame the bloody journalists, except I know it's my own fault.'

'Britten uses tonal music,' Jacqueline said. 'And Shostakovitch.'

'So they do,' Riley whispered.

'And you're not interested in them?'

'Frankly, no.'

'Why,' Bernard asked, 'should you cut yourself from the majority of musicians, even?'

'If I could write music that would appeal to the football crowd, and win respectful attention from a few skilled men, I would, but it isn't possible. Never has been.' He spoke slowly, especially tentative with 'respectful attention', smiling thinly at the phrase.

'Handel?' Bernard said.

'Good point. Wasn't he ruined, though?' he smiled. 'I write the sort of music that I want to hear, to be heard, at this point in time, at this state of my learning, my developing personality, my creative talent, blah-blah, of myself. If nobody else wants to hear the stuff, that will affect me, I suppose. It might stop me composing. It hasn't yet. It may. That's a nightmare I keep out of the way by scribbling even more notes down.'

'But,' Bernard said, 'you've no guarantee of immortality, even short-term prestige. Somebody who's writing intelligible semi-traditional stuff is just as likely to be respected in a hundred years' time as you peep-and-gloop boys.'

'What I'm interested in saying, I'm doing for myself and a few others whose knowledge and opinions I esteem.'

'Because they coincide with your own?'

'Exactly. Exactly.'

There was no vehemence about Riley. He argued as if he admitted your intelligence, was prepared to pass time socially trying to explain adequately, but knew that all was quite irrelevant to himself. Bernard was impressed by the fanaticism. Nothing budged the man. He worked, he considered, he decided, but all elsewhere, distantly, utterly inviolate, musically.

'Why do you blame the journalists?' Jacqueline asked.

'They control the means of publicity. They decide what

most of you think. And they're not interested in real talent, let alone genius. They want a story, eye-catching trivia. If it's a choice between real craftsman's music and a load of slush written at your dying mother's bedside, they'll choose the second.' Bernard flushed. 'I don't blame them. They've got to live.'

'Bernard's mother is dying,' Jacqueline said.

Both men looked at her. Bernard, flayed with embarrassment, hardly believed that she'd said these words. Riley's white hands were together between his knees.

'I didn't know. What of?' The voice was so low that there was no rudeness.

'Cancer.'

'No hope?' Riley said. He sighed; his body was reduced.

'No.'

'My mother died two years ago.'

'Did that make any difference to your work?' Jacqueline spoke with the plummy voice of the lady-interviewer. Riley looked up in anguish, then nodded, very solemnly, at Bernard.

'I was a mother's boy.' He got down from his chair, posed on the back. 'My parents were both music teachers. My elder brother died. They pumped music into me from the cradle. My younger sister's no bent at all in that direction. I think by the time she came, they were both too busy indoctrinating me.'

'Is that bad?' Jacqueline asked.

'It's the only way, in my view. It's a cruel process, because you miss so much, you're one-sided, but you can't expect a person who's outstanding in talent, to put it at its lowest, to be ordinary.'

'I don't see why not.' Jacqueline, again. 'Because you're a musical genius, it doesn't mean you can't be quite a good father, or a moderate carpenter or a charming lover.'

'You might, in fact, be all those things just because you have this . . .' Bernard started.

'You don't begin to understand what genius is,' Riley spoke

huskily, lightly. 'A genius to you is somebody who punches a piano about on television.'

'That's not fair.'

'I exaggerate, I agree. But the greatness of, oh, Beethoven, if he had it, was not that he was arrested as a tramp or didn't raise his hat to the King or did chuck his boots at his landlady, it was that he could direct hours of infinitely superior musical thought to his job, composing. This is unusual, both the concentration and the quality of the thought, and it may lead to eccentric behaviour, but the first, not the absurd antics, marks the genius. And I hate the bugger.'

'But wouldn't you say it's a fact,' Bernard interrupted, 'that because Mozart knew humanity and its suffering, that Beethoven loved liberty, hated tyrants, their music is the greater?'

'As far as I'm concerned Mozart could have known nothing but tittle-tattle, and Beethoven loved nothing but fish-and-chips. It's the musical, understand, musical quality that counts. Nothing else. Oh, I'm sure Beethoven would have voted Labour and marched with the C.N.D., and God bless him. But the great god Bach would have taken the *Daily Telegraph* with the best of them. So what?'

'Then,' Bernard said, 'your journalists, wallowing in the ephemeral, the eye-catching, pulp for the idiots, might for all we know turn up the supreme genius of our age. If subject-matter doesn't count, only quality.'

'And God might be a bloody turnip,' Riley said.

They all laughed. Bernard was pleased, preening himself, that he'd won the argument. And yet he could not get beyond Riley's confidence, these arrogant assertions. Perhaps he was like a mystic, certain over what seems absurd, convinced by paradox. The only possibility that could gravel Riley would be the recognition of a musician more skilled, more daring, more successful than he was. Bernard smiled; the man's attitude was not obviously conducive to pleasure in another's superiority. Why should he have thought that? Riley had merely stated his credo; he believed in music. The great

Haydn had generously acknowledged Mozart's genius. Wasn't he a bit of a simpleton? Not musically, and it was, according to Riley, in notes, chords, rhythms, tone-colours that a musician's profundity existed.

'I must go,' Riley said.

'Should you be composing?' Jacqueline.

'No. I've done my bit for the day. I've got a room at the university. Armstrong, the prof, has given me a little place, right out of the way, at the end of a corridor full of store cupboards. It's quiet and I can look out over trees. There's just a table and a piano. He wouldn't let them put a telephone in, and it's quite out of bounds to everybody when I put the "engaged" sign up on the door at the end of the corridor. Oh, he's a great chap is my gaffer. It means I can do two or three hours every working day, and twenty-four in the holidays.'

'Is that enough?' Bernard asked.

'No, not at present.'

'Do you use the piano to compose?' Jacqueline asked.

'No, not much. I like improvising, sometimes. Once a week. Letting my fingers play boss. I've had the odd idea from that. Not often. Of course, you can't stop thinking about what you've got in mind.' He laughed. 'Obvious. Obvious as the words. I'm always going over what I've just done, or trying to get done.'

'Now? This minute?'

'No. Not really. Nagging a bit.'

'Will you play us something?' Jacqueline said. Riley seemed agreeable. 'That carol? "The Nativity"? It frightened me in a way.'

Riley made no comment, sat down at the piano, began. He slipped through the curious tune above the note clusters. In its small way it seemed eloquent, Bernard decided, finished, polished, but unintelligible.

'I'll give you my latest variation,' Riley whispered.

His fingers burst into a toccata, a fine running sound, tumbling. The notes dazzled, but punched, and worked irregularly into twists of elemental sound which momentarily halted the helter-skelter then flailed it on. The effect was, to Bernard, physical, on the nerves. As far as he could tell, and the quick clanging left little time for ratiocination, he drew no aesthetic satisfaction, had no sense of shape, or direction. And yet it was not the mere rhythm of the carriage-wheel, the machine-gun, the hangover, the dentist's drill. This was a considered attack on the body. The small man was directing a fierce jet of notes out of the piano, and the listener was left flattened, beaten. And yet there wasn't a great deal of noise. The climaxes were fortissimo, but short, rare. The music seared, burnt one down like a blow-lamp, blackened. Riley stopped, was examining the nails on his left hand.

'Didn't play it very well,' he said. 'Too hard for me. Should be faster.'

'Great.' Jacqueline.

'Did you see, hear any, er, er, design in it?'

'No,' Bernard said. 'It affected me. Physically. It was like holding on to some powerful machine, oh, some hose-pipe lashing about.'

'Uuuh.' Riley made a double chin, stuck his bottom lip out. 'The top part was in mirror-canon with the bass, and the three other middle voices which joined irregularly were in strict canon with each other.'

'I thought the top part seemed quicker than the bass.' Jacqueline.

'Oh, yes.' Riley seemed delighted. 'The bottom went half-speed to the treble, quaver to semi-quaver.'

'So the upper was repeated, came twice over?' Bernard said, after a moment.

'That's right. Good. Good. But the intervening middle voices appeared at different times, for variation. In fact, in the repeat, middle parts were sometimes placed outside the main two, higher, above, you know, and poking down through the bass.'

They looked blank.

'You probably didn't notice because my playing was so

bloody awful. I can hear it, but I can't do it.' He laughed, delighted, jam-stealing.

Bernard sipped his drink. From the description this sounded like cerebral composing, but the effect was physical, nerve-stripping. Riley chipped at notes, idly.

'Must be off,' he said, 'if I'm to find Tom. Thanks for the drink.'

He went quickly through the door, so that Jacqueline had to follow him. Bernard moved to the window, watched them walk the garden path, turn right for the garage entrance. Riley was making haste.

When she returned Bernard was holding a book.

'He's very attractive,' she announced.

'Very.'

'Don't you think so, then?'

In some ways Riley was like Jacqueline, small, fair, quiet, sharp, shifting.

'He reminds me a bit of you,' Bernard said. 'He could be your brother.'

'Likes don't attract.'

'As a matter of fact they do.' He sounded put out, school-masterly. 'If you observe closely, you'll see that husbands and wives have a great deal in common, physically and tempera-mentally.'

'I know they say that old married couples grow to look like each other.'

'They're alike to start with. It's only the exceptions, lanky man, short wife, who draw attention to themselves.'

'Am I like you?' she asked.

'I should think so.'

He was doubtful. They seemed unlike more often than not, but perhaps the resemblances were temporarily hidden. By her former marriage, his uncertainty.

'Anyway, I think he's attractive.' It was silly of her to repeat this. Even in his sulkiness he noted how unwise she was. 'What's his wife like?'

'How should I know?'

'Don't you see her up at the university sometimes?'

'No.' He was short. 'I don't often see him. The music building's miles away.'

'I bet she's small, like him.'

He did not answer this, but slapped the book closed and returned it to the shelf. Jacqueline was humming, ruminatively, rubbing a hand caressingly along the edge of the writing bureau. Bernard was angry, unhappy, dredging in his mind for causes of the despondency. She'd complimented Riley on his music; she'd found him attractive, said so. And here her fiancé was reduced to this sodden misery. It was ridiculous.

'My mother was asking about you,' she said.

'Oh.'

'She came to see me. She wanted to know what work you were going to do. And when.'

'And what did you say?'

'I told her that you'd try to get a university post. And if you didn't you'd perhaps be a schoolmaster, or at a training college.'

'And she said?' Why did he not relax? This wasn't new.

'Oh. Nothing much.'

'I don't believe that.'

She jabbed the palm of her hand once or twice against the top corner of the bureau, looked across, her mouth shaped to whistle, her eyes smiling. He glowered, scraped his thumbnail with his bottom teeth.

'Oh, well, then. The usual. It's not good to start married life on Ike's money.'

'Uh?'

'I said I'd see.' The small voice was happy. 'I'd be prepared to wait for you.'

'But not since you've seen Riley?'

'What?'

Why had he said that damn-fool thing?

'Nothing. Nothing,' he mumbled.

'What did you say?'

'Not since you've seen Riley.'

'What difference does that make?' she said, turning away.

'None, that I know.'

'You're a fool, sometimes,' she said. 'You really are.'

'Doubtless. I'm sorry.' There was a long pause.

'In a way, Bernard, she's right.'

'Is that just your manner of telling me that you want to call the marriage off?'

She looked, long enough, as though the phraseology puzzled her.

'No. It isn't.'

'That's what it sounded like.'

'If you will be so damned childish,' she said, 'you'd better go home. There's no use in talking.'

'Is that what you want?'

'Don't be silly.'

He did not speak, sat there, miserable, staring down at the pattern on the carpet, a spiral nebula. When he tried to finish off the dregs of his beer his throat contracted so that he choked. She sat up straighter, tidied the envelopes, tucked her glasses away into the case. Everything about her was spruce, spry, perky. Neither spoke.

'Would you like a hot drink?' she said in the end.

'No, thank you.'

'I'm going to have one.' She waited for him, cocked an eyebrow, but when he did not answer went from the room. As he waited, his muscles twitched and he glowered. He imagined himself playing tennis against her; standing up to the net he volleyed the ball cruelly at her body. The vehemence of his imagination surprised him, the leap of blood at the racket's swing, but only after he'd played the shot over, varying the angle but not power nor intention, some three or four times.

She returned, clattering cup and saucer. When she sipped, the noise riled him. She put the cup on her chair-arm.

'How was your mother last night?' she asked.

'She'd be the same.' He was surprised. Nobody went.

'I thought your father went every night.'

'They asked him not to. She might . . . suspect . . .'

'Yes. That's sensible.'

His throat was tight. He bit hard into his thumbnail, relishing the pain.

'How's your father taking it?'

'He seems normal, now.' He scraped fingers across his chin. 'It must be awful, after all this time, knowing she's going to die. I mean, they've been together, they remember, and she's condemned. He's just waiting. I don't know how he manages to say anything when he gets there.'

'You go to see her,' she said. 'What do you talk about?'

'I just tell her what I'm doing. At the university. She always liked that. You can't do any more.'

'Then,' she said, 'I expect your father does the same.'

He saw the force of her argument, but it seemed cold to him, repulsive. He needed comfort, not common sense.

'You should know,' he said. 'You had a husband die.'

This was a forbidden subject; he had banned it.

'Yes,' she said, noncommittally, picking up her cup and saucer.

'You should know,' he said aggressively.

'I should know,' she answered. She finished her cocoa.

'I wish you'd come and see my mother again,' he began. 'And Dad. They've only seen you once, and they enjoyed that.'

'Well, I'm busy with this festival, but I expect it could be arranged. When shall we say?'

'Tomorrow. Dad and I are . . .'

'I'll take you in the car. What time shall I collect you?'

'Why not come round for tea?'

'Knees under the table?' She laughed. 'That's what Ike used to say, when I took him to see my parents. "Getting my knees under t'table." ' She laughed again, louder, brassier. 'They didn't approve of him either.'

'What was wrong?'

'I was only nineteen. I hadn't left school very long. And Ike was a man. He looked strong. And spoke old. Daddy didn't like anybody who'd made as much money, and as quickly as he had.' She considered Bernard. 'He frightened me, in a way.'

'Why did you marry him?'

'Attraction.' She giggled. 'Seduction.'

He blushed, hating himself. She seemed not to mind, spun her cup delicately round in the saucer.

'You mean you went to bed with him before you were married.'

'Yes.'

He considered her, the fair hair, the small, fine nostrils, the white hand at the cup. At the moment he could neither hold nor understand himself; the world was a conspiracy, a dark cabal against him. He could do little against weakness. Nothing was understandable; all was a puzzling structure of incomprehension; life, bent on reducing him, offered a series of accurate mirrors, each reflecting his inadequacy. The room was changed. There were books here, but not to be read; pictures painted by the blind for the blind; the check curtains moved, but were dissociated from him. And Jacqueline was there; like twisted metal, a wreck, a write-off. His cheeks burnt fire-red.

She, coolly it seemed, took the cup and saucer from the room.

Rising, he lurched towards the window. In a pot she had a plant there, its green stem growing thicker towards the top, divided into inch-long sections. The leaves, dark-green and polished, edged with purple-brown obscene seed-children, plantlets, thrust strongest upwards at the top, like horns, green-metal, piratical, viking-hard. What was it called? The leaf was cold, dull, thick; a couple of the plantlets fell away.

He'd learnt something; that was unpleasant and salutory.

She returned, walked smartly into his arms and kissed him. He held her, pulling her in, fondling her buttocks. The room did not exist beyond his closed eyes; what was, her mouth on his, her body against his. This minor physical contact stilled him, satisfied him for the moment so that he wanted no more. To deny the consummation of love seemed right, richer than the great act itself. Perhaps that was only sense; he held her, kissed her like an expert. He would have mounted her, fumbling, groping, guilty. This was recognised, unconsciously, under the soft pressure of her lips, the clothed heaviness of her breasts. Else a great prince in prison lies. I have no option, in these circumstances, except to send you to jail.

As he walked back he smelt her face-powder on his lapels. One of the lime-trees bordering the main road had been replaced. The corporation had put a rickety metal fence round the young tree, and there seemed something important, to him, in this. He touched the thin palings, measured the two strides of the pavement, placed both hands on the dull stone wall, checked the two yards of garden behind that and its one dollop of privet and clumps of rooted grass, smiling.

> 'And now in age I bud again;
>   After so many deaths I live and write;
>   I smell once more the dew and rain
>   And relish versing,'

he recited, marching.

He laughed at himself, and waved to a staggerer outside the Vernon Inn.

'Ey up, me o'd duck,' the drunk shouted. 'I'm gooin' courtin'.'

They were both alive.

11

EVENING SUNLIGHT glowed, bathed an irregularly shaped section of the floor near the bow-window of the ward.

Mrs. Allsop tapped listlessly at the newspaper on the bed-clothes. She felt the faint discomfort of her spectacles chafing the bridge of her nose, and lifted her hand to effect relief. All about her was lassitude. She could see clearly enough, hear, smell, imagine, direct her mind to this problem or that memory, but never for long. Lethargy caged her.

Visitors were coming in, with that prepared brightness of face. Mrs. Allsop listened momentarily to the scrape of chairs; one or two greeted her, with a raised hand, a word. She heard, but acted as if her attention were almost immediately switched elsewhere, into a not unpleasant limbo.

'Fire at Newstead Abbey,' she read.

She recalled the great glassless Gothic window, sky-filled, and the green gardens. The fire must have been indoors, somewhere. Vague, vague. Some fly-blown books. A fire-place where David Livingstone split his head open playing blind man's buff. She could not recall the rooms with any clarity, and the smudged memory melted into a present with-out definition, a loss of time where the window's sunshine was painted, and the voices sounded and a clock chimed but were meaningless.

Ivy Allsop was in no pain.

She moved restlessly, more from habit than discomfort. When the aches had begun, had spread, she had learnt to move, to earn a little respite in a fresh position. But not now; she was weak, so feeble as to be near a hurt, but without the hot scouring, that kneading deep inside. The newspaper crackled. She brought herself fumblingly to the print, smoothing with her fingers. Her eyes caught 'The Hill' in a small headline. That was the name of the parish magazine, because the church stood on a hillock over the river valley.

The church; it was sunny there, April, fluffed clouds in blue.

> How sweet the breath beneath the hill
> Of Sharon's dewy rose.

That was a hymn. It neither surprised nor touched. She remembered it as a pianist's fingers remember a well-practised scale, unemotionally. But she had a favourite. They used to sing it on Sunday mornings, when her father's friend, Job Towle, preached; he'd chant it in a high, coarse voice. Rose. Old Job's waxed moustache and quiff.

> The roseate hues of early dawn,
> The brightness of the day.

Castle Rising. The Hill. For a second she felt a jolt of heart's pain, and a tear dropped, slithered, shone unwiped. She looked back at *The Post*. It wasn't 'hill', but 'mill'. 'The Mill Now Re-painted.' Interest drifted off. She wiped her cheeks and looked at the curious stain where the ceiling and wall joined. Voices were about their work; low intimate chatter brought in from the outside world. Every nerve in her body was taut, alert, searching for pain. There was none. For months her body had been a gauge, registering the twinge, the flash of agony. Now it measured nothing, except the dread she'd felt, the quiescence of drugs. Her legs were like string, but without hurt, nothing burnt. A wind flung up the grey-white curtains, rattled the sash window. She touched her glasses, glanced hopelessly at the paper, dropped back to the pillow.

Without curiosity she considered whether her family would come. Bernard. Bernard. Now, now, there, then, she wanted his visits. Excited interest surged, flagged. Her son. And Ernest. He was too fussy, trotting round the bed, paring apples, peeling oranges, ministering. Visitors should sit still, talk of professors. Mary would be doing exams. That used to worry her; the girl must have a good breakfast, be in bed in good time, and as the mother went through the morning's work, her heart would turn over as now and then she thought of the racing fountain-pens answering those typed, duplicated sheets on Henry II, ox-bow bends, enlargement of object. Now these were nothing. The words 'examination', 'daughter' were understood, but meant nothing. Mrs. Allsop felt the sadness of this, the blank, the emptying of herself, the voiding of what she had believed and again tears flushed her eyes. Yet while her eyes still brimmed, the dulled mind had pitched elsewhere, died again into passivity.

'How are you, duck?'

The woman in the flannel hat; visited the old lady; always inquired, as she picked at the big turquoise coat-buttons.

Mrs. Allsop disliked the familiar 'duck'; dying alters no prejudices. She smiled, answered that she was doing nicely. This was the most frequent question, had been for months. She thought back to the onset of the disease, and her fear, her self-indulgence, outbreaks of ill-temper. And the doctor's comfort she hankered for, and got. 'Cancer? Who's talking about cancer? Nothing of the kind, Mrs. Allsop. Internal operation. You women.' She and her husband had gone to the hospital by bus. Fear wiped pain out. She trembled a little now, as she remembered. There casually in the rain in the street, judging the joints in the butchers' shops and hearing the water rattle into drains, and an hour later she was in bed, in hospital, in their clothes, warm, on her own, puzzled, listening to the traffic beyond the lawn and trees and towering wall.

'I think y'are looking a bit more yourself,' the woman said.

Mrs. Allsop did not reply. She was a worrier, concerned with the future, and this place, these medicines had not altered her. The period of worry was shortened. She faced the problem as she did at home, deliberately, but the doubt did not nag, was curtailed. Now, as the flannel-woman moved away, Ivy Allsop remembered the morning of the operation, the visit of the anaesthetist, tension yielding as a sense of well-being prevailed, the trolley-march in corridors and lifts. Her dizziness, desolation as back in her bed she tried to talk sickly to her husband who said, 'You'll be more yourself tomorrow.'

Again, with no sense of transfer, she was in a waking doze.

There was a crow of laughter from along the ward, and an apprehensive silence. She heard; no impression. A nurse passed her bed; the red-faced one, Irish.

'They'll be coming,' she shouted.

'Cummin', 'dey'll'. That weaker left eye spouted a tear at this comfort, and hebetude was reassumed. She wondered what Nurse Maguire was doing. That young woman with the blood transfusions, the frightening apparatus.

Bernard hurried down the ward.

'What did I tell you?' Maguire said. 'Sonny boy's here.' She stopped to shift the patient, impersonally, like dusting a china dog. 'There. Give him a smile, then. I would if he was mine. I would that.'

'She's cheerful,' Bernard said.

'Is your dad coming?' She didn't want to know, but hated waste of words about nurses, trivialities. At least she should be given choice of subject-matter.

'He's here, he's here,' Bernard smiled broadly. 'And Jacqueline.'

'Oh, oh.'

'And Jessica.' She was a joke; he didn't say 'aunt'.

'They won't let you all in together.'

He sat down and began to talk. This ritual of sending in a harbinger touched him; he wondered if she noticed. Quickly, with questions, she got him round to the university. As he had walked the corridors, fearful of change for the worse in his mother, the George Herbert lines, which had dinned round his head from the other night, sang back. He'd heard them first from Meredith.

'How's Professor Meredith?' She pronounced it properly, Welsh fashion.

'All right. He's had a bit of stomach chill. He was really off for a day or two. I couldn't do anything right for him. You talk about sour. He's a real hypochondriac with his bottles and tablets. And then one morning I asked him how things were, and he slapped his midriff and shouted at the top of his voice

> "And now in age I bud again;
> After so many deaths I live and write;
> I smell once more the dew and rain
> And relish versing. Ah, my only light,
> It cannot be
> That I am he
> On whom Thy tempests fell at night.

"That's Herbert," he said to me. "You didn't know that, Bernard, did you?" He took a copy from his shelves. "In my day, we learnt the poetry of the masters of the language. You boys are document-grubbers." ' Bernard enjoyed the accent; docooment, no iotation.

'Very nice,' she said. 'And you remembered it.'

'It's called "The Flower". George Herbert's a great religious poet of the seventeenth century.'

'He wrote,' she said, ' "Let all the world in every corner sing." '

'Did he?' Surprised. That Sunday School bellow? His mind switched to his anecdote. Had he told it before? It happened at least a fortnight ago. Furtively he looked at his mother who was staring ahead.

'What is it?' he asked, holding her hand.

'What's what? Nothing.'

'What were you looking at?'

'Looking? I wasn't looking at anything.' The intonation was that he remembered from childhood, when she had been in a good mood and was amused at some unexpected question he'd posed. The voice chuckled. He was delighted.

The others were coming in. Jacqueline first, Jessica one step behind and trailing, humble, cap literally in hand, his father.

'Here they are,' Bernard said.

'Mrs. Allsop.' Jacqueline's voice throbbed. 'How are you?' Concert-contralto. The mother smiled wanly, holding a claw out. The other two added greetings while Bernard drew chairs up.

'We shall be in trouble; four of you in here,' Mrs. Allsop said.

'We'll meet it when it comes.' Jessica.

'Now, love, what would you like? Orange? Apple? Pear? They're a bit ripe.'

She smiled at her husband, told him not to fuss before she turned and inquired after Jessica.

The reply was noncommittal, rambling, for the visitor was concentrating on her sister-in-law's face. There was nothing inhuman about the woman; she could not resist her pleasure in standing on her own feet while this favoured person, this know-all, was on her back and nearly dead. Mrs. Henshaw would not have admitted this; it was unchristian, and at a deeper level she feared it would initiate some killing disease. She was merely, at the present, more pleased than sorry. She would, tomorrow, parade the becoming words to neighbours, put on black and weep at the funeral next week or in three months, but she had learnt twenty years back that her brother's wife was handsomer, more intelligent, handier, better liked than she was. Her long account of Horace Henshaw's health and ineffectiveness droned on; only Jacqueline listened. Bernard stopped the rigmarole with a pointless anecdote about a cat he had seen chasing a rabbit in the university park. Mr. Allsop put plaintive, disregarded questions about fruit.

Jacqueline Ridell sat uncomfortably, trying not to stare at the scoured wrinkles on Bernard's mother's face. In herself, she became satisfied that she was doing good. But she ought not to be asked to do, to say anything. She did not pity the bag of bones who was Bernard's mother. The wrinkles, the transparent skin, the yellow eyes, the listless fidgeting argued against the figure's humanity so that Jacqueline was surprised to hear a coherent remark in a recognisable voice. With the same slight nauseating shock one's eye travelled down the bone-fine finger to stay on a nail that would have graced a young girl's plump hand. For a moment or two she had been intrigued with the back-door whine of this aunt who took such pains to denigrate her husband. Was this Jessica's method of passing time, of entertaining her sister-in-law? Jacqueline did not know, hated herself. Only one of them came out with credit, Mr. Allsop, and they all ignored him.

'Have you decided when the wedding will be?'

The question was directed at her, through the dry lips. She started. They all watched. It seemed as if every conversation round the ward broke off.

'We had considered Christmas,' the girl said.

They had; idly with twenty other dates.

'We want to wait until you're out,' Bernard said. His mother nodded. Was that necessary? To gush, in lies?

'Don't bother about me. You've your lives to live.'

'Oh, no,' Jacqueline answered. 'We want you there.'

'You've got to get better.' Jessica.

'There's no improvement. None at all.'

They were shocked.

'Who said so? The doctor?' Bernard.

'No. I know myself. I know how I feel.'

'Has the doctor told you there's no improvement?' Bernard's tone was hectoring, forcible with anxiety.

'No.'

'Well, there you are then.'

'You mustn't say that, Mother,' Mr. Allsop said.

'We want you out for the wedding. So you hurry up.'

'Yes, please,' Jacqueline backed Bernard.

'You often feel at your worst before you're better, so it's no use trusting your feelings,' Jessica said. 'You're in good hands. They know what they're about.'

Mrs. Allsop had allowed her eyes to close as if she were praying. They waited. She did not move.

'Are you all right, Mother?' Mr. Allsop. No answer. They sat watching her, in the quiet, dying, without a movement of the interlocked skeleton's fingers. After frozen minutes, she shrugged, opened her eyes, said:

'I think perhaps I will have a portion of orange, Ernest.'

' "Portion",' Jacqueline thought. What a word to die with. Allsop, delighted, was busy, scraping with a knife at the pith of an orange he'd already peeled. Bernard rummaged in the locker for a serviette. Jessica sat the straighter, like a *Punch* charwoman, elbows out.

Mrs. Allsop took the quarter from her husband with a grunt of thanks.

He stood back, unsmiling, obsequious. He did not know what he wanted, but he now became tired of his wife's dying. The idea was fixed; he was used to it; he had prepared himself. When, finally, he found himself a widower, there would be, he expected, some outburst of grief, some unplumbed depth of sorrow, but he had had enough waiting. Like his sister, he would not consciously admit that it was time his wife died. Sometimes he thought back to incidents with tenderness. She had been the stronger, but now and again he had insisted and she had yielded. When Bernard was teething, keeping them both awake, she had shouted hysterically that she was going back to her parents', that he and the baby were killing her. His reason was wasted; in the end, temper broke and he shook her until she was mastered. Something like a year later while they were on holiday, they spent a day walking, leaving the child with her mother. They had paused on the edge of a wood; as he clasped his arms round her, looking over the blue-wooded hills, the stretches of corn, the drought-brown of August hedges, he'd been shaken with sexual desire. She was shocked; he had insisted, bundled her behind the bushes, ripped her knickers down. Nine years later, when Mary was beginning to walk, the child, a handful, threw a tantrum and suddenly his wife had slapped the screaming brat with a book she'd snatched up. This was unusual; she was patient, careful, considerate, an admirable mother. He'd wrested the book from her, flung it, so that it jangled, he remembered, the piano keyboard and she'd fallen back, howling into a chair. The baby, he did not forget, had picked herself up and laid her head comfortingly in the mother's lap.

It was odd he recalled these, and with tenderness.

As she sucked at the orange, he half-stood, helpful. During most of her life she had made the decisions for other people. He was, for example, master in his garden, but she gave the judgement whether or not the peas were worth picking or more carrots were to be grown next year. Now, he thought back to his victories, and with real love for her. She had been energetic, knew her mind, and had yielded to him some dozen or so times in their life and this was valuable at this moment when she sourly mouthed at an orange quarter. She should die, put him face to face with his grief, his loneliness, but not while he was remembering how he'd won now and again. He pushed his clean handkerchief towards her mouth.

Bernard began another anecdote. It concerned one Ben Mowlton, the Reader in Ancient History, a learned and absent-minded man. One of the feeble jokes current amongst undergraduates was that he grew so immersed in his work that he forgot the state of his bladder and had to rush for the lavatory in crisis. Certainly his progress there was more hurried than that on his return. The girls said it was because he was shy about natural functions, but those who attended his lectures thought this unlikely. One day, and Bernard had not retailed any of this closet chatter, Dr. Mowlton was dawdling along the corridor when he stopped one of his students and asked him where he was rushing to; the boy replied that he was late for the doctor's own seminar. Today, the description of Mowlton's amazement, his flight for his note-books, his incredulity at the half-dozen faces gaping in his room, was wasted. The Allsops, brother and sister, did not even pretend to twist their lips into a smile; Jacqueline's attention was directed at a factory half a mile away and the mother, propped up, pushed a half-chewed piece of orange about her plate.

They became aware of a disturbance further down the ward.

Jacqueline turned, rudely. Jessica tilted her nose. It sounded as if someone were breathing very heavily, hoarsely, a snort of noise from a trapped criminal, in films. Talk stopped in the place. Now they recognised the sound: sobbing. Allsop stood, ready to run the menial errand that authority would demand, but nobody moved. The crying squealed louder. There was, apart from it, complete silence; people stared in unrestrained curiosity. This is what Bernard feared on his visits, a death, a relapse, some physical horror, a blatant crack-up.

A scatter of urgent talk broke from a bed half-way down the ward on the other side.

A girl was standing. Her straight hair hung to her shoulders and a huge, polished fringe allowed only a triangle of face to be seen. She stood, in a white sleeveless blouse and a belted black skirt, groping. The hands moved haphazardly and as she swayed under the lacquered hair she sobbed. Suddenly she dashed an arm at her face as if to knock her own head and screamed into the back of her hand. The noise was harsh, big, whooping. A middle-aged woman waddled round from the other side of the bed, put an arm about the girl's shoulders. Before they started for the door Bernard noticed that the woman straightened her hat with the left hand. Just as they began to move the girl shrieked again and then the pair trotted out. The younger woman's buttocks swayed above her clacking high heels.

Bernard looked back at his mother.

She had wriggled deeper into the bed, but was still holding the plate. At the first noise she had stared with the rest. The wrinkled eyes had been like a hen's in a rictus. But, very shortly, she had returned to the messy piece of orange and her fingers.

Chatter hummed again. Within five minutes the middle-aged woman returned. At Mrs. Allsop's bed Jessica was talking in a slow drawl about the instability of young people and their lack of consideration. There was much more un-organised illustrative material. Her sister-in-law paid not the slightest attention. Allsop took the plate from under his wife's hands, wiped her fingers, but she gave no sign. Jessica continued, at Jacqueline, in a low voice that both whined and hectored.

'Are you tired?' Bernard asked. The lecture was continuing. His mother nodded absently.

'Lie down, then. Dad and I will settle you.'

The pair of them helped her down flat on her back, removed the bed-jacket, spectacles, flannelled mouth and eyes. Jessica had made a token pause but now was at it again, quietly fierce, to Jacqueline alone, ignoring the rest.

'Are you comfortable?'

'Yes.'

'Are you going to sleep?' Allsop, bending over. She nodded.

'Go home now. Sleep.'

'You want us to go, Ivy?' Nod. 'Is there anything you'd like, for me to bring you, you know?' She shook her head.

'My mother's tired. She wants us to go now.' Bernard. Jessica stopped, affronted, and clapped the metal lips of her handbag together. She looked about her as if she had lost something, stood up, said:

'Well, then. Yes. Time we went. Yes. Now you look after yourself, Ivy. And don't forget, anything you want, just let me know.'

'I'd like my health and strength.' Feebly.

'I can't give you that. I would if I could.'

'I know you would. I don't want anything else.'

Mrs. Allsop closed her eyes. She opened them again as she spoke to Jacqueline whom she thanked in a courteous sentence. Bernard took his mother's hand as he bent to her, and she put an arm heavily about his neck. Next she kissed her husband and sister-in-law perfunctorily. Jessica made another search, on the bedclothes, the floor-space, moving her chair, and they filed out.

'She's no better,' Jessica said, immediately they were on the corridor. Nobody answered that. 'She's still in her right mind. It's amazing, isn't it? D'you know, there was a woman who lived up our street . . .'

This was addressed to Jacqueline, the favoured.

The girl walked on, staring ahead, utterly down.

12

B ERNARD SAT reading the *Evening Post*.

He had worked all day in his cubby-hole at the university, not arriving home until after seven. Now, with a cup of tea, he was enjoying a ritual with the evening paper that never had been quite superseded by television-watching. He didn't read systematically, but let his eye dart here, stay as critically on an advertisement for a second-hand guitar or scooter as on the front-page court case or political tangle. Out in the yard he could hear his father talking. The old man had mashed Bernard's pot, had washed the dishes, cleaned up, shooed Mary upstairs to her homework and was now on his way to the garden. Some crony must have called, and the son was glad. He'd little to say to his father but knew his loneliness and was delighted when something happened to relieve it. He wished Allsop had been more sociable, a member of one of the men's clubs, even the allotment-holders' association, but the old chap had remained satisfied with his home, and that was that. His wife had not even been able to get him to her chapel, except at Harvest Festival or Anniversary. But in these last months, while the mother had been worse, people had stopped to talk, had refused to shift when he was most laconic, forced their consideration on him whether he wanted it or not. And Bernard thought it had affected him; he was less taciturn, could turn a sentence on the weather or the dahlias or the Test Match as well as the next man.

Now, vaguely, the son could hear the voices outside, but unrecognisable. That old bore Whittaker, Tom Westmoreland or Willy Flood and his stooping son. He nodded with satisfaction, went back to his paper, read how Amanda Ellis, aged six, had collected a mile of pennies. If a penny has a diameter of one inch . . . ? Or was it a ha'penny? His mind staggered into arithmetical contortions. The back door was pushed open, sticking as usual, and the voices became more insistent.

'Bernard, here's Mr. Butler to see you.'

Tom with a fool job, Bernard thought. He was mistaken. The white head and red jaw of the senior Butler were presented.

'Hello, sir.'

'Mr. Butler would like to talk to you.' He motioned the visitor to a chair, while his son noisily wrapped his newspaper away.

'How is, is, your, the, er, wife?' Butler asked, grunting. He had been talking for at least five minutes outside. Just remembered?

'No better,' Allsop answered steadily. 'She'll never be any better, I'm afraid.'

Butler lowered his jowl into his collar.

'Well, then, I'll leave you to it.' Allsop raised a rustic forefinger. Bernard crossed his legs, looked inquiringly at his visitor.

'You well?' Butler mumbled, stroking his Kaiser Wilhelm hair. 'Ah. Then. Now. I thought I'd come to see you.' His words were gobbled, indistinct. 'You see, my wife and I have been talking it over and, in the end, it only seemed fair, proper, to visit you here, tell you what we had on our minds.'

There was a proconsular air about the man. He spoke straight at his hearer; his blue, bloodshot eyes did not wander. A finger was lodged in what would have been a pocket, had he worn a waistcoat. Bernard edged forward, uneasy.

'I'll be quite blunt with you, now. That's my way. I'm used to it. I found it generally pays.' He stopped, blubbered his lips as if he found himself short of a drink, the acceptable social mode of pausing. 'To be quite frank, I, that's my wife and I, think that, er, well, are not convinced that you and Jacqueline are suited, er, exactly.' He stopped again, snapped, 'I'd like your views.'

Bernard was taken aback, did not reply.

'Oh, I see, I see,' Butler continued. 'We've talked this out. We're not convinced. I know it's not a light matter and I didn't come here without considerable thought.'

'On your own account?' Bernard's voice was cold, small, in contrast to his fear, the contracting shock.

'Account? I don't understand you.'

'Did you speak to anyone else?' Again the steadiness.

'My wife. I told you that. Yes. My wife.'

'Jacqueline?'

'Jacqueline? Do you mean did we consult Jacqueline?' Butler looked quite blown at the suggestion. 'No, sir, we did not.'

There was a pause during which Butler breathed loudly, shifted from ham to ham in his chair so that it creaked. Bernard was afraid, physically cowed, shrunken in his fingers, his thighs, his shoulders.

'Why?' he said. His voice cracked on the word which toppled like a clayey stone into water. 'Will you tell me why you think we aren't suited?' Better, more controlled. Further rolling from Butler, magisterial handling of his jowls, out-breathings.

'It's a long story,' he answered, after a time. 'Complicated. I don't know how much she's told you about her first marriage. She has confided in you, I expect.' She had not. Butler did not wait for confirmation. 'They did not get on. I am putting it mildly, on purpose. I blamed Ike Ridell at the time. I still do. Nothing but good about the dead and so forth, but I can't forgive him for what he did to my daughter.' He puffed, wallowed. 'We used to talk about it then, my wife and I. "It's none of our business," she'd say. "You'll only make matters worse. Grin and abide." They didn't match. You knew that, of course.'

Still Bernard kept his mouth shut.

'She was too young, in fact. I thought so, at the time, but there's no telling some people. She knew her mind. She loved him, and that was that. But it wasn't all honey and roses. He wanted his way, because that's what he was used to. If anybody was a boss it was young Ridell. In business you develop certain methods; you wouldn't know, but I've been about the world, mixed with them, good and bad. And people like him, go-getters, profit-makers, are ruthless. They'd go to the wall otherwise.'

Butler heaved himself upright in the chair, banged his hands down to clasp the wooden arms.

'And she wouldn't have it. Don't allow that quiet, meek-and-mild face to take you in. She's obstinate, if she thinks she's being imposed on. He was generous. I'll give him that. She could do pretty well as she liked, except that she had to appear at certain of his social functions. He was proud of her; they made a fine pair. But on those occasions she had to be ready, and by that he meant beautifully dressed and so on, the money was there, and exactly when he said. These weren't frequent. Not more than once a fortnight. Otherwise, she could do as she pleased. In the ordinary way he'd try to get home for the evening meal, but it wasn't always possible. Money doesn't follow you round like a dog. You've got to chase it when and where it shows up. And if he got back and found her out, not often at first, I may tell you, he didn't complain. Only these formal occasions. But she wouldn't have it. She'd make him late, try to fluster him, pretend she'd forgotten. She was inexperienced and so on, but she could do that all right. She wasn't blameless. You might well think she was asking for trouble.'

Bernard felt cooler and angrier.

'He lost his temper, threatened to beat her. That made matters worse. Again, to give him his credit, he saw that it was so, but he just couldn't contain himself and once or twice it did come to blows. Well, that's that. I don't want to go over it again. To tell you the honest truth I don't like to think about it even now.' Nor did Bernard. He thought fighting mad, unlike himself, as he sat, so that he missed the next sentences of Butler's argument. When he was calmer, listening again, he heard: 'It was horrible. My wife, well, I won't, you can imagine, dreadful, dreadful.'

'Are you afraid that I shall, er, er, do something similar?' Bernard asked. It seemed ridiculous.

'No, sir. I am not. I'll be frank with you in that I was glad when Ridell died. He might have been a loss to the city and its industry and all the rest of it, as they said at the time, but he was no loss to me. I'm talking frankly. I always do. I've no time for the mealy-mouthed. As far as I was concerned he was a swine.'

'From what I can make out,' Bernard intervened, foolishly again, doing nobody good, merely asserting his presence, 'she was very upset when he died.'

Butler pulled a sour face, coughed.

'What do you expect? They were married. Death's a matter of importance. Have you never . . . ?' He stopped, remembering Mrs. Allsop. 'Well, yes, now. Yes. Now, where you come in.' He smiled, ponderously but friendly like a solicitor announcing a bequest. 'It's more than a year now and we can say she's got over . . . the other, er . . . You appear. Now I'm going to put this to you as I see it. You may not like it, and you can say so. You appear on the scene. Decent young chap. Clever. With a bit about you. You can talk, I expect. But you were quiet. You didn't throw your weight about. The opposite. You can see the attraction, can't you? All he wasn't. Culture. Knowledge. I've nothing against these. I'm an engineer, roughed it.' Bernard grinned. The man was a caricature, as he puffed on about his experience of a world of men. This led after five minutes' rapid reminiscence back to reiteration of his remarks about the attraction of a quiet, modest, literate person. 'Now I've said all this you can see where it's leading. This marriage may be as disastrous as the last.'

'What makes you think that?'

'My dear young man, I've just explained at length.' Butler glowered, annoyed.

'You've just pointed out that I am the opposite of a husband she did not get on with. It seems neither logical nor anything else to deduce from that that this marriage will be unsuccessful.'

'It's the quick . . . the quick choice. Headlong rush into it.' Butler was floundering.

'I grant that you can't conclude that the marriage will be a success, but the thing to do is to look at me, my qualities and so on.'

'I have. And, moreover, this time I am determined to speak before it's too late.'

'Yes,' said Bernard. 'I can see that I'm not as formidable as Ridell.'

It took some seconds for Butler to grasp this. He knotted his forehead.

'There's no need for you to take it like that.'

'Mr. Butler.' Bernard was beginning to enjoy himself. The physical ache had disappeared; he saw his visitor as a fool. 'I'll tell you that I'm not quite satisfied with your explanation.'

'Why not?' Fast.

'Aren't you too positive? If you'd have said that the last marriage was unsuccessful, and that you'd like me to be careful, not to rush things, to be especially considerate of Jacqueline, to give her time to know her mind I should have seen the sense of it. But this "You're no good for her" doesn't convince me. It's . . .'

'What you've just said is exactly what I've been trying to say.' Butler looked genuinely glad. Bernard was shaken. Was that true? Had the man been unable to communicate except in his clumsy, hectoring fashion?

'Well, that's sensible,' Bernard conceded. 'I thought that there was some other motive. For instance, you might have concluded that all I want is Jacqueline's money.'

'You've thought about it, then?'

'Of course I have.

Butler frowned, slapped pig-fingers on the chair-arm.

'I don't like that,' he said. 'I'll tell you straight.'

Bernard shook his head.

'I wonder what Jacqueline would say if she knew you were here.'

'Nothing. She'd know I wouldn't take these steps without her interests at heart.' He flapped his jowls, frowned deeply, slumped forward.

'She mightn't be very pleased that you hadn't consulted her.'

'She knows very well,' Butler said, 'that she made a hash of it last time.'

'People deceive themselves.'

'Maybe so, maybe so. But I don't think she does. She remembers only too well . . .'

'We tend to forget the unpleasant.'

'Do we? Do we?' These two were barked out in a kind of breathless desperation. 'I don't know. There are some things I wish I could forget. And one of them is seeing her, my own daughter, with her face streaked with tears standing in that damned hall of her house and saying over and over again, "I can't come home, Daddy. I'm married to him. I can't." I pleaded, I can tell you. She wouldn't budge.'

Bernard was generously moved. Notwithstanding the clichés, the far-back gobbling, get-the-men-on-parade, sarn't-major voice, Butler had hung out his anxiety, like a signal, and Bernard read it. His imagination fumbled at the picture of the weeping Jacqueline and he hated the world.

'I tell you what,' he said, 'we'll do to set your mind at rest.' He felt as he talked to the older man like some newly appointed prefect about to deliver his first homily to a fag, completely capable and a hypocrite. 'One or the other of us, you or me, as you like, will go to see her and discuss this so that she knows exactly what she's about. Preferable if you go, but I will, if you want it that way. Together, if you like.'

'Well . . .' Grudging.

'We'd explain exactly. . . . Or you'll explain exactly all your doubts and, er, provisos,' words were running away with him, 'to her.'

'Well, no. That's not quite the point.'

Bernard's irritation flashed. The man was not reasonable. He wanted flat capitulation. 'I am not fit to marry your daughter nor have the honour to lick your boots, please sir, your humble and obedient servant, sir, sir, sir.'

'What is the point, then?'

'It's difficult to put, put one's finger on it exactly.' Butler stopped, bubbling, on the expression, pressing his fat-fold over his tie and patting his hair. 'Somehow, I just do not feel that this marriage is going to prove, er, successful. That's all.'

Bernard was angry now.

'Why not?'

'I've done my best to explain.' The judicial expression, the finger-tips, well-scrubbed, rather delicate, together, the peering through the eyebrows, the heavy breathing as if in exasperation at stupidity all seemed uncertain, assumed, almost practised, and inadequately at that. 'The circumstances that I have outlined. . . .'

'Mr. Butler.' The visitor jerked as if he had been kicked. 'All this is nothing but prejudice.' Bernard became solemn. 'If you have anything against me, come out with it now. I'll listen. Be just as frank as you like.'

'I have explained to you . . .'

'You haven't. That's utterly wrong.'

Butler was bent double, forwards, his right hand placed, almost at random, across his face, dwarfed. He moved up, squared his shoulders. His eyes bulged, dull marbles.

'I will not be spoken to, young man, like that by you or by anybody else.'

Bernard shrugged.

'Mr. Butler, I've every sympathy with you. I really have. But look, what have you got against me? All it boils down to is that you don't want your daughter to marry again, or at least, just now. If I were a millionaire or a rajah, I suppose I'd do, but as I'm not you see me as an awkward devil who's egging her on to do something silly.'

'Exactly.'

Bernard was displeased. Whatever he said was taken by Butler as supporting evidence. He wasted his time.

'Your argument only holds, though, if the premise is correct.' This like his last speech was prim; he'd won the argument and was now merely goading his opponent for pleasure. 'You argue from the idea that she shouldn't re-marry. I tell you that is quite false.' He ought to have wagged his finger in the man's face. 'Thus I refute it.'

'I thought I could get you to see reason.' Butler puffed out a little breath with the words. 'You are, young man, you, you are selfish about this.' The door opened. Mr. Allsop walked in. 'You've no consideration for anybody except yourself. That's putting it bluntly.'

'You're not going to say that.' Allsop.

He was wearing a laddered cardigan held by one button. He wore no collar; his hair spiked out untidily and he was carrying his gardening gloves. The two seated men looked up at him.

A big silence.

'What's he saying, Bernard?' The voice was flustered.

'It's all right, Dad.'

'No, it's not. He gave me some sort of explanation of what he was doing, what he wanted when we were out there in the yard. I believe in allowing any man his say, and I let him come in. Anyway, you're old enough to stand up for yourself. But he's not going to sit there in my house blackguarding my son. You won't find a better wherever you look or when. And I'm speaking, Mr. Butler, from what I know, from personal knowledge. You've just said to him what you've come to say, I don't doubt, and now I've come in to say to you what he won't say for himself.'

'This was an amicable argument, Dad.'

'It didn't sound like it to me. Bernard's a hard-working

boy. He didn't get a first-class honours degree in history idling about. He worked. All day. Every day. And moreover, he'd give a hand at home. While my wife's been ill, I don't know what I should have done without him. He's stood by me, thick and thin. When I didn't know whether I was on my head or my heels, he'd be there with a steady word or action. I'll tell you something, Mr. Butler.' He shambled forward round the table to stand on the hearthrug between the two. There was a smudge of mud across his cheek. The arms, where the cardigan was rolled, were bone-thin, long-haired. 'This last six months I've been through hell. I wouldn't want any man to know let alone feel what I've had to put up with. But if one thing's helped me to keep sane it's been the behaviour of my children. This boy here, in his quiet way, has been like a brother to me. And the girl. Many's the time I've felt like cutting my throat, and he's come in with a cup of tea or cocoa or whatever it is and started asking about this and that in the garden. And he's no interest in it. But he's remembered enough to start me talking and take my mind off. That's the sort he is, and that's the reason that neither you nor anybody else is going to sit in this house blackening his character.'

Bernard listened, proud, embarrassed. But his pride was bogus in that he did not believe his father was settling anywhere near the truth. Butler manufactured fiction about his daughter; Allsop's defence of his son was spurious. Both liars were united in sincerity.

He had never heard his father talk like this before. The old man was unassertive; willing to underwrite his wife's opinion or decision. Now and again some political issue would squeeze a few sentences out of him, but these were offered diffidently and only in front of his immediate family. This performance would be more typical of Mrs. Allsop. To Bernard's mind it smacked of back-wall controversy or confession. This was the sort of emotional statement that he'd overheard from women. 'She were real good to me. A saint, d'you know. I says to our mester, "I don't care who she is an' what she's done, if ever there was a saint o' God on that day, it were her." '

The old man's aggression was worked out on his garden paths or his plants. But this, racked by his wife's illness, the frustrations of waiting, had pricked him into this outburst. Bernard smiled. In the same way, perhaps, Butler's lips had been unlocked; God knows what personal inadequacy had kicked him here to take it out of his daughter's young man. Very likely it was nothing of the sort; his wife had bullied him into coming and that was why he had been so feeble. Bernard preferred the feminine approach of his father. But the other man had swerved into that vein, with his 'tear-streaked face' and his daughter's refusal. Suddenly, and he judged sentimentally, the son felt sorry for them both, wanted a reconciliation.

Butler had pursed his lips and with a flat hand was patting his silver waves.

'I'm sure you're right, Mr. Allsop,' he said, quietly. 'And just as you speak for your son, I must defend my daughter.'

'Not at his expense.'

'No. I didn't put it well. I'm not used to this sort of work. I'm too used to handing out orders. It's been my job and I see that that's not the approach here. Mr. Allsop, I apologise unreservedly both to you and to your son.'

'There's no need.'

'Yes. There is. And I shall take Bernard's advice. I'll go round, tell Jacqueline what I've done. Clear matters up.'

Mr. Allsop inclined his head, and smiled, rather insipidly, at his son.

'Good,' he said. 'I spoke out of turn myself. Get us a drink, Bernard. What would you like, Mr. Butler?'

'Very nice of you. Well, I'll have whisky, if you . . .'

'I didn't mean that kind.' Allsop spoke quite simply. 'We don't keep strong drink, er, well medicine. I mean tea or coffee or cocoa, something of the sort.' He smiled again, false teeth falsely even.

Butler was confused. He had his hands pulling on his trousers' legs.

'I'll have,' he said, 'just what, whatever you're having.'

'Tea, then,' Allsop answered. 'Bernard'll mash, while I clean the garden off my hands.'

13

Dr. Riley came across Bernard in the university refectory and invited him to go for a day's walking in Derbyshire.

Bernard accepted at once. He was bored by his research; being at present reading and fact-sifting, 'lad's work'. The fancy theories of Collingwood about the correct question did not apply; he read with elementary queries before him: is this relevant? Might it be so? He had done a great deal, was pleased with progress, could probably boast, as Meredith said cheering him, that he knew more about that decade in this part of the world than any other historian living. But it irked him. This was antiquarianism; he wanted to have to use his brains.

Jacqueline, too, was distant. She'd two preoccupations. The first was a holiday, planned months before, on the Costa Brava with her parents. The preparations were enormous and intense. Maps, friends, brochures, agents were endlessly consulted; books of reference fairly tumbled; long arguments tangled how every minute should be spent. Mrs. Butler would down tools in her kitchen, dash to her plans and notes, and nudge the holiday an inch further before she rang her daughter whom she kept, willingly, for half an hour at the phone. Father was dragged in. He had 'good ideas' and 'corrections', but soon lost interest. An hour a week was as much as he was prepared to spend planning a holiday where, as Jacqueline frankly told her fiancé, they'd lie in all probability most of the time under a striped umbrella, sucking pints of orange juice through straws. Bernard, however, got the impression that they were issuing the passports, booking the berths, building the hotel, piloting the plane and fanning the sun. Jacqueline's second interest was her brother's festival; she seemed to do five unpaid half-days of clerking on that every week.

She was vague, therefore; infinitely pleasant but not concentrating on the young man's affairs, so that when Riley made his proposal Bernard accepted. They were to meet at the Midland Station early. Riley was leaving his car to his wife and family, a sacrifice, it seemed. On the train they exchanged Christian names, said little else. The elder man stared out of the window, chin in hand. Once they had alighted in Bakewell and had set off down the road, he became more cheerful, chattered about Tom Butler.

It was difficult to make out whether he despised or admired. Butler had talent, at driving others to work; Butler could perform miracles, provided somebody else did the grind; he'd conjure assistants from all over the city, and get the credit, and paid work, all to himself. Riley, bouncing along in his khaki shorts, with his rucksack and white legs, seemed to enjoy these antitheses; they appeared with the regularity of a schoolboy's cheer-boo jangle. 'We're building a house (boo!), a public house (hooray!); only one bar (boo), a hundred yards long (hooray!). We shan't sell beer (boo!); we'll give it away (hooray!).'

There was nothing intense now about the man. He had the manner that Bernard disliked in young lecturers on their beery nights-out with their students, matey scandalising. There was nothing he hated more than some chemist drunkenly spelling out to an equally boozed third-year man what a bastard the prof., called by his christian name, had turned out to be over the publication of some stuff he'd slaved his guts out to get done because . . . Same again, Landlord.

Riley rattled on. His talk was inconsequential and cheerful. Bernard, remembering the dedicated musician, had been apprehensive and felt deflated at the moment listening to this jangle. Not that Riley was lacking in intelligence. He was rather interesting about Jacqueline. She was bright enough, like her brother; they got it from the mother. The old man, for all his talk of far-flung empah and forty years' experience, was a failure. He'd never built anything very big and he'd never made substantial money. That's why she'd married Ikey Ridell and why, he was disarmingly blunt, Riley couldn't make out what she was up to getting engaged to a pen-pushing historian.

'Mark you,' Riley said. 'She's attractive. I fancy her myself.' He ushered this out at the blue-grey hills in his breathless voice, almost as if dictating, so that no one could take offence.

'You're a married man.' Mock naive.

'There's not a married man in England between thirty and forty who doesn't fancy some other bird. My wife's a good woman. I'm glad I married her. But we've got four kids. A weary shag every fourth Friday in Lent. A man likes a girl dressed up for him, out to attract him, not somebody cribbing like the clappers because he's home half an hour later than he said he'd be.'

'Do you . . . ? Do you go off with . . . ?'

'Other women? None o' your business, my lad.' He laughed throatily. 'And when I'm down to work I don't stick to a regular timetable, and that's what a family of four squealers requires. So I find myself without a meal, or with a burnt offering the God of bloody Israel couldn't recognise, and my wife going up the wall and shouting the roof off. But I'm lucky. I can work. And Armstrong's confirmed me here in my job. I'm grateful. Not many'd do that. I know. I've had the sack. Twice. Sir E. Walter Purley, he was my last prof. "If you can't deliver lectures at the set hours, Dr. Riley, you'd better take yourself off elsewhere. This is an institution dedicated to teaching and learning. You attempt neither." '

'Was he any good? I've heard him on the wireless. . . .'

'Oh,' Riley answered, 'he'd be clever academically when

he was about twenty-five, and very attractive then, I'd guess. But he's just a dried-up old prick now. Doesn't know a semiquaver from a dose of clap. And jealous.'

'Of you?'

'Yes.' Riley, still clomping the heavy boots down, slapped his khaki-drill behind. 'He'd just enough talent left to see I'd got something he'd never even had. Didn't like it.'

'Isn't Armstrong the same?'

'No. Never anything creative there. Administrator. He's told me what I've got to do in one-syllable words. I do it, well or badly, and he provides me with plenty of space and time to compose in return. I'm lucky. There aren't many Frankie Armstrongs about.'

'What are you writing now?'

'I never talk about the work I'm on with.' Snap. Like that.

'Are you satisfied with life?' Bernard asked, embarrassed at the rebuff.

'That's exactly what I'm not. When people come up to me and say, "I wish I'd your creative gifts", I could pole-axe 'em. I wish they bloody well had. You're creative because of other matters, and one is, well, Christ, I don't know how to describe it, but I'd say it was a yearning, that's a bloody wet word for it, for anything you haven't got. Let's think.' He scratched his head violently. 'Imagine a Welsh choir, giving it seven sorts. I hate the bloody sounds and sights of it. Every bastard one of 'em a soloist, twisting his neck sore to blast his neighbour's soul and singing reputation. And yet I want to know what they're on with. I can tell the tune's nineteenth-century orange-squash and vinegar, but the words, Welsh words to make their black eyes start out of their head. If I knew the language, I'd probably see that they were as trivial as the tune. But I don't. It's not some drivelling lyric about sunshine on the green hills by some nonconformist person dressed up as a bloody Arab for the eisteddfod, it's mystery, what I don't know.'

'But that only includes . . .'

'What?'

'I mean,' Bernard said, 'that you only want to be, to take part in things you approve of.'

'No. I've just said I dislike Welsh choirs.'

'May I suggest that's untrue?' Bernard giggled at his daring.

'Damn me.' Riley laughed. 'You're sharp. You'll be at home with the high-table brigade.' He spat histrionically. 'You might be right.'

'You wouldn't want to be blind or a criminal or, er, dying?'

'I see. For a short time, if it were reversible. See what I mean?'

They walked hard for a couple of hours and stopped at a pub. Here Riley was abstemious; he drank a pint and a half while he ate his pork-pie and sandwiches. Inside he hardly spoke, no outdoor garrulity, asking rather formally, as if to get on better terms, about Bernard's work. His eating had a prodigious quality; he chewed enormously so that his closed mouth seemed to orbit round his face. When they'd finished he suggested they start again and Bernard, who, no drinker, had been dreading a session, was pleased.

Ten minutes further on Riley said:

'This is where we stop.'

'What for?'

'Sleep.'

They climbed over a dry-stone wall, picked a corner in the sunshine, and lay flat down. Riley, rucksack under his head, was out at once, but Bernard found the ground hard, the flies troublesome. At two-fifteen, however, it was the older man, prancing, heaving his shoulder-straps about, who woke his companion.

'Straight up,' Riley said. 'No roads for us.'

They sauntered, dazed still, up the clumpy field, clambered walls and worked their way out to rough moorland. The valley to their left was wider now, with road, river and occasional houses, but at each side on the crest rock stood bare, like a grey untidy cock's comb.

'That's the objective,' Riley said, finger out at the highest of the peaks. 'About a couple of miles.'

The going was harsher, in the sun with the grey stone closer to the surface, hardly hidden by the heather, ling, thin grass. Riley had now stopped chattering, though he still flapped his arms like an ugly bird.

'This is the life,' he said.

They staggered across three or four fields, ran foul of rusty barbed-wire; once Bernard stumbled, fell heavily, knocked the breath out. Riley stopped then, wiped his glasses.

'Is it a race?' Bernard. Riley wiped sweat off.

They began again; cloud crossed the sun and wind whipped their faces, pleasantly. The uneven ground, the frequent obstacles, the uncertain pace kept the younger man constantly in discomfort. He skidded again, found himself cut with a stitch. Riley was blowing hard.

'Steady on,' said Bernard, stopping.

Riley looked wild, arms flailing, fingers working but he stood there, legs apart, glaring over the valley. After a moment's sitting, Bernard found it cold, shuddered, but refused to move. The sun emerged and he felt refreshed.

'Right.'

Riley nodded, stepped away, skidded and slid a yard or two down the fierce slope. He sprang up, swore as he marched, batted at his buttocks. Now, at last, they found themselves near the peak, their objective. They plugged up rough grass, one in one, until knees ached and breath tore. At the top of this a rock-cliff reared, scarred, grey, twisted, wind-banged.

'Sit down,' Riley said, and undid one of his boots, tightened the lace. Below a car slowly toddled the road. Bernard with no head for heights pushed his back against the rock as he sat, drove the heels of his shoes into the thin earth. The breeze swung chilly.

'Ready?' Riley said. 'We'll go up to the top.'

'Up the cliff?'

'Yes. There's a way. Not climbing really. All right?'

Bernard nodded, hopeless. Riley trotted about. 'Haven't

quite got the place.' His companion sat down again; the cliff above him was vertical, might even boast an overhang. Riley was swearing in a blustering way, like a child drawing attention to new shoes by marching with dead-straight swinging arms. Pointless. He came back.

'Can't find it,' he said.

'Doesn't matter.'

'It's hereabouts. I've done this times. Look again.'

Bernard sat, miserable. He was cold, out of the sun, frightened; the soles of his thin town shoes looked wet-grey, cardboard. There was a howl from the other man. Bernard got up.

Riley was, perhaps, fifty yards off, rubbing his hands, pointing.

'This is the bastard.'

He pointed at a great piece of fallen stone, ten feet or more long, sloping at an angle of forty-five degrees. He jumped on to this, his nailed boots scraping, turned, called. Bernard followed. At the end of the fragment they moved on to the rock proper and went rapidly upwards and left on a series of six or eight natural steps, each two feet high and no more than six inches out. Bernard came up to Riley who stood on a small platform a yard square, twenty feet above the place from which they had started.

'Be careful here,' Riley said, and swung so that his rucksack struck the other man a clumsy blow. 'Not dangerous, but . . .' He reached up to a ledge, seven foot higher, scrabbled with his toes, levered his elbows, and awkwardly dragged himself up.

'I'll wait for you,' he said. 'There's a bit of a path now.'

Bernard reached up to the ledge, fitted his fingers, lifted his right foot, slithered it about until he made a foothold, dragged the left, moved it about on rock that seemed mirror-smooth. The pain in his fingers was excruciating. He heaved like hell on his hands; jabbed his left toe into the wall. For the moment he moved upwards, powerfully, but energy died, both feet tickled loose and he fell. His shoes hit the platform, three feet below, with a jolt that screwed the bones up into his pelvis.

Breath was knocked out of him and he felt sick. There was some sort of despair about the whole thing; next time he'd slip again in the same ignominious way, but over the edge of the platform and down the unfriendly face.

'I'll give you a pull,' Riley called.

Bernard raised his right foot, found the same hold. Above, his companion seized his wrist, began to drag brutally. He lifted the left leg, kicked the rock, found a knob. Riley was hauling with violence now; forearms and knees judged, scraped painfully. It seemed as if both legs dangled loose and only the torturing heaving on one wrist until the artery throbbed and leapt, near bursting, kept him there. His right foot gripped; his left knee knocked the ledge; again he was stuck, couldn't shift. If Riley let go, he'd topple back, flop off. It didn't seem to matter. Another jerk; the knee banged the rough corner, was miraculously on the ledge.

He was bruised, but his clothes were untorn. He wanted to hang on to his mate, scream, drag both hysterically off the perch, madly down, to the daft safety of the field forty feet below.

'You all right?'

Bernard nodded. He couldn't speak. The trembling in his legs was like language, the vocabulary of panic. His face was turned inwards to the rock.

'We go along this path, ledge affair here. Wait until I've turned the corner and then come.'

The path was clear, perhaps ten feet long and between twelve and three inches wide. The wall above was vertical, as was the drop below. Riley marched on, took a step or two, turned, faced the rock, edged sideways quite quickly, his hands about shoulder height. Just before he turned, at right angles, out of sight, he called:

'It's easier from now on.'

Bernard loathed himself. His body was water, dirty useless fluid. He did not dare step on the path. With a fierce shrug he pulled his shoulder-bag upwards; he wanted to weep. Forty, fifty feet. Might not be killed. He turned inwards on to the path, stood trembling, hands touching the unfriendly cold, the mild roughness of the rock in front. Forcing himself, he began to edge sideways, inch by inch. His legs were stiff as if any relaxation would scatter their power, topple him down. Frightened as he was he hoped Riley wasn't watching him. A fearful glance leftwards showed he'd progressed a yard. He was winning, in spite of fear which twisted his testicles, flushed his bowels. A phrase hummed in his head: 'The bold anfractuous rocks'. He'd no idea where it was from, but repeated it, drummed it out silently like a charm, a prayer. 'The bold anfractuous rocks, bold anfractuous, anfractuous, anfractuous.' He was moving better, more firmly, six inches at a time. Anfractuous. The fright was there, the drag of the space below, apprehension as to what he'd meet round the corner, but he was travelling, was in some small warm control of himself. 'Anfractuous rocks.' He'd manage it. Squinted right, nearly there, moving still, anfractuous, curse it, had a leg round, on a wide place, flat where you could stand or turn round. To the top there were steps, not difficult, with bits of grass, curling brambles and Riley, on the edge, shouting, 'Straight up.'

Bernard went hard. His thin shoes were scuffed, but he pulled uncaring, no, rushed faster, took no notice of scratches, stood at last in the wind, which buffeted his face.

'Good?' Riley asked.

'Good.' He grinned, felt sick, sat down, examined his shoes, undid and retied a lace before slowly scanning the bottom of the valley below, under the rock he could not see, the road and river at the intersection of the friendly green slope of the fields.

'Enjoy it?' Riley.

'Not bad.' What if he suggested they descend the same way, so that he'd edge, farting, along the path, muttering, in full disgraceful view of his companion? He could not.

'Were you frightened?' God. God.

'A bit. On that ledge.'

Riley was sitting now, a penknife in hand, poking the mud from his boots. He was concentrated, eyes staring in the pale face, hair mop-like, glasses awry. When he spoke it was downwards, at the ground.

'The first time I did this I was terrified. Two of them had to push me, bodily, like a sack, up to the path. I was a school-kid then, in the sixth form. I've been back at intervals to try it. I came on my own, got here, and walked away, made myself come back. It took me an hour to do what we did in two minutes.'

'I often wonder about these mountaineers,' Bernard said. 'Aren't they scared?'

'They can't be as scared as I was or they wouldn't do what they do. They're all athletes, of course, nowadays. But they can't feel the fear. I'm petrified at the top of a ladder.'

'I suppose if you succeed, you're more confident next time.'

'Yes,' Riley said. 'That's so with me. I have a sort of ghost of the fear, the beginnings of a tremor, when I do this now. Sometimes I quite long for the terror back again.'

'Why don't you go somewhere else, harder?'

'Don't talk like a bloody fool. It's the old story. I want what I haven't got. I'll tell you.' He leaned back, yawned for what seemed minutes. 'I didn't marry the first girl I was really in love with. And now, I'm quite shaken, literally tousled and tossed by a—the wish that I'd done so. If I think, I realise that I made the right choice, that my wife's as good as I'm likely to get, and yet there I am like a great stretched cock.' He collapsed, flat, crossed his boots. 'That's me. I've got to live with it.'

'Is it your music?'

'Music? I don't know. I suppose I tantalise myself, keep my nerves pretty raw. I do without meals, starve myself of fags to get straight with my work.' He snatched angrily at a blade of grass, pushed it between his teeth, chewed.

'What do you want?'

'Success. Money. Just the same as anybody else.'

'Not self-respect,' Bernard said. 'The sense of a job well done.'

'Sense of balls.'

The sun came out, and they lay in a sheltered hollow, with eyes closed, enjoying the orange-red warmth. There was no suggestion about further climbing, and they walked leisurely to the station six miles off, drank tea, travelled back in a carriage crowded with six-formers with hiking boots, two pairs of socks, anoraks and screeched jokes.

14

MARY ALLSOP began the school holidays in annoyance. There had been some talk, since April, of her accompanying Jacqueline and the Butlers to Spain. It was difficult to determine how serious this was; perhaps it was only a further paper-complication to add to Mrs. Butler's pleasure in plotting the holiday. At any rate, one letter had reached Mr. Allsop about the project, and he'd made several phone calls. In the end the scheme fell through when Jacqueline put it tentatively to her mother than Mrs. Allsop might die while they were abroad. It was useless to argue; Mrs. Butler got it into her head that Mary would have to be rushed back for the funeral, probably in hysterics. When Allsop denied this, said steadily that it would be better for Mary to stop where she was in the eventuality, Mrs. Butler was shaken, saw herself dealing with moral delinquents and came up with some off-hand excuse about inability to obtain accommodation at this late hour and left it.

Mary was disappointed and angry.

Her family were wet. Not only had she this dying mother, a cause of embarrassing, clumsy kindness from the mistresses, but also a father who had no car, never sailed, could not swim, was not on committees, was never featured in the papers, hardly appeared in the street except at the same boring, unvaried times. True, she had a brother who was, had done well, at the university, but he might have done better for her if he'd been at Oxford or Cambridge. Soon, it seemed long enough to her, he might be a doctor of philosophy, but that was hardly glamorous.

Then he had suddenly acquired a really attractive fiancée, a young widow, wealthy, marvellous, elegantly dressed, car, house, posh accent, well known, the bundle. Here again, she rarely met Jacqueline, but the engagement had been well examined over the local tea-cups and her noncommittal, throw-away attitude was much admired in the school. Sixth-formers sometimes made a point of walking with her. Thus the projected holiday in Spain, with all its appeal words, air-line, car ferry, passport, booking, *Yo no tengo un libro, señor*, expunged pretty well every social envy she'd ever suffered. She was angry, therefore, when Mrs. Butler put a stop to the idea, deeply disappointed, but crushed her rage, had her excuse pat for her schoolmates, made it appear that she had deliber-ately chosen herself to forego the trip because of her mother's illness. Her hints that further similar jaunts were already preparing called out no obvious disbelief.

But her frustrations boiled when Aunt Jessica offered in exchange a week at Yarmouth.

Allsop mentioned it over tea. He advanced no preparatory material, merely said that Jessica proposed to write to Mrs. Gittings and ask if she could fit another one in, somewhere, on a camp-bed. He used the aunt's blunt words. There was a silence.

'I don't want to go.'

Her father, who had not expected this, and Bernard, who had not been listening, looked at her after the hot little sentence.

'It'll be a change,' Allsop said mildly.

'I don't want to go.'

'Your aunt has been kind enough to . . .'

'I'm not going.'

A shocked stop. Mary had not intended the rudeness; it erupted from her disappointment. Her father drooped shame-faced, shifty; Bernard drummed the table, whistled sound-lessly. She blushed and crammed her errant mouth with bread and butter. They should know better.

Aunt Jessica's week in Yarmouth was a joke, even to Allsop. She went every year, same week, second in August, same house. The landlady was an old crony, had lived twenty-five, thirty years ago next door to the Henshaws for a few months and wrote letters that combined business, 'a double room, h & c, as per advt, 10 gns. the week', with backyard chat 'I hope Horace is as well as can be expected and that his chest isn't too bad. The air here will do him good. The weather's been glorious.' Jessica, once installed, got up at six, helped prepare breakfast, exchanging news, views and com-plaints with Mrs. Gittings and her girls. There followed a performance in the bedroom, clearing up, dressing up and if the weather was fine husband and wife sat in a deck-chair or idled near a band or parked on seats in a public garden, saying nothing to each other, but if luck held falling into animated conversation with strangers. Once or twice they walked the pier and, on a single occasion, dropped on suddenly, they risked a half-hour trip in a motor-boat. After lunch a 'lay down' on the bed was followed by a shortened version of the morning's schedule, and by half past four Jessica would be back at the house, in the kitchen, with her apron on, helping to cook the dinner they'd fuss over at six and in full conver-sational spate with the lady of the house. During this time, Horace Henshaw would be left on his own, by the sea front. This was the source of ribald suggestions from the Allsop family, for even the mother thought this legitimate amuse-ment, if kept within bounds. It was the only time Ernest Allsop showed any sign of humour, and curiously enough it resembled that of the vulgar seaside postcards he never bought. Horace had a 'glegg', a dialect word spiced it up, at the bosoms of bathing beauties; that was how it was put, for if one had mistaken the tone and said 'stared at girls' buttocks, breasts, belly buttons' immediately the game would have been wrecked. As with the cards, one kept within the convention. Horace 'swigged' surreptitious bottles of beer; presumably in his innocence, Allsop thought the Yarmouth pubs were open at five in the afternoon. He fell in, by calculation, with bad company, lost his money (Jessica never allowed him any), was arrested by the police, had his moustache shaved off, dived from the end of the pier. When at the end of the holiday Jessica gave her full account and some mention was made of her husband or he interpolated some laconic phrase the Allsops, especially the two men, were all ears for anything that could be twisted into corroboration of these fictional adventures. Horace had a wonderful quarter of an hour the previous year when he told how some drunk had handed him a small bottle of whisky at four-thirty on a seat in front of some laurel bushes. Bernard had concocted a yarn about a bottle of John Haig only the day before, and when Horace woodenly confirmed the brand name the whole family were in stitches. Even Aunt Jessica laughed, and failed three times to interrupt her husband's bewildered triumph. After dinner, the Henshaws walked the front for an hour and sat till ten either in the kitchen if Mrs. Gittings weren't too busy or otherwise in the lounge.

The whole holiday was ridiculous, and Mary knew they should have known.

Allsop cleared his throat.

'It'll be a change for you.' Mary did not answer. 'I think your aunt's very good to have offered. She wouldn't really relish . . .'

The girl sniffed, very loudly, her face puckered and tears spilled down, thickly. The two men looked at her and away; Allsop grimaced like a man who has been struck.

'Don't, er, er, upset yourself, love,' he muttered, half rising.

The tears tumbled. Mary made no noise, seemed to hold her features, her body in stillness which only the eyes belied.

'It's all right,' the father said. 'You needn't. . . . If you don't want to. . . . I thought you'd like it. We're away all day, and . . .'

She gave a yelp, a little scream, got up, scrambled out of the room. Allsop, helpless, broke a piece off his bread, spoke to Bernard without a glance.

'I don't see why she need carry on like that. I only . . .'

Bernard was furious.

'Shut up,' he snapped. His voice was a bark, a caw, cracked. Allsop lifted his head, sucked in breath, and put white hands on either side of his plate. Bernard chewed as best he could; the father did not move, whipped under the rebuke. His son imagined the peaky face, the carefully parted hair, the clerk's suit with a scatter of scurf on the collar which would be brushed away just before he left. And what had fifty years' decency brought this man? A daughter in tears, a son who spoke to him as if he were a cur, a wife damn near dead. On the credit side, a pen-pushing regular job and a garden, full of plants that didn't answer back and which could be replaced for a shilling or two when they died.

'Pass the pepper, please,' Bernard said. He could just speak. The white right hand moved, hovered near the cruet, lifted, passed.

'Thanks.' He sprinkled his tomato. 'Sorry, Dad.'

Allsop nodded, acknowledging.

Thus the holidays started dismally for Mary. She was angry and hurt, but her mood varied. Sometimes she kicked the furniture; at others she decided to be saintly, repay evil with good, polish the house, prepare a complicated, delicious tea for the two men. They did not notice. A piece of cheese hacked from the pound still half wrapped in its grease-proof paper and shoved between two slices from a white cut loaf was just as acceptable as any delicacy the cookery manual, the domestic science course and a whole afternoon's slaving could manage.

She mooched about. Eric Parkes was away, in Devon; he sent a picture-card which she'd picked up a hundred times. In the morning she cleaned the house, cooked or shopped and read; in the afternoon she walked, hoping to meet anybody who'd say something; in the evening she visited the library regularly, read, wriggled in front of the television set, went out for a long stroll at bedtime. She played a game or two of tennis with a girl in her form, repaired her bicycle, rode out into the country, was miserable everywhere.

When she was completely at a loose end, she'd catch a bus into the city, hang about the shops, visit exhibitions, bore herself to death in the castle. She had to do this without thought. Her mother had drilled it into her that a bus-journey costing money somebody had earned was only taken with a purpose; one did not buy a bar of chocolate without long consideration; even a wild generosity into the missionary box was frowned on as undisciplined. The girl had, therefore, to commit herself, by handing her fare to the conductor, before guilt set in and prevented the unnecessary trip.

On one such afternoon when it had turned colder and there was an autumnal mist of rain in the air, she had traipsed the length of two enormous shop-fronts and had jostled her way through the interior of the second, she made her way to the Central Library. One might see somebody, something; a handsome Indian student whose face would be fixed in one's memory for life and forgotten in three days, a bearded rabbi, a tramp, a high-school boy who looked up from his papers and laughed at one with his eyes so that it was anti-climax to take down *History of Nottinghamshire* and have to read it.

Today, in the drive, one heel back on the cycle racks, stood Joan Seymour, straight hair straight down on to the shabby shoulders of a leather jacket, eyelids sick sea-green. She was in the sixth form, clever but unsatisfactory; she made no attempt to hide the nicotine smears on her fingers. She had never spoken to Mary before.

'Where're you going so fast?' she said.

'Just inside. To look at the books.'

'I'm waiting for somebody. An' if he doesn't hurry up, I shan't be waiting much longer.'

Mary nodded. She'd nous enough not to commit herself. Joan Seymour made some movements registering restlessness and settled back against the nearest cycle seat.

'Is it yours?' Mary asked, pointing at the bike, a new lady's model.

'A bike?' She punched the seat. 'Catch me on this.' Though the intonation was scornful, Mary had the impression that the other girl wanted, was delighted, to talk to her. Perhaps the young man, she guessed, was a smasher and Joan wanted an admiring crowd, even of one third-former, when he emerged. 'What's new up your road?'

'Nothing much.'

'Seen anybody?' There seemed point behind the question, though Mary could not place it. 'Know anything?'

'No.'

'You're some help.' Seymour rubbed her blotting-paper-pink lips, scratched at the black line round her eyelids, hauled at the belly of her slacks and stared, her chin round and double with thought. 'You haven't heard then?'

Mary waited.

'About Deirdre Fenton?'

Mary suddenly contracted into a mass tight-packed round her navel. Deirdre Fenton, the girl Eric was interested in, the one he'd chuck her over for at any time at any second's notice.

'What's she done?'

'She's going to get married.'

'She hasn't done her A levels yet.'

Seymour sniggered, lifted a heel, adjusted her shoe. The white socks were dirty.

'She's done something else.'

'Uh?'

'She's got to get married.'

Deirdre was blonde, fair, clean, with hair like a shining helmet, and a smile, stepping from the big cars. She had money, crisp clothes, two baths a day, deep and scented. Everything about her was luxurious, paid for, envied everywhere; but the cleanness, the palpable beauty of unwrinkled stockings, pressed pleats, curled eyelashes, nails with un-scratched varnish. She was a picture and she'd done what was dirty or had let men, a man, do what was dirty to her, inside her. A blush spread the length of Mary's body, hot red on her face, her breast, her temples, her pudenda.

'Who's she marrying?' The question was casual, gave no inkling of chaos boiling.

'Some man from Woodborough. Malcolm somebody. He's old. Twenty-five, they say. Nasty type.'

'Does she want to marry . . . him?'

'Want?' Seymour snorted. 'He's as good as any other.' She bit at the grubby corner of a thumb-nail. 'Well breeched.' She did not bother that Mary couldn't understand the ex-pression. Her face was sallow, disfigured with holes of pores, blackheads, and yet she was assured of herself and her attraction.

Mary, dazed still, fumbled through her shock, staring at the leaded Victorian Gothic windows, the passers-by with their bundles of books, thin brief-cases, the great purple-black brick wall of a factory over the patch of lawn. Eric Parkes? Would he know? He was on holiday splashing in the sea with brown-bodied girls in bikinis and sun-glasses. Should she write?

The thought was checked. She was getting her own back. He'd always preferred Deirdre. Even to the extent of making Mary think as he did about the other girl. This cleanliness, 'blanched beauty' he called it, was an idea he'd inculcated. Eric talked to her as if he were talking to himself, apart, whispering, for nobody elsewhere, trying words which were to be forgotten until some definitive formula was achieved. But she listened. Every word, cutting with jealousy, goading her raw, was taken in, stored poisonously. 'She is the slim moon's lovely ghost,' he quoted, and though he was talking about poetry she knew he'd meant Deirdre. And one day he'd come out with it, plain. She said a word or two about the other one, hating, hoping to draw him into some admission.

He was too careful; he spoke off-handedly, scientifically, scouting for evidence. And she'd not resisted telling him that Deirdre bleached her hair. Stroking his chin, sticking his lips out, he considered, not letting on whether or not he knew. And in the end he'd nodded and said it suited her, the colour and texture of her skin, the blue eyes, the style of clothes. She did right. Mary was dashed by his thin manner which did not hide his infatuation. After a time of awkward silence when she'd blushed and torn secretly at her handkerchief he started to sing, breathy towards his own feet:

> 'Have you seen but a bright lily grow
> Before rude hands have touched it?
> Have you mark'd but the fall of the snow
> Before the soil hath smutch'd it?
> Have you felt the wool of the beaver?
>   Or swan's down ever?'

He'd stopped there, though she knew how it went on. They sang it at school. 'O so white, O so soft, O so sweet is she.' Mary said, mumbling, 'Do you love her, then?' and there was no answer. 'You do,' she'd said, and his face was washed violently red, a deep flush so that he had to jump up to hide it, and had lifted her off the ground, one, two, three, spinning her round, twisting her, his flying hands dancing her, with strength, knockabout gentleness, till she had to squeal to him to stop and there was an excuse for his redness and lack of breath. Mary Evangeline Allsop. Deirdre Lynn Fenton. The soil had smutched it.

'How do you know all this?'

'Pat Baskill saw them,' Joan Seymour said. 'In town, on a Saturday morning. She knows them, plays tennis. They told her. Deirdre was crying, she said. Malcolm was engaged to somebody else. Ever such a nice girl; works up at the hospital.'

'What does she say?'

'How in hell do I know?'

The young man came from the library; he had a university scarf wrapped below his boils.

Seymour kept him parading a minute before they moved off arm-in-arm.

Mary stood shaken, but soon recovered. Later she tried the effect of the announcement on herself. At first there was a jolt of embarrassment as she thought, 'Deirdre Fenton is pregnant.' Then the feeling became less painful, with the faint pleasure of an accomplished dare. Even the word 'pregnant', once shunned, became easily thought of like 'womb' in the hymn or on page 73 of the biology text-book. Once she could hardly keep from looking it up; now 'womb' was as charged emotionally as 'tibia' or 'fibula'.

When the Butlers came back from Spain, Jacqueline invited Mary over to her house, where she did a good deal of cooking and spirited work on the duplicator for the festival. The child found this utterly attractive since Mrs. Ridell did not make demands, allowed experiments in cookery, within reason, and encouraged Mary to chase about the house. To be truthful, Jacqueline did not find the child attractive; she seemed slow, without ideas, painfully modest, lumpish and provincial. Therefore Mrs. Ridell talked to her as grown-up to grown-up, hoping to shock or stimulate. This was so different from the long dull hours in the empty house that Mary never noticed her hostess's irritation or boredom. She went twice a week, Tuesday and Thursday, walked the garden, seemed mistress of the place and lived the high life.

Mary mentioned that Eric Parkes had returned from holiday.

'Bring him along on Thursday for lunch.'

'Oh, I don't know. I don't know whether he'd come.' Ambivalence slapped her down. Would he? For a meal? What would he tell his parents?

'You like him, don't you?'

'He's all right.'

'All right?' Jacqueline mocked. 'He's a gorgeous dish, isn't he now? Admit it.'

'I don't know whether I'll see him.'

'Send him a letter then. I'm not short of notepaper. Now's the time.'

'I don't know what to say.'

The writing materials were put before her and she was left to it. The elder corrected, approved a rough draft, which was copied and posted immediately. Eric accepted in two polite notes.

On Thursday, Mary pelted to the house at nine-thirty to find Jacqueline still in bed. Once, however, she was up, something of the mother was apparent. She outlined the plan of campaign. Mary stepped out of her pretty cotton frock and new stockings, donned a housecoat before she was set on to a couple of hours' hard cleaning. She did this without a hitch. The rooms shone, were satisfyingly neat; she'd a good eye, knew where to put furniture or ornaments, how far to close curtains, what to touch and what to leave. At eleven-thirty she was sent to have a bath, an unheard luxury at that time of the morning, was given a short twenty minutes before Jacqueline was up hammering at the door. Again she was embarrassed, dripping naked, having fumbled at the bolt, as the quick eye of the older woman appraised her flesh.

'Come on, slow-coach. I thought you'd be out and dry.'

The room was large, light, with a wide porcelain bath and silver-cushioned stools before a wall-length mirror. The bath-towel was enormous, furry and, unexpected this, hot.

'I've come to make you up, so get a move on.' Mary stood with the towel round her, back to the mirror. 'Your hair looks nice, but I'll use this ribbon.' Sharp tugs with the comb, a thumb pressed in, brutally. Jacqueline was aburst with energy. 'Stop fidgeting with that towel and co-operate. You're like some pearly queen there.' She snatched the towel away, flung it in the corner. It seemed wrong to the girl, blasphemous, to have to stand stark naked in broad daylight while this dynamo of a woman jerked her head this way, that, and the silk of a sleeve or the rough skirt touched the bare nipple or belly, brushed thighs and the secret hairs until she wanted to squirm away in shamed pleasure.

'That's you, then.'

'You haven't done my—my mouth.'

'That's not being touched. Get your clothes on and watch your hair when you put your frock over. I'll be back in a minute to finish you off.'

The eyes had been darkened, and lined so that they seemed larger, bigger. Oriental, liquid, Mary thought, pools. It changed her face into a woman's where the cheek-bones stood prominently out, and the curl of white ribbon was flaunted. She hurried, forgetting her nakedness as she covered it, in delight to see the completion. She was still rapt with the mirror when Jacqueline came back, for five more minutes' violence with the comb.

'Now go and sit in the drawing-room till I've had my bath.' Two, one after the other, deep, hot, like that, no trouble, no skimping. 'Keep your ear open for the kitchen. I don't want anything to boil over. Nothing should, but you never know. And don't run about. Sit still if you can. I'll put the perfume on when I get down. You'd soak yourself.' A real push in the small of the back, a mother's clout.

Mary queened it downstairs, posturing at every polished surface. She was someone else, even felt a certain stiffness about herself as if she hadn't yet learnt the new, dazzling part. Jacqueline was wonderful.

When the hostess came down, she glanced with approval at the demure Mary, well back, straight-backed in windsor chair. At least she looked presentable, now she was still, not talking. But the stricken look on her face when she opened the bathroom door. It was as if she had been pushed stripped into the street. Jacqueline had gone upstairs thinking the child would have been out, dried and dressed, but that was no excuse for back-street prudery. And she never came out with an amusing word, couldn't even thank you audibly. Mary smiled, and the woman paused before smiling back. Perhaps, she considered, she was looking on this fourteen-year-old, this hoyden, as a rival. She'd have a good figure if she could use it, but she stood as awkwardly as a monkey with diarrhoea. Poor little bitch.

Eric arrived at twelve-thirty, overawed, carrying a bunch of flowers which he presented brightly to Jacqueline. She handed them over to Mary who scuttled off for a vase. Eric, ill at ease, but determined, sipped a largish glass of sherry, and nodded every time Mrs. Ridell spoke. She was instantly amused, and reconciled to Mary's coltishness. This, this shaver, Father's word, was the one she'd wished to snatch from little sister. She laughed. Eric Parkes had a way with him; he was never short of a remark; he smiled, all teeth in his brown face, as he spoke; he'd break any wench's little heart for her for fourpence. But his talk; the Midland accent breaking its neck to become accepted southern standard and the prissy anecdotes, boring as scrag-end mutton, beginning, 'I have a friend' or 'We met a man in Paignton' designed to show he knew the world and its fly ways. Mary, the poppet, was open-mouthed. Jacqueline had forgotten that girls could be so obvious in their infatuation, so blatant, and that young men could be so damned blind to it. She'd been like that, herself; belly-yearning for a pimply boy with blond waves who played cricket and mouthed words of such gravamen as, 'Should have put him on the other end two overs earlier before he'd got his eye in.' God, she squirmed even now. The human race.

They ate; Eric talked. Jacqueline, without satisfaction, noted that the majority of his observations were directed at her and that Mary accepted this as natural. At washing-up time he was in his element, adopting a facetious, bossy tone, taking over the operation, bursting into mock opera, insistent on donning, fooling with, an apron. He probably imagined himself as utterly successful; she saw him coldly as a mark one (obsolete) Sunday School teacher relaxing at the annual bun-fight. But if Mary liked it, fair enough.

Mary was embarrassed, again, hating his chatter. He wasn't

like that, all wit and finger-nails. She wanted him quiet, saying nothing, speaking a line of poetry, close to her, touching her, lost for words. That was Eric, not this university boy with his palaver and poise.

When they'd finished in the kitchen, Jacqueline said sharply, 'Now go and sit down, you two. I've got to shoot out for an hour or so this afternoon.' This wasn't true. She'd no idea why she'd said so. 'I'll be back about four.' To Eric. 'You are staying for tea, aren't you? Yes, don't argue,' before he'd a chance to answer.

Jacqueline ostentatiously banged the back door and the two were left in the drawing-room, in armchairs, very uncomfortable.

'Sit here. Or walk round the garden.'

'Come into the ga-harden, Maud,' he bawled, shutting his eyes and clasping his hands in front of his groin. They walked quietly out. Beyond the rough stone walls they could hear the rattle of the Saturday street. Here they moved along the paths, pausing before the flowers or shrubs, unable to name them, in postures of admiration.

'They're asters. I do know that,' Mary said. He did not contradict.

'It's a marvellous, big garden,' he said. 'Who does it? Milady?' Both giggled.

'No. She has a gardener.'

'That must cost her a pretty penny.'

On the stone path, among the black-currant bushes which were ludicrously draped with raggy lengths of lace curtain, he took her hand.

'I'd like to live here,' he said. 'It's more like an estate than a garden.'

'It is nice.' She spoke as if she owned it.

They sat on a plank across two gross flower-pots by the far wall, laughing at the conversation in the street, basking in the sunshine. On their return into the house, he put an arm round her, pulled her in, kissed her ear, fondled the right breast.

'Do you know something?' His bright tone covered his

lack of confidence. 'I've never seen you with make-up before.'

'You've not looked very hard.'

'Suits you.'

He had both hands cupped round her breasts, fidgeting, masterful, not loving her. Pleased and annoyed, she broke away. It was cooler indoors after the baking heat outside, and she was afraid. They were in a house, together, alone; there was no telling what he might start. She shivered, made for the dining-room. He threw himself back into his armchair, bottom lip drooping, hand picking at a fold in the chair cover, sulking. They didn't speak, didn't look at each other. He, wanting to fondle her, was annoyed that he'd begun so clumsily; she did not know what she wanted.

After some minutes he rose, stretched, looked into a bookcase without much curiosity and then sat on the floor at Mary's feet his head back on her knees. She jerked rigid at the touch, relaxed, put a hand in his hair, massaged with finger-tips.

'Um. Nice,' he said, eyes shut. In a few minutes he turned slightly and put his arm round her calves, clasping them hard so that she could feel the hardness of bone in his left forearm. Her eyes closed. Very slowly he unloosed his grip, shifted his head slackly so that it lay supported partly by the chair-arm, partly by her thigh, and stroked, tickled her knees. The movement was done in circles, at first with one finger as if to suggest by its formality of pattern that nothing was meant, that he touched her as one fiddled with a special pencil or empty ash-tray. At the feel of his hand she was stiff, again, bolt upright, as though listening for some small distant sound. Tension was so great that for some seconds she seemed incapable of either hearing or seeing, a tiny stretch of consciousness was prised out of her life. Almost with surprise she noticed her fingers in his hair, did nothing about it.

'Nice,' he muttered, but she did not answer.

They could hear the clock, and very faintly the street-shouts. Somewhere, in the house, a hum, an electric note, buzzed. All was cool, blue, shadowed, carpeted; outside the bushes were sun-drenched and the far wall invisible behind the thickness of green.

'Are you happy?' he said.

'Yes.'

He was heavy on her lap, and his fingers fumbled about her knees, like a wasp drunk with jam so that she wanted to bat him off. His head pressed harder, uncomfortably awkward, but vulnerable, to be desired. She touched his closed eyelids.

'Mary.'

'Yes.'

'You're nice.' He spoke into the thick of her flesh. And now his hand had moved, was under her frock, but still, flat on the top of her stocking and the outside of her thigh. She waited, and round her the room, the garden, town, sky seemed to be watching, expectant, anxious, hopeful, ashamed. 'No finger moves without disturbing stars.' That was a line he'd quoted more than once. His hand was hot and cold, and she trembled with a fierce watery pleasure-in-pain. Now he was kneeling, with the right arm across her, his face down, hard downwards in her lap as if not to see what he was about, and his left hand there, unmoving, ready to leap, to menace, disgrace, disfigure as it lay, crouched, on stocking, smooth flesh, suspender. She could hear her own breathing; body seemed gently pulled about, outwards, scattered away from the threatening hand that did nothing, that murdered her confidence, raped her love, blasted her with joy.

It shifted, minutely, delicately. Like an army.

She waited until the next stirring, leaning down, thumped his bowed shoulders with her fists. His hand was withdrawn, fast as a sword-flash, but he knelt where he was, face down in her.

'No,' she said. 'No.'

'Why not?' Soft. Leering.

'It's wrong.' She flushed. He kneeled upright now, straight-back, patted his hair with his two hands, very stern, concerned with his appearance. Then suddenly he shrugged, dismissing her and her qualms. The gesture angered her so that dazed, incoherent of thought as she was, she spoke to hurt him.

'I'm not Deirdre Fenton, you know.'

He left that until he had found a more comfortable position, accommodating himself with his back to her and the chair, his legs stretched out and across, his arms folded.

'What's she got to do with it?'

'Haven't you heard?'

'Heard what?' He was apprehensive, and she made him wait, crossing her legs, rasping the stockings, adjusting the frock-hem. She tried her sentence through in her mind, knowing victory.

'She's got to get married.'

His face grew white, green-white; his lips were sucked in as if he were about to vomit. The head seemed unsteady, a puppet's on elastic. She had not expected so violent a change, physically, had not realised how words could kill. The right hand placed arrogantly thumb forward under the armpit dropped loose, wavered, scattered alms, collapsed. A gulp belched out of him.

'Who said so?'

'Joan Seymour. Pat Baskill saw her, and this man, and Deirdre told her. The man, Malcolm, I think she said, was engaged before to somebody else.'

She thought he'd cry. Eyes seemed stretched, mouth shaken, uncertain. The cheesy pallor of his face changed redder as he breathed loudly like an injured dog. She sat back, watching, loathing his collapse. For the moment she'd expected him to crawl about the floor, a poisoned spider, angularly writhing. In the end he gobbled in his throat, pushed himself up, and slouched for his chair. She hated him, feeble, impotent, flaccid, shrinking inside his clothes, crippled, a coward.

He moved his mouth.

'Is it true?' The voice croaked.

'That's what they told me.'

'You didn't see her?'

'No, I didn't.' There was a pause, very long, before Mary

163

spoke again. 'Do you think it's true?'

His head creaked up like a rusty crank; he gaped, was silent.

'Do you think it's true?' she repeated cruelly.

'How do I know?'

His voice was shrill; his head jerked. Suddenly he closed his eyes and lay back in the chair, face upward. Now colour was normal, breathing inaudible. Again she stared, afraid at the protracted silence, and his stillness, his uncommon ease. When he roused himself he stood straight up, and leaned, hands clasped, on the back of his chair.

'It's bad luck,' he said. The social voice. He was smiling, brushing at the front of his trousers. He hoisted these, came over, sat on the arm of her chair and said:

'You didn't think I'd do anything like that to you, did you?'

His arm was across her shoulders.

'You wouldn't get the chance,' she mumbled, looking away, hot, flurried. His fingers chucked her chin.

'You don't think much of me, then?'

No answer was given. Uncomfortably trapped, Mary tried not to move, either towards him or away.

'What's wrong with you?' he said. He turned her head round, with no violence, not unkindly. 'What was I doing?' She dropped her eyes. 'Come on. What was I doing that you didn't like?'

'You know.'

'What was I doing?'

'Trying to touch me.' Her voice disappeared.

'I'm touching you now.' He stroked her face, not heavily, but without passion as one uses a lather brush. At the pleasure-less movement she was shamed again so that she hated him, would have abandoned the place, the company. 'You're nice,' he said. She stiffened. 'That's true,' he said, leaving her, walking without fuss to the window. 'It is, in fact, perfectly incontrovertibly true. You, Miss Mary E. Allsop, are adjudged by me, the world, the flesh, the devil, the glorious company of the Apostles, the noble army of martyrs, as nice, delightful, wholly charming.' He hummed to himself. 'What does the defendant say?'

Nothing. Hunched. Reduced. Sulking. Dirty.

'I'm paying you a compliment, miss,' he said, turning round, teeth revealed.

'Shut up.'

'That's no way to talk. "Shut up!"'

'What about Deirdre Fenton, then?' she said.

'Not before time. She asked for it.'

'You liked her.'

'And now,' he said, 'I like you. Just for this afternoon, mark you. A transient, brief, passing, ephemeral moment in the bottomless abyss of time. . . .'

She began to cry. He took her in his arms.

Jacqueline Ridell completed her shopping and drove round to rout Bernard from his work at home. He looked absently wild, in jeans, a flapping shirt open from neck to navel, hair tousled.

'Have you been asleep?' she said.

'I'm working.'

'Don't believe it.'

'Right. Come and see.' He led her upstairs.

There was bravado about him. At her house he'd wander through the bedrooms at his ease; they seemed inviolable, like hospital wards, hygienic, utilitarian, in spite of curtains, bright carpets, modern coverlets. Here he was leading her upstairs for the first time, into his middle, largest room. By the window was a heavy old-fashioned table of nearly-room width thick with his papers. At the back of the table the piles were orderly but near his chair there was a certain derangement.

'Not much system,' she said.

'All organised,' he boasted, and tapped the metal filing cabinet. 'This little lot,' he moved a sheet or two among the half-confusion at the front, 'will be straightened out when I finish and I'll know exactly where to start next time.'

'My, my. Well, do it now, because you're coming back to tea.'

'I'd intended to do another hour.' He sounded half-hearted.

'You've had that.'

'What about Dad's meal? He'll come back . . .'

'We'll lay it before we go,' she said. 'Don't make excuses. Pack up and shut up.' She sat down on his bed. 'I'm a bossy bugger,' she announced, and watched for the effect of the word. None. He was in his chair, deftly sorting sheet from sheet, weighting each pile with an ink-pot, a pencil-case, a small book, a fossil-encrusted rock. 'This bed's hard. Is it where you sleep?'

'What do you think?'

'Um.' She swung her feet up, lay back, arms folded behind her head on the pillow. 'Come and flop alongside.'

He was wary of the small voice; it scratched, but after a decent interval marshalling his papers he did as he was told. There he lay, without much room, flank to flank, staring up at the ceiling with its lump near the window and hair-cracks across the middle.

'Kiss, then,' she ordered. They tangled, but he felt her detachment in spite of the welcome of her mouth and the fierce arms. It was as if, all the time, she observed him for a detailed diary; he'd no evidence and, quite possibly, the feeling was born of his own inadequacy. Perhaps, since she did not allow the final coupling, he was reminded of his own inexperience, her deeper knowledge, his ultimate failure to assert himself, and this left him uncertain, *in statu pupillari* to her. He threw himself on top, trying to establish his manhood with violence. She did not repulse him, lay under him, conveyed love and wordlessly refused him his way. In a frenzy of kissing, he wanted to force her through the bed, ravish her with weight, the power of gravity.

'You're heavy,' she said, in the end. 'Roll off, darling.'

'You don't like it.'

'That's what you think.' She smiled; small wrinkles appeared by the blue eyes, marring and completing perfection. Then, she grew older than he was, surer.

'God,' he said, 'I could do things to you.'

'You've squashed me flat already.'

'I'd blow you up, you woman.'

'Naughty, naughty. Get off.' He kissed her hard so that she took his head in her hands and would not let him raise it until his breath was gone. Even she, for the moment, sagged stunned, but she was soon nattily smiling, composed again. This time at her push he moved, sprawled alongside, panting. She sat up, kissed his navel and tugged mischievously at the line of hair below. The stab of pain jolted him upright, and he seized her by the frock, tugged, twisted her, through a quarter turn, back, forwards, towards, away turbulently, side, back, side, back, slapping the mattress. The wild violence of the exercise numbed him within seconds; he was exhausted, frightened at his reaction, which had caught him unawares, revealed animality he neither knew nor liked, flogged him soft.

He dropped back to the bed, weak with fatigue, eyes shut in orange darkness. She did not move for a while. Half-relieved he heard her put feet to floor and say, utterly cool:

'So it's like that, eh?'

He turned, feeble, belly drained. She was standing there, face towards him, hands quickly busy under her dress.

'You've ruined my suspender belt,' she said, 'you mad ape.'

He watched her neat movements, of hands, of body and the momentary stillness to discover if the correct adjustment had been achieved. 'That's better,' she said, without embarrassment. 'I can walk now without twisting my blood.' Blubbering his lips, he slewed round to sit on the side of the bed. Very neatly, she came to him, sat by him.

'I know how you feel,' she said. Her right hand was thrust across, into his waistband, on the flesh, and forced down briefly to rest mildly, to hold his genitals. Frozen in joy he stared at a vague reflection of themselves in a picture of a cottage and garden. 'We'll get married at Christmas,' she said. 'How about that?'

Her hand was removed; she had now walked away.

'Yes,' he said.

'Please.' Her voice was business-like, a teacher or nanny's correction from habit. 'Come on, now. Tuck your shirt in.'

While they were preparing Allsop's tea-table, and Bernard had delayed this by another bout of kissing, she said, straightening knives he had laid:

'You know, darling, your room was very like you.'

Dazed with pleasure, barely listening, he managed an interrogatory noise.

'Not much personality about it.' She giggled.

'Oh?'

'You're not cross,' she asked, 'are you? For instance, you put books any old how on your shelves. There's no attempt at . . .'

'I put them handiest for reading.' This was quite untrue. He'd outgrown most of them so that they merely collected dust unopened. 'That's what books are for. Not decoration.'

'And the wallpaper. Plain. Utilitarian. Methodist. Puritan.'

He and his mother had done the paper-hanging together the summer before he'd gone up to the university. She'd chosen it, and the pair of them had enjoyed themselves. Mary had been out at school, Father working. Five years ago. And she had been perfectly well then, and excited because he was to start his adult life, and delighted to share this chore with him, boss him, impress on him she could still show him a wrinkle or two for all his brains. They'd laughed. Like a brother and sister. He'd never known her so relaxed and warm. And the paper had worn well, had hardly faded. Better than she had.

'What do you want?' In fact, until Jacqueline had criticised it, he'd never thought of the walls, aesthetically, or anyhow. His mother had been healthy then, as well as he, and she here, felt now. She wasn't old. She was going to die. In the confusion it occurred to him, like a message flashed on a screen, that they'd only looked at their mother's death from their own point of view. Never from her own. Did she want to die? Rebel as she lay there? Curse the pain? Reject God? Spot and blast their selfishness? Their? Their? His own. He had not considered her, only himself. Perhaps at this moment his father or even Mary, who never said a word about it, were imaginatively sharing, suffering on, that death-bed while he consulted his own convenience as usual.

Dashed, he shifted a cup, fiddled blindly in a drawer for the tea-cosy.

Wallpaper; brown, speckled wallpaper. 'Hen's egg' his mother had called it. She would never see it again. Perhaps she remembered it and that sunny, paint-drenched September week five years back. People died, he'd heard, much as they had lived, used the same form of words they always had, recalled as they did in health. He wondered if it meant anything to her, now. Or was it merely a small pleasure denied, but disregarded in the ultimate displeasure of death? She should live longer. Another twenty years, papering bedrooms, spoiling grandsons.

His head turned.

Jacqueline was stock-still, by the mantelpiece, the back of her head darkly reflected in the oval mirror, a small watchful entity. She had touched him today, novelly, on his nakedness.

He gasped, as if he'd broken out from a thrashing sea, a quicksand, from under the killing wheels of a juggernaut, from lightning, all death. He was saddened still, reduced in energy, but inside him as he looked at this girl a core of joy burnt. Love burst. He was mentally ashamed that it was so, but transformed, himself beyond himself. In love.

They took hands. She seemed self-absorbed, quiet; he had no notion whether or not she shared his joy. They finished preparation for tea, touching one the other as they passed, not talking and it was not until they were seated in the car outside the wall of Jacqueline's house that she spoke.

Her words were dry, trivial.

'Now we'll entertain the young bloods,' she said. He nodded, made as if to get out when she put a hand on his arm.

'Who's this Parkes boy?' she asked. He explained. 'Are

these two serious? Young love and so forth?'

'I don't know.' Her phrase jarred. 'I've pulled her leg often enough about him, but I don't know whether it means anything. Mary doesn't confide in me. My guess is that she'll be embarrassed when I turn up.'

'He's the proper little headmaster, isn't he?'

'Oh? Just says "How do you do?" and then listens.'

'Oh, no. He's got it all weighed up. Dandle your baby or cosset your grandma. That's little Eric.'

'You don't like him?'

'He's a squashy banana.' She pulled violently on his arm, surprising him. 'I love you.' She punched his ribs, got out.

15

THE FIRST WEEK or two of September were wintry, with cold nights and fog early on.

Mrs. Allsop was still alive. Thin as death she drifted in and out of consciousness, not changing, able to lift the gaunt fingers, move the hole of a mouth, recognise. Sometimes, now, she cried, without obvious cause. They'd be talking to her and she'd be listening, answering, half-attentive, until her eyes would open to allow tears to splash down the wrecked face. She did not seem to mind, or notice, and when her husband bent across the bed to wipe her cheeks she made no acknowledgement, though she would mutter thanks if he had put her spectacles on or propped the paper for her to glimpse. She sighed, often, and in the pushing out of her breath any life in her existed most clearly; there was exertion there, life asserting itself. She was expected to die at any time.

Bernard had a wild idea. He wanted to take her propped up in blankets in Jacqueline's car and show her all the places she'd known. Her house, the street, the gardens, the Common, shops with the same women pushing in and out, the stone chapel with its slate roof and spire and the quiet purple dark up the worn steps, the park, gold-thick in autumn. Would she notice? Did these mean anything now? Perhaps if her thoughts went backward at all they reached to her childhood. She didn't originate from this part of the world, but from a farm in Leicestershire, a place quite unknown to him, but which, for all he knew, was exactly as she had left it as a girl, or, more likely, was changed, built over, scored by macadam roads, red houses, its clay trenched, the trees uprooted. He did not know. She could speak still and she nodded when he told her that the date of his wedding was fixed. She smiled even, and then said in that little quibbling voice that had nagged through his life:

'Before you finish at the university?'

'Yes, Mother. There's no disadvantage, really.'

She nodded again, stared shortly at her husband, closed her eyes.

'So we want you to get well so you'll be there.' He patched his voice with brightness, but she did not respond, did not care.

Mary went back to school.

In the hall, on the first morning, serious with the prefects, stood Deirdre Fenton. She was paler, slightly thinner, but peerlessly at ease in the navy school uniform. Nobody said a word, though Mary thought Joan Seymour looked guiltily away each time they passed. Routine established itself, French and chemistry, hockey and school dinners, slouching for the bus, time-wasting, along back-streets, new mistresses, old mistresses in different clothes, the school captain straining-calm on the rostrum. And Deirdre Fenton standing in the hall, knowing something that the Head did not, or the A-level examiners. Mary shivered.

Jacqueline found herself more excited over the festival than her wedding. Smart verse-posters had appeared, tickets changed hands. Tom grew cock-a-hoop while the promoters coined money. She'd been invited, as Tom's sister and chief unpaid skivvy, to meetings, cocktail parties, exploratory gatherings, councils. These were odd, and attractive; drinking was heavy and the personnel well known to readers, say, of *Radio Times*. But these famous people were no better-looking, no more eloquent or witty or quick than people she knew already. It was, honesty compelled the admission, a delight to find that this producer of genius did not shave properly or that a young poet stank of whisky and could not pronounce his r's or that the brilliant pontificator in the Sundays was as incapable of answering a question about Ronsard or Corbière or St. John Perse as anybody else. God. The world of the tongue.

She enjoyed the disappointment of these encounters, talked about them to her mother. She did her best to humour Mrs. Butler who, she knew, was opposed to the fixing of the wedding, and had said so at once. The mother did not, however, waste time in repetition. First she got at Tom, who told the world that the old girl was an interfering bitch, but confessed to his sister that he couldn't see anything in Bernard for the simple reason that there was nothing there to bloody well see, so what? Mr. Butler was pressed into service. He needed little urging. Like a good many unprincipled, vacillating people, he liked to imagine that he ruled his life by logic. Therefore, now and again, he'd apply some simple, useless little set of rules and draw some equally vacuous, irrelevant conclusion from them. Bernard Allsop had not got a job. He'd therefore live on his wife's money. Anybody who did that was a fortune-hunter, or worse. Ergo, give him a wide berth.

He put his syllogism times without number to Jacqueline, but with force and satisfaction. It was unanswerable. She could believe him. He'd a knowledge of men and the world; he'd seen that sort of chap, decent enough on the surface, plausible as you like, but as the twig was bent the tree was inclined. Take young Simpson Reid, now, in the Indian Engineers. There followed a Somerset Maugham slice of oriental spice and occidental idiocy.

In the end, Jacqueline told him to shut up.

He was angry at that, but frightened. Very likely she had sounded exactly like her mother, and the poor father found the only person who'd ever appeared to take any notice of him rejecting him off-hand. He looked pathetic, drooped, said she could trust him.

'Now listen, Daddy. The date is fixed. We are going to get married whatever you say or think. So just reconcile yourself to it. And while you're at it, you might report to Mummy what I've just told you.'

'Don't speak like that,' he huffed. 'You've no right. After all, we're your parents.'

'I've every right. I'm in my own house and you and Mother are interfering. And you know it. So you might just as well make up your minds that I shall please myself.'

'Now, Jacky. It's for your own good. We don't . . .'

'Don't be silly.'

She snapped, felt ashamed, became sarcastic. He lost his temper, exploded, spluttered, was sorry. There was something handsome about him with the rising wings of silver hair, the turkey-cock jowls, the insubstantial claims to experience. She despised her father, disliked him sometimes, but pitied and loved him. Big a fool as he was, he was part of her world. Nor could he conceal his admiration for her. He touched her, like an orphanage child with a new doll, to establish possession, to express pride, to draw the attention of a hostile world to good fortune. Even at her exasperation she could not dismiss a barbaric remainder of affection. Father Butler. My father is a fool. She knew this but could not feel it.

As the festival approached, she became more apprehensive. She noticed that she could not sit so easily now with a book; after five minutes she'd lose track, jump up to do something, nothing. Or she'd catch herself, almost with guilt, feeling slightly sick. Her flesh goose-pimpled more easily, at her fear. But it was nothing to do with her. She'd no money invested. If she suffered such tremors it ought to be over her wedding.

Tom Butler was expansive. Ten minutes of his company

warmed her. Friends were lavish in his praise. He'd done marvels; to get a festival together in this short time. There wasn't another man in the town, country, world (according to the drink) who could have seen the possibilities, built round two events, the Playhouse Shakespeare and Ionescu, and the university's three concerts, this battlement, this edifice, this cultural cathedral. Only he would have coaxed artistes down, spotted they'd a blank date. At such ridiculous notice, admirers said, he brought down people one normally booked for two or three years ahead.

And yet this talk was febrile; it concealed, she thought, anxiety. This recital was not taking, ten seats sold and that was a five-hundred-pound loss. But Butler, or one of his lieutenants, legion, and infinitely variable, with long hair and dirt, naval beards, bald-heads, business tycoons, smart executives, bank managers, horsey or bedworthy women, county and four-ale bar, would adopt this scheme to fill the place, approach this society, that philanthropist, try this scheme, ring that paper, visit this pub, drink free in that drawing-room.

The festival tangled.

Jacqueline did not know when someone she'd never seen before in her life would poll up, demand five hundred circulars that evening, and stop, pleading life and death urgency until they were done. She'd sit down and cut the stencil, wondering what difference five hundred copies of this trivial message would make. There was too much of her mother's sharp sense about her for her to be sure that if she duplicated five, no fifty, thousand copies, of this stuff, not ten guineas' worth of profit would accrue, but she typed, and hoped, her father's girl. She represented, she told herself, rationalising her rash optimism, publicity in a small way, but in a world of entertainment where the meretricious or journalistic could be inflated into accepted classics, where some ordinary man, ham-handed, mentally crippled, could be, almost by chance, kicked upstairs into the millionaire bracket by the mass-bashing media, and solely on account of his clumsiness, his gawky stupidity, his everyday face. Miracles happened. These men turned the world upside down. Gruff schoolmasters became television personalities; guitar strummers were mobbed; hacks were worshipped; the hum-drum grew godlike. Jacqueline tapped on. 'This talented young cellist was recently described by Rostropovitch as the finest exponent of . . .' 'There is no doubt that this thea-trical entertainment will shock you, if entertainment it can be called. When five years ago this masterpiece was tacked together in a Californian railyard . . .' She asked her brother if anyone would lose money.

'Of course,' he said. 'This has all been done too fast.'

'Will you?'

'Me? I haven't got any to start with.'

She felt guilty, edgy; temper flared easily.

Bernard earned the rough side of her tongue when he told her one evening to stop fooling with her duplicator. The machine she was trying to mend stood on a wooden bench in a whitewashed cellar. It was cold down there. She was fagged out, wanted to give up.

'Mind your own business,' she said.

'Let me have a try.'

'No.' Her voice squealed; her hands slapped his forearm away. 'You leave me alone.'

'I just wanted to help.'

'Go away, will you?'

He went up the stone steps, but by the time he reached the top he was convinced that she was crying. He turned. She was. He paused, swung his foot, came down again.

'Let me do it, please,' he said.

She lifted her face and howled, a baby's sound. As he put his arm around her she thumped him on the chest, hard, a knuckle-bang.

'Jackie.'

'Go away,' she said, cried louder, a rough squeal of misery. 'Go away.'

'Why should I?' He laughed, half-heartedly, and pulled her

to him as she turned away. She kicked backwards and her heel bit metal-sharp into his shin. The pain exploded, toppled him, nearly floored him.

'You little bitch.'

He stepped towards her as she dodged behind the heavy joiner's bench.

'You leave me alone.' Her voice was a gabble, a gramophone record played too fast, high, inhuman. 'You leave me alone.' He stood still, shocked by the back-street wail, lifted his trouser-leg where a trickle of blood showed small on a dent in the shin. Soreness scraped. 'You leave me alone. You keep your hands to yourself.'

She was bending forward, squinting at him, mouth tight, face podgy with tears and dust. The skin was blotched, puffy, half fat, half punctured, rubber-slimy. Her eyes flicked from him to the duplicator; a nerve wobbled in her neck, which was corded, scraggy, a hen's craw.

'Don't you hit me,' she shouted. 'You leave me alone.'

'I wouldn't touch you with a barge-pole,' he said, going for the steps. As he turned, he knocked a pile of her duplicated sheets which slapped to the ground. He walked on, furious, but flung back, bent, picked the papers up, straightened them clumsily and replaced them on the bench. She was bending over, still, like a weasel, a stoat, one of those tooth-mad, red-eyed devils in a stinking cage. Her sobbing grunted, snuffled. A tear, or snot, hung at the end of her nose.

'I'm sorry,' he said. She did not answer. 'I'm sorry, Jackie.' That pig-noise. 'I was trying to help.' He took a clean handkerchief out of his pocket and passed it over to her. Surprisingly, she held a hand out, wiped her face. He looked away, examined a small wooden butter barrel which stood perched on a chair with a sawn-off back in a corner, deal-plain under the bare electric bulb.

He heard her move.

She handed his handkerchief over. In the yellow light, reflected roughly back from the walls, she looked pale but composed. There was no vestige of trouble on the smooth features; her hair was wild, but attractively so, and the expression on her face one of whimsical curiosity, that of a mother watching a child embark on a new, safe project.

'I'm a fool,' he said.

She did not speak, stood there. This puzzled him. She was herself now, poised, calm, but she did not speak. Very slowly she took up one of her duplicated sheets, appeared to read it, sighed, put it back. He smiled, tentatively. She put a hand on the rounded top of the duplicator, almost posturing. 'Hear ye, Israel.' But she did not speak.

Silence bristled. Her nail scratched the metal cover.

'I'm sorry,' he said again, almost ashamed now.

'Yes.'

'I really was trying to help.'

'All right. This thing's been going wrong all day. It got me down. I was silly.' Her voice was level. 'I thought you were going to hit me or push me or something.'

'Why should I do that?' he asked.

Her eyes opened wide, then narrowed. That was comical. She removed her hand from the cover, rounded the bench, put her arm through his.

'This damn festival's killing me. Don't ask me why, either.'

'You're sure it's that?'

'Yes,' she said. 'What else should it be?'

'Our wedding.'

'Oh, that.'

' "Oh, that." Is that how it is? Your father's very anti, isn't he?'

'We don't pay any attention to him,' she said. 'You know as well as I do. He's put up to it. And that reminds me. Don't let me boss you about like that when we get married, will you?' She might have been serious. 'Dad's too nice.'

'He always seems so confident.'

'Oh? The Anglo Indian bark? He never did very well, really. He made a living and Mother had a bit of money of her own, well, more than a bit, really, a lot, and was a marvellous manager. And now he talks and emends,' she smiled, 'what happened.' She coughed.

'But he doesn't seem diffident.'

'No, he's always had this parade-ground way with him. To cover the inadequacy, perhaps. He wasn't a bad engineer, but he wouldn't take a risk.'

'That's an advantage, I should have thought. I wouldn't want to cross a bridge that some rash calculator had knocked together anyhow.'

'No, no.' She was close to him now. 'He just didn't go for jobs he was capable of, kept himself out of the way, never extended himself.'

'That's not a bad thing, either.'

'For some people. Not him.'

'You don't think very highly of the poor old chap, do you?'

She considered the floor. The ache in his bruised shin twisted into pain, throbbed, disappeared.

'I'm talking like this,' she said, very slowly and moved away from him. The cream dress wrinkled, shifted, smoothed itself to her. On her left hand was a smudge of purple, heliotrope, from the machine. 'As if I know all about it. Until I left home I took him at his own assessment. I had as much money as the other girls at school, our house and car were as good as those of my friends. Well, with one or two exceptions. And he'd always talk to me. He loved explaining, oh, scientific principles, or why he'd done such and such a thing on such and such an occasion. There was one tale of how he'd stopped a murder, actually prevented it, while he was on holiday in Italy. And another, how he'd improvised some means of blowing a cathedral organ in Bombay or Madras or somewhere. There were twenty Indians running up and down with ropes, I think he said.' She showed her delight.

'Are these stories true?' Bernard asked.

'I've no more idea than you have. Does it matter? He was a good father and that's what counts. He was away a lot when I was small, but he sent presents. Mind you, he wasn't responsible for me as my mother was. He never punished me.

178

So I took him at his own valuation. It seems ridiculous now, but there it is. And it wasn't until I married . . . Oh, Ike made some remark about him, said he wouldn't put him in charge of an ice-cream barrow, something of the sort. I was cross, defended him. And then Ike began to tell me how much Daddy had earned, who his employers were, and how he'd been given the sack once and how he'd had to retire, sick, from some big motor-road job. He'd got it all worked out. Figures, dates, names. The lot. And,' her voice was slower, 'he said if I didn't believe it, he'd write me down one or two questions to ask for myself.' She seemed dazed. 'He wasn't usually like that, really. He could be nasty, but not in that way.'

They were alienated from Bernard's territory. A husband underscoring a father's gross failure. Bernard was apprehensive, despising himself for his narrow knowledge. He should have said something now, to dispel Ike's dominant image, to restore Butler's. Instead he merely hated awkwardly, childishly, the part of her life he could not share.

'I was naive. Once he'd said that, I put two and two together. And I asked my mother. She talked more than she should. Probably she resented the fact that he didn't get into the big money as her father did. She claimed that Daddy really had talent, both as an engineer and in administration, but that he hadn't the character to go with it. "He wouldn't exert himself for anybody," she said. "If he had a drink in front of him that he was enjoying, he wouldn't leave it and get on with his work. He'd call for another one." '

'Did she hold it against him?' he asked.

'I suppose so. They led a queer life, you see, what with his being abroad and out on location. And another thing was that he'd started off with her father's firm, been one of the bright young men, but had gone off on his own. She thought that if he'd stuck, Grandpa would have kept him working, and rich.' A great pause, both numbed.

'I don't know why we're talking down here in the cold,' Bernard said, in the end.

'Because I can't mend this damned thing.' She slapped the cover of the duplicator. 'My great-grandfather, my grandfather and Daddy were all engineers, and look at me.'

They began to walk away, up the cold steps, Jacqueline in front.

'Tom makes money,' she said. 'He's worth a tidy packet.'

'And?'

'It matters to them. Tom's all my mother wanted in that way. Talented. Quick. And rich. But then, he's not married, and hasn't got a family.'

'She wants that?'

'Don't you go getting ideas, young man,' she said, mockprim. 'I don't know why I'm telling you all this. You've got enough troubles of your own.'

'Such as?' He laughed.

They were in the hall now, with the cellar door locked behind them. She turned, face white, mouth sick, in incredulity.

'Your mother,' she said.

He'd never thought. He shrugged, easily dismissing his remorse.

'That reminds me.' He began fussily to outline his scheme for taking his mother on a ride round the places she knew. 'What do you think?'

She didn't answer.

'Well?'

'Have you asked the hospital authorities?' She spoke without enthusiasm.

'Well, no.'

'It might cause no end of trouble. Upset her. Make her violently ill. Give 'em extra unnecessary work. I don't know.'

'I never thought of it that way.'

'You ask them.'

He was dashed by her words, her stance. She'd inherited her mother's coldness. He would have dropped the idea there and then, but on the next day she asked, efficiency expert, if he'd made inquiries at the hospital.

When he approached the ward sister, she screwed her forehead, looked elsewhere. She was a pretty, thin-lipped girl.

'You would like to take your mother for a ride round the town, Mr. Allsop? Do you realise what condition she is in?'

'I know she's going to die.'

No answer to that; blue eyes focussed elsewhere.

'I thought,' he began again, 'that it might make her happier, that it couldn't really do any, much harm.' Silly, to himself.

'You'd have to get permission from Dr. Williams.' She stroked her stiff skirt.

'When can I see him?'

'It would be better to write.'

He composed the letter with difficulty, rewriting three times. It took him more than an hour to make exactly sure he was saying what he meant. He heard nothing until nearly a week later when the ward sister caught him on his way out.

'Dr. Williams doesn't think it's a good idea.'

'He's read my letter?'

'Yes. It would only do harm.' Blue, stony eyes stared. The cold face was still. 'I'm sorry, Mr. Allsop. But we don't want to cause Mother any anxiety.'

There was the answer. Mother. From faceless Williams and blue-eyed efficiency. It's bad enough to die, without help from amateurs. He dragged himself away, reduced, dwarfed, a slapped child. When he reported to Jacqueline she nodded with the same terseness, the identical thinness of lip he had noted in the ward sister.

In the youth club Eric Parkes cornered Mary. He was big, haughty, rude.

The record-player banged hell across the room; pointed toes tapped.

'That's a marvellous story you were spreading,' he said.

'What story?'

'About Deirdre Fenton.' She knew, trembled, felt herself curdle with weakness, grow insignificant, filthy.

'She's back at school.'

'So I hear. And so much for your gossip.' His voice lacerated. 'I'd keep my mouth shut if I were you.' He moved away, shoulders set.

Mary crept back to the girls, to squat on a table, out of the way.

'You look white,' Maureen said. 'You all right, duck?'

Mary nodded, swallowed, cried in the lavatory, went home to cry again.

16

THE FESTIVAL fortnight began in mid-October. The Theatre brought its production of *King Lear* forward a week and opened to every bigwig in the county on Saturday evening. It went magnificently, craggy, howling with a kind of stone-age polish. On Sunday afternoon the same notables, sober now, joined the pious in a Festival Service at St. Mary's. There were lush parties through the week-end and the four events of Monday night were well attended.

Tom Butler stood back, explaining at length why there would be a financial failure. According to him, no one had taken his advice, and the organisers had allowed the pressure to ease in the final three weeks.

'It's obvious,' he claimed at any one of the parties, slopping the whisky round his tumbler, 'that in mid-October you don't get a holiday crowd. What you have here is a population of nearly half a million. You therefore lay on a festival which will pull some thousands of them in for two small weeks. You excite them with publicity, you get names to stand about in the bars and foyers, you insert a television camera or two and flood the local papers. Result, a nice little money-making investment. Emphasis, mark you, on little. The *Lear* was on, anyway, and so was at least one of Riley's concerts. I built round that. I, we, you, if you like, did well. We've packed the place with telegenic faces, practically free.' He'd glare, drink deep as a horse, cough and say, 'But they don't know a side-street huckster from a supermarket millionaire. They think they've got the Edinburgh. In this place. In October. Well.' Gargle. 'I'm glad it's not my money.'

In spite of this hoarse jeremiad, the theatre was crowded; it would have been, anyway; the Theatre Guild put on a rape-study that brought every student within miles scalding in and the concerts were twice as well attended as they would have been had they been delivered at monthly intervals. Some of the fringe delights made money. The Festival Club was packed stinking until one every night in a sort of miners' institute Saturday. In a promenade atmosphere, all stood or sat on the floor after the organisers packed chairs and tables away as room-consuming, anybody with a loud enough voice and the courage of his convictions could mount the tiny platform at the far end from the doors and the bar and declare his intentions.

A drunken poet ran *Lear* down.

'This is a hoax. That's a young man's bawling against the universe. No octogenarian has that sort of energy, not even Verdi or Sophocles. And yet you sit there with your jaws sagging.'

They were off.

At one of the St. Mary's concerts there was a scene. The Tudor Singers had done faultless motets, a mass by John Shepherd and had begun on a modern group. After Vaughan Williams and Kodaly they performed a bit of spiky Riley, rehearsed past perfection in a month, and had just started a Hymn to the Holy Spirit by a nameless organist at one of the Oxford colleges, with a smattering of clashing seconds, triplets and a stumble into five-four when an old man, in a dilapidated coat, had stood, rammed a hat on his bald head and shouted, 'Stop that blasphemy, stop that blasphemy, stop that blasphemy.' His voice banged like a megaphone, breath control marvellous. 'Stop that blasphemy.' The choir moved on, mp to mf to pp, molto legato. A sidesman glided towards the man, called him 'sir', asked him to remember where he was, but the sentence hammered on. The hymn concluded, 'Ho-o-o-oh-oh-ly Para-(fff)clete', organ D Major, swell reeds squawking. The interrupter removed his hat, sat down, muttered through the last item, shuffled to the door where he vaguely enunciated 'the chords, the chords' to embarrassed ladies.

The local papers failed to record the incident.

At the Festival Club the young men tipped their bottled beer and shouted culture, demonstrating that the next biggest hoax to *Lear* was Britten's *War Requiem*, which was castigated because it was too difficult for a performance by local forces and not worth doing anyway. Two local novelists were accused of trying to prostitute the talents they palpably lacked. A curious type with long curls was forcibly prevented from reading a page or two from *The Naked Luncheon*; elderly ladies hurried out to complain. Letters about the savage behaviour of young men, and (alas) women on whom the state was lavishing money 'dearly earned by rate-payer and tax-payer alike', and which veered after a brief, formal reference to the 'almost incredible scenes of uncouth behaviour' into diatribes on the sexual morals of these animals on the foul mouths of young blackguards and the disgrace to the fair name and reputation of this delightful city yours etc. doubled the length of the evening paper's correspondence column for a fortnight.

The Press rushed at the club. Youth stood justified.

'This is no country for old men,' the hack wrote. 'Here the young men stand outspoken, but in defence of what they believe. They want no generation of the mealy-mouthed. Ideas are bandied, are flattened, are exalted here, but ideas reign. People talk about music, art, culture as if these matter. Sometimes the expression is shocking, coarse, unprintable; sometimes the notions propounded are heretical in the extreme. But here is a generation which thinks, and no one who has the good name and reputation of this fair city at heart can . . .'

Tom Butler was delighted.

'That club's the best thing in the place. Kids' corner. You won't find anybody very drunk and they're whacking the daylights out of cultural discussions. Half of 'em don't know a string quartet from a soliloquy, but they're listening and expecting an explosion. That's culture, not paying a guinea to hear somebody you're indifferent to scrape through the Bach G Major cello Suite.'

He took Bernard and Jacqueline in half-way through the first week. The premises were Victorian, with great stone-barred bow-windows and white rooms, all crowded, noise minimal at this time, ten-thirty, and no one up on the plat-form setting the world right. They found themselves room on a kind of wall-bench, cushioned at the end with a heap of duffel-coats and college scarves; two nervous Indians and a raw-boned girl, in a kind of loose gym slip or maternity smock, massive legs in black stockings straight out, smiled in silence, communicated by hand signs. Butler had the beer up in no time.

'I should have thought Riley would have been here,' Bernard said.

'Riley?'

'Image-busting.'

'Riley?' Butler was maddeningly tasting his drink. 'I don't think you know much about life, my young friend.'

'Here we go,' said Jacqueline.

'Bill Riley shoots his mouth off now and again. I don't say he doesn't act in an ill-advised way from time to time. That Simpson girl, for instance. But basically,' pause for further sipping, 'he's a musical composer, a serious, dedicated artist. When he's got the sheets of manuscript paper in front of him he's a somebody and he knows it. And because he knows it, you don't find him round places like this every night of the week. You'd think I was mad if I expected historians to chase women or drink themselves to death or start riots just because they were historians. It takes as long to write a symphony as a historical monograph, and it's a damn sight harder work.'

'It wasn't on grounds of his profession,' Bernard said. 'His personality was what led me to suppose that . . .'

'God,' Butler said. 'He's energetic, but it's channelled, sublimated into his music, not spilt over every beer-table or pair of knickers handy.'

'Steady on, Freud,' Jacqueline interrupted. 'Don't be so damned bossy, or vulgar.'

'My dear little sister . . .'

'Bernard's right,' she said. 'If one's energetic, and he is, he'll show it, wherever he is.'

'You, my child, are as illogical as this fiancé of yours. If Riley were here, in his usual form, he'd be whanging round like a jumping-cracker. I am not contesting this. I merely contradicted our young friend's assertion that he expected the gentleman to be here. It wouldn't surprise me if he walked in, any more than the appearance of, let's say, the bishop would; or the town clerk; after all, we're here. But I don't expect him any more than I expect the higher clergy or the senior administrators.'

Bernard felt squashed. As Butler's half-hoarse posh voice droned on, depression spread. His beer was cold, gassy, dug down his gullet like a skewer. The rattle of conversation and glasses, the bar lamps, the incessant movements of bodies seemed pointless. What was all this?

At tea-time yesterday, when Mary had gone upstairs to start her homework, Allsop had said:

'I don't think your mother'll be here long, now.'

'Why? Was she worse last night?' He had not even inquired.

'No. Not that I could see. It was something she said.'

'Oh.'

The father's hands were on his knees, as if he were frozen in the middle of some game. O'Grady says. His face, grey in the dim light, was ditched with shadow.

'She said, "I don't know what'll happen to Mary." And she looked at me, did sort of struggle up. "When I'm gone."

I said, "You're not gone yet, Ivy" and she said, "You've got to face it." And cried a bit.'

'Oh.'

'She went off then. Dazed, you know. I think sometimes that they, er, er, have a—a presentiment, don't you? They know. I'm sure they do.'

'No.'

'I think she did, Bernard.'

The voice was solemn, humdrum, impressive. It was as if the man reported from the grave, became dignified with a corpse's numen. Bernard shivered. Reason gave no comfort at such a time.

'It's a pity it had to end like this.'

There was no answer, either, to that. Bernard was not even sure his father meant anything, or just decorated a sigh with coherent words.

'Did she seem worse, then?'

'No. As usual.' No recognition that this had been answered once.

'What did they say?'

'I didn't see anybody. The sister wasn't there, and the young one was rushing about.'

'Doing what?' Fatuity.

'Oh, carrying flowers, once, when I saw her. I expect they've plenty to do.'

The lines in Allsop's face were dark. He sighed, heaved himself up and began to clear the table, clumsy-shouldered, like an ox.

'Don't you do this, Dad. You get ready to go.' Allsop obeyed.

'I don't know what she'll say.' He made for the door. 'I dread it, sometimes.' The pained lines round his mouth crinkled into embarrassment.

Bernard seemed, to himself, frozen, as if areas of sensibility had been disconnected. He went unwillingly with Jacqueline to see *Lear*. He did not talk, felt winter in his spine. There was nothing in the warm smell, the spicy fug of the theatre, to liven him. They drank sherry, bitter as the sea, and as cold. He hunched himself in his seat, grudgingly stood to let late-comers pass, loathed the rapid chatter, the necks, the shining hair of the women, their perfume. It was one vast parrot-chatter of a hell, to nag at his coldness, his isolation. These were extras, assembled at wildest expense, to smile, nod, breathe, greet, to portray life round the corpse of feeling that was himself.

The curtain rose, on gold, on silver, the tang of grease-paint. Words were exchanged. Generous plumminess and a well-groomed beard.

> 'Of all these bounds, even from this line to this,
> With shadowy forests and with champains rich'd
> With plenteous rivers and wide-skirted meads
> We make thee lady.'

Bernard stared, uncomprehending, as if the language had been dead, Lear's original. The tableau moved, Cordelia ruined, Kent dismissed. He sat dumb in his plush seat, letting his eye strike for stage to auditorium, drift back, king to crowd, glare to dimness.

Time was wasted, here.

Suddenly, without his noticing, Shakespeare's words scored, took charge, and he was intent, was Lear cursing, Kent flyting. Warmth grew in him, excitement. Now he recognised that he was sitting amongst sober suits, but it made no difference, he was himself in another, so that the interval, straight on Gloucester's blinding, jarred him with surprise. A huge blue curtain fell, into folds, where madness and sin had raged. 'I'll fetch some flax and whites of eggs To apply to his bleeding face.' And down dropped the safety curtain, khaki-dun.

Jacqueline signalled him out to the coffee bar. They passed people they knew, lifting coffee-cups, smiling, bowing heads. These were unreal, zombies, with Gloucester's bloodied eyes trampled. He caught sight of his face in the mirror; it was red with his hair fuzzed up. There was no difference between his expression and that of the others; a kind of petty grimness, a determination not to lose a place in the queue or a reputation for politeness. Two coffees. Help yourself to sugar, sir. No, sir. Not tonight.

He was motionless, his back to the tiers of photographs, stirring. Jacqueline did not speak. Something of his own misery returned, his inadequacy. A young woman forged across towards him. He knew her face, he thought; could not put a name to it.

'Hello,' the young woman said, banging her coffee-cup against her saucer. 'He doesn't remember me,' to Jacqueline. 'Railton. The party. The studio-place.'

'I don't remember your name,' Jacqueline said rudely.

'Clay. Bettina Clay.'

'Oh, I knew your Christian name. Jean Pinkett's friend.'

'Jean Thompson, now.'

'I know you,' Bernard said. 'The party, where Riley played that Nativity. You and another girl. I thought you were sisters.' He'd no idea why he'd come sputtering out with that. Jacqueline was not pleased and he preoccupied, elsewhere. 'And let him smell his way to Dover.' Well. 'How are you?'

'Have you heard about Jean?' The question was directed at Jacqueline with teenage-girl keenness.

'No.'

'She was at school with you, wasn't she?'

'Yes, she was.'

'Her husband's left her.'

'Oh.'

They stood there, three people with sweet coffee.

'Wasn't he at the Railton affair?' Bernard said, after a pause. 'Pale fellow, with teeth.'

'Yes. He was. He always seemed very attentive. But he went off, last week, left her stranded.'

'Who did he go with?'

'Nobody knows. There is some talk of a woman. But

nobody knows, really. Jean never suspected anything. That's the mystery.'

'How's she taking it?' Jacqueline asked, dry voice.

'She's gone to her parents. It's made her ill. And her mother. She's a semi-invalid, anyway. The mother, I mean.'

'Was it expected?'

'No. Nobody dreamed.'

'Poor woman,' Jacqueline said. 'But she was always a bit accident-prone.'

Mrs. Clay looked down her nose. They stood together but spoke hardly at all. In the end, with curt goodbyes, they parted.

'Somebody should tell that woman,' Jacqueline said.

'About what?'

'Her dress and her hair. They just don't go.'

The lights dimmed; this time Bernard was tumbled back on to the heath with Gloucester, Kent and Lear, in a mad sanity of imagination. Cordelia broke his heart for him; the tragedy cleared him at once of his own preoccupations. 'Pray you undo this button.' He was alone, a fighting man here, head alive with fury, cursing the world. Cleansed? Purged? Anger buzzed inside him, sourly, like a late-summer wasp. Somebody must pay for those great deaths. The clearance of scum was no recompense; Shakespeare knew that. Lear and Cordelia died, and thousands have died a little, in them, added minutely, each according to his sensibility, a dram in the scale balancing those great deaths. These died, these two, and left men twitching in the jaw, scowling round with the powerful energy of hunters, cannibals, headmen. 'Break heart. I prithee break.' And mine. Nobody could bear this, shift this burden and remain the same. A thousand people would creep out of this theatre, all changed, reduced, part-sacrificed, oblations to Shakespeare's greedy man of a talent, a genius. 'The oldest have borne most.' Scuttle off. Cripples out. In the twinkling of an eye. 'The weight of this sad time we must obey.'

Once outside, they sat in her car which was parked in a

side street. She wound the window right down.

'Fresh air's good,' she said. 'That place gets stuffy. You begin to smell bodies.' She turned on the car light and moved her face about to peer into a hand-mirror. 'I thought John was good,' she remarked, when her scrutiny was near ending. The Christian name annoyed him; it was the in-phraseology, the clique-clack of a provincial city. She didn't know the actor apart from his work, but made out she did. Or perhaps she'd met him once amongst a hundred others in her brother's company. And now he was John, when he did well. Bernard made no comment, stared through the windscreen at the iron railings that separated Georgian fronts from the street.

'It was marvellous,' he said, detesting the word. Not that he could do better.

'I suppose it was. Well done. Can't think it's much of a play.'

'Why not?'

'When people are tortured they scream,' she said; 'they cry and grunt like animals. They aren't making great pronouncements.'

'You've got to accept the convention.'

'I don't. You're moved by it. I'm not. I think it's artificial. You don't.'

He could neither understand nor control the shaking anger in him. She sounded so prim, and it was as if she had deliberately set out to wreck the—the what? Enjoyment? Uplift? Exaltation? He said nothing, but she wouldn't leave it.

'I don't understand half the stuff for a start.'

'That's your fault, then.'

'Come, come.' Mock-governess. 'I can think what I like. Free country, you know. Why should we have to consult notes and read books? There are plenty of good things I can understand without all that.'

'How can you judge if you can't understand?'

'I understand enough to know the other part isn't worth my time. That's called criticism. Making a choice after consideration.'

'If it's not prejudice, it's idleness,' he said.

'Somebody's getting cross.'

'No. I am not.'

'If you can't argue without getting your hair off, we'd better shut up.'

'Can you tell me the name of any book or a play you claim to understand and which is good?' He spoke in a clipped sixth-form-master style, lips frozen.

'Oh, I don't know.'

'That won't do. You've made a claim. Substantiate it.'

'All right,' she said. 'Somerset Maugham then.'

'My God.'

'You haven't read any.' She laughed, unserious, untouched, and pressed the self-starter. As the car moved away he kept quiet, admiring her skill, as his mind festered over her stupidity.

'Are you coming back for an hour?' she said.

'No thanks.' At his politest. 'Home, James.'

'You're cross.'

'I'm not. I want to see me dad before he goes to bed.'

'Me dad,' she mimicked.

'Yes. I'm worried. About him and my mother.' Correct pronunciation this time.

'I'm sorry,' she said, and touched his knee with her left hand. He did not move. There was little traffic along the orange-bright roads with their blue-cold side-streets, but she drove slowly.

'Here you are then,' she said, outside his house.

'Are you coming in?'

'No, thanks.'

He watched the rear lights which dipped over the hill to reappear on the next; as she was about to turn left he saw her switch the headlamps on, sweep the corner. Now she'd gone he stood dejected, wished himself elsewhere. *Lear* meant nothing on this cold stretch of road, to the man at the wheel of the lorry rattling past, to Mrs. Benniston who had just pulled her bedroom blind, to him. Depression numbed him as he stood disconsolate by his own front gate. In the distance he heard the rumble of an approaching train. Disappointed in himself, he put his hand on the iron gate, swinging it, waiting. He shivered at the cold touch of the metal. The damned train was taking long enough, detaining him here in the street at this time. He was determined to see it. Now it thumped closer, into the station, under the bridge, hammering the rails, flinging blocks of sound to hit, thud on the houses and echo, pulsing back. They'd got the fire-box open and the glare reddened the underbelly of the flying smoke. Waggons clashed by, metal jangling on metal, powered, overpowering. The guard's van rattled past, comically, and its red lamps swayed off, like Jacqueline's, were gone. He shuffled up the path, in the dumps, into the cheerless house. He had seen a goods train.

His father was still up, reading, an empty cup by him in the hearth. Allsop looked up, smoothed the paper on his knee.

'Hello,' Bernard said. 'How's Mother?'

He hardly waited for the reassuring answer he expected, but pulled his jacket off. No change. All this had happened before; violently ill one night, back to—what, normality? the next. Quiet dying?

'Very poorly, I'm afraid.'

It took some seconds before he grasped what was said.

'I'm sorry.'

'She was hardly conscious. Breathing very heavily. I suppose really it was a sort of death-rattle. I don't know. She indicated from time to time that she wanted a drink. There was a vessel there with a spout.' Death-rattle, indicate, vessel. His father sighed with animal vigour. 'It wasn't very nice, I can tell you.'

'No. Shall I get some tea?'

'She might go at any time. They'll ring.' His father's nostrils flared wide. 'No, thanks. Not now. I've had a drink.'

Bernard lumped himself into a chair.

'Mary in bed?' His father nodded. 'Have you told her?'

'Yes. I did. I thought I'd better. I don't know . . .'

'Was she upset?'

Allsop knitted his brows, trying to recall.

'She didn't say much. They never do.' He brushed his hair back from his forehead with white fingers. 'To tell you the truth, Bernard, she seemed more interested in, oh,' he floundered, frowning, touching himself, 'asking permission to go out with some young man.'

'Really?' The word brayed in its artificial accent. 'Where?'

'To see *Julius Caesar*, was it? Something of the sort, at the university. Young Parkes had asked her to go with him.'

'What did you say?'

Allsop hitched his trousers, straightened both socks.

'I said she could. It's next Saturday. Part of some festival, I think she said.' He looked up. 'By then her mother might be dead.' He quietly scratched his calf, face forward, thin hair grey, bleached in the yellow light. 'It looks like it,' he said. 'It looks like it.'

'Yes.' Bernard leaned, with his hands clasped between his knees, awkwardly, on the back of his chair. Now he was lost. Every remark of his father's had been calmly made, dully, and the old man sat there, pale, but no different, himself, an ordinary man. Outside, another goods train thumped past; the driver would be watching ahead, steadily, as the fireman swayed, stoking the glaring box. They had problems as they thrashed those hundreds of metallic tons along the line. Their kith and kin had died, had run away, had withered in heart, had twisted bowels with fear or disgust.

'We'd better be getting aloft,' Allsop said, standing. He lifted the cup from the hearth and as he carried it, it rattled gobbling in the saucer.

'Yes. Anything I can do, Dad?'

'No. You'd better tell Jacqueline. I've told Jessie. Called in. She wants to go tomorrow. She's a good sort.' Bernard followed his father into the kitchen where he swilled the pots mechanically under the hot tap. 'It doesn't seem fair.' Was that said in the splashing? 'Ending like this. I used to wonder about it at one time, and wish I could go first. Now you get numbed to it.' With the back of a wet hand Allsop wiped a tear from his face. It seemed natural, here, in this place, lined with the bright plates, saucepans, basins his mother had bought. The son took a tea-towel, dried the saucer and cup his father had been holding. 'I've made a bit of a splash,' Allsop said, dabbing with a dish-cloth. 'I'll put the kettle on. I think I could do with a hot water-bottle. It's a bit cool.'

'Let me do it.'

The old man allowed it.

17

THE FINAL concert of the festival was a performance of Handel's *Messiah*. This was to be done with a small choir, an eighteenth-century orchestra, a chamber organ with all the solos rewritten in florid operatic style. Riley's fellow-lecturer at the university, Rollo Wykes-Thomas, had completed the score a year previously and as soon as the festival was mooted Frank Armstrong, the professor, had begun to organise. The difficulties were enormous; first there was a choir of about forty, with reserves, to be trained in a work which they all would claim to be able to sing 'on their heads'. And this with the month of August blank. They decided that they would use and augment a professional orchestra; by incredible luck they found this could be managed with a week's rehearsal. Armstrong and his wife, another indomitable, got the money for this by writing round to local firms and brazenly saying exactly what was wanted. Big business liked the approach, paid. Rehearsals for choir, and young soloists, began in June. Armstrong issued his ukases: one hundred per cent attendance or out, full member and reserve alike. Doubters said this would reduce the decent singers in the district to a choir of twelve within a fortnight; in fact, of the hundred and twenty tested, in a week, by Wykes-Thomas, the professor and the assistant-lecturers, Armstrong would not allow Riley to break off from his own work, nearly a hundred stayed the course.

'You're a marvellous eighteenth-century scholar, Rollo,' Armstrong said, 'but you couldn't organise a visit to the lavatory.'

'That doesn't need . . .'

'Doesn't need, doesn't need,' Yorkshire accent powerful. 'My lad, that's the trouble with half the people in England today. Doesn't need.'

Armstrong's commandos created a stir, so that in the end there were to be three performances, on Thursday, Friday and Saturday. A record company was interested, and the B.B.C. were to make a tape. All the money to cover expenses, and the cost grew enormous, was in the bank by the middle of September.

'The cash is in,' Armstrong told Wykes-Thomas. 'Now make something of it. You've got to convince people who believe they knew *Messiah*, note for note, before you were born. They'll foam at the mouth to hear four equal parts, for a start; what they like is a million sopranos, a thousand bosoms wobbling contralto, ten thousand false teeth on the bass and a few tenors shifting phlegm. They'll throw bricks in the choruses to hear all the notes Handel actually put down; they've never had 'em yet. Never. And when they hear that bloody swooping and diving you're written in the solos, they'll tear the place down. Now you make sure, lad, absolutely bloody certain, in fact, that what they're having kittens about is what you want 'em to hear. Drill. Drill. More drill. Don't forget. There's nobody in your choir above fifty years of age, but even that means thirty years of ingrained rubbish to be erased. No backsliding when they see all that soap and shining eye-glasses. You won't hear the last, I'll promise you. But if they're going to have you, and me, and everybody else within a mile, limb from limb, we'll make 'em hear what we want 'em to hear first.'

Thomas agreed and slaved. Armstrong collected more

money, stopped the work of the music department for at least a fortnight, once in June, once in September, to get the copying done and harried Butler to organise a series of letters to the Press.

'Armstrong's a marvel,' Butler told Bernard. 'He doesn't leave a bloody thing to chance. It wouldn't surprise me if he didn't raise Handel from the bloody dead to play the organ for him.'

Bernard and Jacqueline had bought expensive seats for the final performance.

Mrs. Allsop was no worse, half-comatose, grimly alive. Her husband went each night and sat at her bedside, saying nothing, not touching, only looking at her irregularly. It was as if he were clamped in some rigor of pain, and he walked the streets home from work or the bus with a blind mind. There was no helping him; he wandered through his unmapped agony on his own, refusing help because he had no idea how to accept. If he had opened himself to sympathy he would have stripped to his own horror and been broken. Now he moved about the house shaven, moderately efficient, a man of habit, teetering on madness.

On the Saturday of *Messiah*, Mary went to *Caesar* with Eric Parkes. She had a day or two before seen a sweater she liked, and had asked her father if she could buy it. He did not listen. Very patiently she explained again, this time describing the texture, the colour, the shop, a curious chromium place with slanted windows called Teen Types. She offered to pay for it with holiday savings she had not touched.

'Yes,' her father said. 'What do you say it is? A skirt?'

'Oh, Daddy. It's a sweater, with . . .' She went through the tale again, lost herself this time, unable to raise enthusiasm for digression. In the middle he stood up, very courteously, walked to the kitchen to turn off the immersion heater. He stayed there, hovering.

'What do you say, Daddy?'

'Say?'

'Can I have it? I'll buy it. I've got enough.'

'Buy it? I don't . . . I haven't got the money here. I'll go to the bank this week-end.'

'I've got my own money.'

'Will that do?' he said.

The child was defeated, stood in the middle of the floor with her mouth open. Her father for all his attention could not understand a word she had said, and she knew it.

'You buy it,' Bernard said, 'and Dad'll give you the money at the week-end.'

'He might think it's too much.'

Bernard named the sum out loud to his father.

'You'll owe that to Mary. All right?' Slowly as to a baby, a foreigner.

'Yes. Yes.' For the first time their father shook his hands in exasperation. 'I know. Don't go on so. It's for a skirt.'

They both laughed, and he opened his eyes and smiled with them. It was as if a split second previously he had been hammered on the skull and would crumple at any time.

Bernard's depression had been growing. After the *Lear* performance he had spent a day wildly arranging in his mind the arguments he should have put to Jacqueline. They were convincing, he thought, but what frightened him was the way in which they reiterated themselves, tippled back, reissued, repeated in a sort of coherent nightmare. Each step of the argument was logical, but endlessly put in a delirium of words. He could think of nothing else; it was important to win her over. His head ached feverishly and the sentences banged. 'Don't you see that if you carry that to its conclusion there would be no drama as we know it, a mere peep show, vitiated by the law of diminishing returns?' 'My dear girl, don't you understand that if you . . . ?'

He worked, dully, and watched his father.

Mr. Allsop blundered about, and one evening as he was painstakingly mending the fire he knocked a live coal into the hearth so that sparks spattered the carpet. These Allsop extinguished quickly, saying as he moved, 'Damn, damn.' Bernard had never heard him swear before. 'Damn.' With the faint smell of burning, the father looked up at his son's face, understood the expression there. He turned his head.

At that moment the depression turned into anger. Somebody should suffer. He remembered how, as a child in the junior school yard, he had watched Jack Sadler, a boy in his class, thumping some girl who, he said, had picked up one of his glass marbles. The fist on her back had thudded and twanged, as if on padded wood and tinfoil. And he had watched, furious for the terrified girl, but afraid to interfere, trembling at the violence of her screaming and the intense regularity of the blows. A teacher had run across, grabbed the boy by his hair, and thrown him full length in the muck. And there was anger again as the women teachers came out to surround the girl, coddle her indoors. There was no such for his father; he floundered on, thumped into a swear-word he was ashamed to use in front of his son, and was punished again.

Bernard went that night to the hospital. It was the best he could do. Mrs. Allsop was drowsy, but conscious. Her speech blurred itself as if her lips and tongue were already dead. He tried to tell her about his work, but found it impossible. What did some cuttings from a newspaper of 1811 mean to her now she was a day or two short of death? He stopped.

'Go on,' she mumbled. 'I'm listening.' The rough sound of the last two words, ah uh-ih, with the section of breath and the eye-flicker, unnerved him. He forced himself to bend closer, to continue. As he sat back, numbed, he watched the nodding of her head, the black opening of her mouth. His father was beginning now.

'Bernard's going to hear the *Messiah*.'

'Ah?'

'The *Messiah*. Bernard's going on Saturday.'

'Ah.' Falling nasal intonation. Her grey hair looked wilder, grew in spite of the cancer, as she moved her head.

'That'll be very nice,' Allsop said.

'Eh.' She half opened her eyes. 'I used to like *Messiah*,' she said. 'Ah ooh uh eye Muh-eye.' Heavy breathing, bad, quick pants. 'I sang in it once. De Montfort Hall.' Bernard couldn't make out what she said.

'She sang it in the De Montfort Hall,' Allsop interpreted. 'In Leicester.'

'When I was a girl.' The effort. 'Eh ah oh uh cuh. Nineteen years old.' She closed herself up from them, breathed more easily.

'She's never forgotten that,' Allsop spoke after an interval, but there was no confirmation from the bed.

Bernard wondered if they had worn white dresses, how they had travelled there, these girls from the outlying villages, what they had chattered about, to which young men, who the conductor was, the soloists? Had the memory any power now, any pleasure, or was it merely a verbal formulation, made frequently enough before and merely repeated here without accompanying pictures or sensations? Parry Jones? Gladys Ripley? William Parsons (bass)? Isobel Baillie? Harty? Sargent? And he was dead now, a corpse, he who'd directed this wreck of a mother through 'And the Glory', 'Worthy is the Lamb'. Somebody else would do it this year, with superbly pointing baton, while they both would be dead, changed, in the twinkling of an eye. That was thirty years ago, only seven years before his own birth. 'For unto us a child is born. Unto us a son is given. And the government shall be upon His shoulder and His name shall be called Wonderful, Counsellor, the Mighty God, the Everlasting Father, the Prince of Peace.' Every mother.

They sat the rest of the half-hour uncomfortably, each trying to signal interest or concern. Even Mrs. Allsop occasionally opened her eyes, nodded, moved her mouth.

'Do you want anything, Mother?' Allsop would ask then, but the inch-long shake checked him. When they wished her good night she barely shifted, was too listless to acknowledge the perfunctory kisses, their powerless affection.

On the Saturday of the *Messiah* performance, Bernard had tried to get Mary to invite Eric Parkes to tea, but she refused, huffily.

'He's not your steady, then?'

'No.' Glazed, sullen look.

'Not serious?'

'Shut up.'

'Just good friends, eh?' he laughed.

'You ought to have more sense at your age.'

He was surprised, recognising that she did not see this as unmeant backchat. The sulky jab of her answers, the hitch of her shoulders, depicted someone he did not know, easily hurt, unsisterly.

The tea was relatively cheerful, with the three together, all the lights in the room on. There was a good starched cloth on the table, pork pie, ham, chocolate cake, meringues. Bernard exchanged views about the football results with his father. Both, in their ignorance, became animated asking for knowledge, offering opinions deferentially. Mary joined in with a detailed account of the life and habits of the local international centre-half. She spoke in a hurrying, colourless voice, but was delighted to give the information. When pressed for sources, she then described the girl who sat next to her in class, who went to see the team without fail every match, travelling with her father in the special bus, wearing the red-and-white scarf and swinging the rattle. She heckled the referee, called to the players by their Christian names, collected autographs and was raising a petition for the reinstatement of the outside-left who was doing marvels in the reserves. In answer to Bernard's question, Mary said that the girl was probably the cleverest in the class and that her father was a plumber.

Allsop suddenly volunteered information about a man he'd met on a street corner and who'd been reserve goalkeeper for England. 'A tall, bow-legged fellow, with a long white face.'

'How old was he?' Bernard asked.

'He'd be over fifty, by then. An ordinary working man.'

They were cheerful together, the younger pair volubly excited. Bernard deliberately tried to keep conversation from flagging, succeeded, was pleased with himself. His father was almost animated and for once took an interest in his food. It was as if they'd been paroled, shortly.

Suddenly Mary, biting celery, said:

'I wonder what my mother's having for tea?'

She'd obviously no idea of the effect of her question, but chattered on about the excellent food that hospital provided, told them a story about the father of another girl of the school who was a cook at the City and had competed against chefs from London hotels and had won. He'd been offered 'no end of jobs', but he refused to move. Allsop and his son sat frozen, the façade demolished. Again Mary did not notice their silence, the expressions; she rattled on, left them to wash the pots, called out to her father as she left that he was to be sure to give her love to her mother.

'Does she know how bad she is?' Bernard said.

'She lives one thing at a time,' Allsop answered. 'Just now it's going out with young Eric Parkes. And I suppose that's right.'

'You can at her age,' Bernard said, bogus.

'It's what I've been doing now for months, living a day at a time.'

That put him into his place, but as he legged it over to Jacqueline's house the exercise revived him. It was cold, and mist hung across the allotments; the beans clustered thickly still round their poles, but a frost would kill them now, at any time, tonight. As he clopped along the road above the river, tunnelled under railway and macadam at this point, the mist moved, low and steam-thick on the fields where the little Leen wound. He pulled his gloves off in the warmth of exercise. Words from *Messiah* had been repeated, re-sung in his head as he had hurried. 'Since by man came death, by man came also the resurrection of the dead. For as in Adam all die, even so in Christ shall all, shall all be made alive.'

He could not rid himself. 'Since by man . . .'

Just over the level crossing he stopped in the darkness. There were lights on in the closed shops, while cars clumped by on the wood-blocked rails. He peered over towards the river, in its shallow trough, but could see nothing—Bernard

Allsop, flibberty-gibbet, malachi stilt-jack, big talk king. What did these words mean? Comfort hung there, in rags. The rotund sound, the sad victory, the rush in the major, the second triumph in a minor key were magnificent in themselves, but shielded him from reality. Perhaps that was the province of great art; to turn one about-face from the world when that was too overwhelming, and to blind one with the darkness when one was over-cheerful, neglecting a neighbour. That was too easy. The academic analysis revealed nothing, shifted nothing. He had only, standing here by a railway line at the junction of two streets, to begin to hum again and the music won, dismissed scrutiny, spoke to his condition. The final statement 'Even so in Christ' rollicked in the minor, reserving the ultimate of power to the trumpet aria in the trumpet's key. But he, Bernard Ernest Allsop, was uplifted, eyes brimming, a man intact after the shattering blast of his mother's dying. 'Shall all,' Handel said, 'shall all be made alive.'

Was he enjoying his part in this imminent death, because he was not involved? He loved his mother, but it was his father who scratched on from day to day. And his dad had no reserves, then, no buttresses of music or words. He resented his father's depth of suffering, but was honest enough to be glad he was not called on to be battered with him. Perhaps it was his youth, his interests, his wider culture. Even as he made the point mentally, he despised himself. This was snobbery, gross, undisguised pleasure in his own superiority. They were to lose a wife, a mother. His father felt it like a man; he dallied with St. Paul and Mynheer Handel. Why not whisky or drugs? He was not grown up; like a child he could be distracted with toys, given a sugar-bun and a kiss, of the highest order, to take the hurt away. Jacqueline, now, she had known death, had learnt it hard. Her husband, whom she thought she hated, who cuffed and clouted her, who'd seduced and married her, was killed, thrashed down dead, was alive, big, uncouth, growing in her mind one minute and the next a body, a pale hunk, a thing. For as in Adam all die. All, all. That hairy-armed? Imperative? All, shall all. Bernard straightened the lapels of his overcoat, walked on, and music sang in his head.

Jacqueline was in her helpless mood.

She teetered about, looking lost, wondering out loud what she had forgotten.

'I'm sure there's something.' She did pretty pirouettes, moved an ornament or two, put her head on one side.

'If you don't get a move on, we're going to be late,' Bernard said, kissing her. She waved her hands in vague reproof. He liked this act.

'Is it cold out?'

'It is.'

'I wonder if this coat's warm enough. We might have quite a walk from the car to the hall. It's not easy to find a place to park.' She rested finger-tips on a mildly wrinkled forehead. He stood close, stroked her.

'You'll ruin me,' she said.

The performance was a disappointment.

First of all, the same people were there. Bernard had no idea why he thought this would not be so, but it displeased him to see the paunchy bank managers, school teachers, know-alls, spinsters, organists and their wives, who'd turn up for any music provided it was not composed after *Elijah*. True, this evening, there was a slight sense of occasion, in that quite a few men wore evening suits, but so did the choral society members for their jamborees.

The choir and orchestra assembled, very compact round the soloists and the chamber-organ. Rollo Wykes-Thomas, the conductor, whacked his baton vigorously up and down and the orchestra double-dotted the 'grave' of the overture. The bite of the strings was good; they seemed to understand the newness. But the main snag was that the soloists had not become world-beaters overnight; they did their best, but sounded what they were, moderately competent young professionals offering a rather ornate version of the very well known. Not that they were embarrassed by the shakes and cadenzas; they lacked the authority to convince. The choir sang with spirit, so that the choruses were more dramatic, with Handel's bandying of the words from part to part real now, decisive, meaningful, but nine-tenths of the audience preferred 'His yoke is easy' or 'Behold the Lamb of God' with a great wall of Victorian organ diapason behind five or six hundred well-tanned voices. This stuff was good, fresh, Handelian perhaps, but dimmed in this big place.

'The real trouble is,' Bernard heard some silver-haired pundit in the interval, 'the lack of climax—Handel's dramatic, and if you take away his great, er, power-points you've reduced him.'

'That chamber-organ,' one school-ma'am said, 'do you like it? It's more like a mouth-organ.'

'That bass,' announced a middle-aged expert in glasses and shabby raincoat, 'has such a wobble in his voice that you can't tell whether he's meant to be singing a trill or not.'

'The trouble with Rollo,' this from a female assistant-lecturer, 'is that he can't get anything across. You'd think he were driving a land-rover over a ploughed field there.'

'You can't alter Handel's tunes,' a choir-master was mouthing, 'for all the fooling. They're wonderful, and they're like the master himself, simple.'

'I don't go for all that bubbling in the oboes and those recorders or whatever they are. They're so damn dull. Makes the thing sound Salvation Army, somehow.'

Jacqueline talked to her brother who was in full evening dress.

'Has it been a success?'

'Oh, yes.' Tom was unbiassed, judicial. 'It's a fine reconstruction by Wykes-Thomas. You'll hear when the B.B.C. take it up.'

'Will they do it?'

'Yes. The Midland chap's here tonight, and he's ambitious. He won't stick in Brum much longer, and this'll be one step out for him, I'd guess.'

Bernard was glad to sit through arias he'd never heard before, but he was not greatly moved. Perhaps Butler and the publicity boys had painted too brightly so that he expected utter, marvellous change. No, that was wrong. Half sourly, he concluded that there was something to be said as far as he was concerned for the Mozart-Prout, Hamilton Harty-Beecham palette, that the thunders of Sinai and little Bethel were preferable to the still small voices of Handel and Dr. Thomas. His taste was depraved. 'Thou art gone up on high. Thou hast led captivity captive and received gifts for men, yea, even for Thine enemies, that the Lord God might dwell among them.' That soared and dipped, wonderfully, inspired nonsense, reassuring mumbo-jumbo to him. He wished he'd never heard anything of the work before, that he'd been paraded here as a tyro. He shuffled in his seat; Jacqueline was smiling as she fanned her cheek with her programme.

And now they were sitting down again after the Hallelujah Chorus. Justice had triumphed, decency, common sense. In spite of an arrangement that needed a programme as large as a paper-back book to explain it, they had stood for Hallelujah. A pouter-pigeon accountant had clattered up, chapel organists, choral society members, and all had struck a blow against modernism, nonsense, spoof, blague, the sacrilegious. They went down proud men, justified women.

Part III, and Sister Dorothea's text, 'I know'. The soprano tripped prettily, it was surely quicker than usual, as if Thomas were expunging the godly hope. Yet the movement forward was right; Bernard began to be caught in it, pressed, urged onwards, climbing, 'For now is Christ risen from the dead'. This mummy was stripped of the grave clothes, wiped clean of Victorian spice, resurrected, made young again, until Handel's own enthusiasm glowed in the fresh voice, steadily striding, proclaiming without rallentando, moving upwards, absolutely sure, convinced. 'I know.' If Thomas had done nothing else, he had touched this miraculously. Bernard dabbed his handkerchief to his eyes, squinted at Jacqueline. The fanning programme shadowed thinly, unshadowed her face.

'Since by man.'

They were away while Bernard was rapt still with the aria. Quick, beating, heavenly, brooking no argument, but leaving him untouched. He could not hope to be healed twice; the illness must recur. He noted the sprightly singing, approved it, but there was nothing like the effect of his own repetition on that misty cobbled road by a soggy field, shops, a lump of chapel, a railway crossing. These choruses were bearable, thank God. All great art is bearable, just. It cannot torture, reduce men to animals, daub them with their own blood and faeces. That happens, has happened, will, but the artist, enduring it, reduced himself by it, asks no one to be rack-smashed with him. Handel, who knew madness, who was perhaps crazed now, foodless, dirty, in his hurry dragging a thumb down the wet ink of his errors, breathless, in tears of exhausted joy, had spoken with the supreme rationality of music. The trumpet sounded, the dead would rise. This was, in fact, badly sung in a hoarse, cobwebbed voice, but Bernard was snatched up again, beyond this young man, with his chin in his collar, the shining instrument, the sweating Wykes-Thomas. For this corruption must put on incorruption.

By the end of the work he had recovered, had missed the ponderous leaden beauty of a choral society 'Worthy is the Lamb', though this choir flicked their voices like fine whips at him, and the counterpoint that Handel's laughing exuberance of intellect had lit round Amen, like a bonfire, a beacon, a furnace, a forest blaze of searing heat, had burnt him out, whole, wholesome, quiet, unable to clap, a little man in a little suit in a little place.

He was still silent in the cold air.

Jacqueline took his arm, warmly, pressed close to him as they walked uphill to the car. She smiled, was happy, loving, as if she had won something. She was, by nature, undemonstrative so that he had usually to translate her abbreviations into a tenderness he hoped was there. Tonight she pressed, excited, gripping his arm, forcing her presence on him physically.

He slid his arm round her back, and kissed her. She pulled

him to her with violence, thrust her tongue deep into his mouth, on this lighted street. When they moved off, they bounced, half running, like school-kids let free.

At the top of the hill, under the grey houses, she grabbed him again, dominated him so that he was marshalled by superior vigour into the position she demanded. Again the soft violence of her mouth melted to his; her teeth jabbed his flesh.

'You're nice,' she said, voice riggish.

They stumbled along to the car, his hands on breast and belly as if to heave her from the ground. Inside, she took out mirror, leaving her door slightly ajar to keep the light on, examined her face, but it was, he thought, by habit.

'No need,' he said. 'You're beautiful.'

He crooked his hand under her left leg, stroked stocking, thigh. Jacqueline returned the mirror to her handbag, tossed her head as if to shake her hair loose again and banged it against his shoulder. Her right hand raked inside overcoat and jacket, had taken a finger's heap of his shirt and pulled it tented away from his nipple. She seemed to be gnawing the material of his overcoat.

'God,' she said. 'God.'

Her driving was careful enough, and she put the car efficiently away as he stood and waited. Inside the house she drew blinds, turned up the heating, hung away her coat as though following a scheduled routine.

'Sherry,' she said.

She poured two thin glasses of Bristol Cream, sipped, tickled the ends of hair over her forehead.

'That was good tonight,' she said. 'The best thing I've heard for years.'

'Yes.' He made the monosyllable purr.

'Well, wasn't it? Won't anything please you?'

'It was very good,' he said, smiling. He raised his glass. 'You please me.'

She strutted across, stood in front of him on the couch, fingered his hair, drew his head towards her. He got rid of his glass. Her hands curled quickly about his skull, brushing his ear, skirting the eyes, outlining his cheek and chin. Suddenly, with a jolt that knocked a grunt of breath out of herself, she jerked his head into her belly, held him pressed, while she caressed his neck.

'Oh, you,' she said, blowing breath, releasing him.

'What's up?' he said, patting the seat. She drank again, joined him, on the couch, threw her arms round him. She was strong. Her mouth cornered his, her breasts thrust hard at him, she tugged the hair at his crown with a violence that pricked tears to his eyes. Now he was pushed back so that she lay on top of him; she moved on him, roughly, as if she were the man, mounting.

'I love you.' Her voice was soft, but fierce. She seemed not to be looking at him; in his flurry of sexual excitement he, dazed momentarily, saw himself as a ladder, a plank-bridge she was crossing to some treasure, life, safety, satiety, up and beyond. She was all strength, her tight dress high on the silk flesh of her thighs, all white, and his. He shook, trembled, seemed reduced, a husk of himself round the central hardness of his sex. Outside him, but close, battering, dominating him, she threw herself, small, tremendous, disciplined to the urge, his mastering mistress.

He lay hard-fleshed, soft-minded, straining, blood beating until he was knocked into a weakness, a gross feebleness of strength, a powerful act of surrender. Now they had rolled so that he was on her. He plucked at the cloth of her frock by her neck, dragged her head up to show he was alive in this fire of death, put a hand awkwardly down the warm flesh of her back. They struggled there, to find comfort where none was until he withdrew his hands and took her head between his palms.

Fighting, she heaved on the knot of his tie, shook it, throttling to rebuke his maladroit movement. His lips found her neck, and he rested there, in the red darkness, panting, resting *in extremis*, scattered, personality in fragments, himself a disintegrated jostle only to be moulded back to humanity by the satisfaction of his loins in this heat-wild thumping woman under him. For a second his eye caught the polished top of a round table, her half-drunk glass of warm-bright wine. His consciousness was snatched away, centred for him on the body beneath, the guiding, dragging, sucking, swallowing glory which would snatch him, puncture his strength, rip his power into weakling joy.

In this minute he was ambivalent.

She was handling him now, until he screeched. Trousers loose, he was open to the world, but denying all with his mind.

'Take me. Take me.' Her voice shone, hot metal.

'No. No.' He squealed his fear.

He was pulled into her, made aware of her strength, a liquid, receptive beauty. In panic he hunched away, wanting, wasting.

'No.' A wail. Why? She was all his, forcing him back, down, in, through. He knew a momentary penetration before he pulled back, ashamed, reduced in his own estimation. He lay on her, out of her way, unsatisfied, astonished, continent, a prude.

Nothing was spoken; like a man thrashed by machinery he sprawled, afraid of what he had done and not done, flat out on her body, ashamed, humiliated, hopeful. She was crying. He pulled her into his arms, grabbing at her. In the wet violence of her sobs he felt her arms tighten about him.

'We shouldn't,' he said. 'We shouldn't.'

She nodded, face miserable, tears flushing.

'Not until we're married,' he whispered.

He held her there, quiescent, tight, only half conscious of what he was about. Her crying seemed not to matter to him, an unimportant physical symptom, like that scrape of her nails down his thigh, smarting now, forgotten shortly. He began to tremble; cold clutched. Quickly he let her head slide back to its cushion, where she lolled, frock rucked into a thick fold. Standing, he poked his own clothes straight and buttoned, knelt at her shoulders. No movement. Though her face was wet she was not crying, might have been asleep, arms naturally, easily, by her side.

He shoved a hand under her shoulder, pushing, without help, then bent, kissed her mouth, sideways. She neither stiffened nor relaxed, as he humped her.

'Wake up,' he said, frightened.

Nothing. His mind froze. He had refused her, rebuffed her body, denied her what she'd often asked, got, overwhelmingly, before, from Ridell. He had niggled, drawn back. For what? His fear? Of what? A child conceived? A revelation of his own inexperience while she could still reject him? Love for her? Unconsummated, technically consummate. He had been, had penetrated briefly; a second's snatch, thrust, that had robbed both, and him, him completely, of their chaste relation. Then? Why? Puritan misgiving? Upbringing? Thou-shalt-not? His own chilled inability to be anything but this sniffing, wet-skinned, canting unbeliever, this smut-daubed sex-in-fingers.

Nothing. She did not move.

He was proud with it, fearing. His mother had won here. She had never openly mentioned sex; she'd hated this naked fornication. Would she? He remembered her dizzily in hospital, forgot her in the race of his mind. William Riley, now, he wouldn't have baulked, have risked, lorded it, would have been lying now, here inside her, at the end of one tether, free in delighted prison. Riley? How did anybody know? Perhaps he'd done well. Ridell had seduced her, pounced and devoured her sex, mastered this mistress, whored through his young wife-to-be. She did not want that. She preferred, perhaps, this timid Bernard, with his trousers down, doing nothing, falling cold, a lily-white boy. She? She? As she lay there. Anger streaked his thoughts. She should move.

He kissed her again, shook her.

'Wake up,' he said.

Nothing, no stir.

This was mad. She was breathing, colour normal; she'd

closed her eyes to him for nothing, shut him out, to punish his presumption or his quailing.

'Wake up,' he said, 'wake up.' Tense, muscles of his jaw tight.

'Why should I?' He started.

She was laughing, her voice far back. She sat up, lifted her frock over her legs, swung her feet to the carpet, heels together neatly, put her shoes down, donned them and reached for the sherry. She raised it to him, ironically, drank, sighed, sipped, smiled like a princess.

'You're a good boy.'

Her hand patted the couch by her side.

'Come on, Fido,' she said. 'Up, boy.'

He obeyed.

'Bernard Allsop, I love you.'

'I love you.'

'I should think so, too.'

He burst to explain, was disturbed, humiliated. What were the words? Action was complete enough.

'I wanted you,' he said. She did not answer at once, considered, toyed with the glass.

'Yes,' she said, a dry voice. That was not the woman who'd writhed under him, had thrust herself blatantly at him. 'That's good.'

'Did you mind?' He coughed. 'My . . . not? Not doing anything? It didn't. I didn't think, know what you . . . wanted.' Wanted? Did he need it in letters ten feet high? God. She showed. Wanted? Wanted? He had drawn back, not she. He. He had winced. 'I'm sorry.'

'I'm glad,' she said, in that same prim voice.

'Why?'

'You're a good boy.'

She jumped up, stalked off, poured herself sherry and stood facing him, stockings smooth, frock uncreased, hair neatish. A gulp at her sherry was revelatory.

They said little more, sat about, kissed mildly in a daze, which he interpreted as happiness. On his way home, he'd refused her offer of a lift, he found himself exalted, a powerful strutting figure, who'd achieved greatly in denial. While he hammered the pavements he was lifted, exulting. The bare lime trees, the overhead lamps, the mist, a clumping pedestrian, all were part of the occasion; he wanted to shake hands, felt close to the gift of tongues, knew the world in a vortex of love.

At home the rooms were chilly; the fire faintly red in the darkness dropped to grey ash when he switched on the light. The table was laid for the morning, with a supper cup laid beside that for breakfast. A note propped on these read, 'Gone to bed. Lock up safely. Dad.' He stood back to the hearth, from which no warmth struck; he tore a piece from a newspaper, a jagged triangle, and fluttered it on the fire's top to see if it would blaze. Slowly it curled at the edges, then flapped into a lick of flame. He filched a biscuit from the tin, crunched it as he stared at, picked up a photograph of Mary; she was standing by the sunflowers her father grew in the end border, in a summer frock, smirking and attractive, smooth-faced, dimpled, round-breasted. He put this down, tested the sideboard's surface for dust, transferred his attention to the studio portrait of his mother. He took this in two hands. She was not ill when this was taken, but she looked thin, with her hair bushy, like a careworn Virginia Woolf, half-listening to some subtlety, half-obsessed by some chore. Mrs. Allsop seemed to reach forward, to peer out, to sniff perhaps, to make absolutely sure. But of what? The camera? The photographer with his patter? There was beauty, a silvery effect, an intelligence, a listening brain, a quietly directing force sketched in the face, but, he could not help the thought, something of a hen's scragginess. That's a son for you. He'd damned himself when he'd seen the first proof. An old boiling-fowl.

Mary, usually laconic, had erupted calmly, 'Why, it looks beautiful.' To hear this from the child in her new grammar-school uniform must have been marvellous. Allsop had become almost talkative, enthusiastic as a television advert.

Mrs. Allsop stood pleased, but did not say so, considered and publicly decided, 'It's too film-starry for me.' 'No, it's a good likeness, I'll say that.' 'No, Dad. No. That's a picture of somebody who's had less housework to do than I have.' And she'd eyed Bernard, the last arbiter, who pronounced it excellent, just like her, as it was, but who knew, niggling, that there was something hen-like about its stretching pose, its unmoving eye.

He wondered what she was doing now. Asleep, perhaps, drugged, drowsy or restless. He had felt, experienced, delved greatly that evening. He was a different man. His hands clenched in pleasure and embarrassment. Jacqueline. Two beautiful women. Both loved and bossed him; both were gifted. In the cold house he moved from door to door, closing, locking, bolting. He made sure that the fire was safe, that each light was out, each window-catch fastened before he went upstairs.

There he hung about on the passage, walking a step or two, standing, miming a man deeply thoughtful. He pushed open his father's door.

'I've locked up, Dad. I'm going to bed now.'

A snuffle from the bed, a toothless mumble of words, a heave on the bed-springs.

'Good night.' He was not answered, did not know why he spoke. After learning himself in Jacqueline's house he needed, perhaps, to be spoken to, like a ghost, to be assured of his insubstantial reality. Shuffling, he moved to Mary's room. An electric night-light was burning. His sister's head was down in the bedclothes, off the pillow. He lifted the sheet from her mouth. By her chin lay a scabby teddy-bear.

On her dressing-table he noticed a piece of paper, which had been folded into the narrow strips of a fan. He straightened it. The evening's programme. The University Players present *Julius Caesar* by William Shakespeare. He opened it, wondering at what stage of the proceedings Mary's fingers had pleated this, and why? In the interval? Over coffee? As Eric Parkes had said 'hello' to the university girls with their scarves and slacks? Perhaps he did it, Eric himself. A little ironical gentility to pass five minutes. 'A fan, madam, to cool your heated beauty.' Bernard took it nearer the night-light, touching, exploratory. Cast in order of appearance. Flavius— a tribune, Frank Holland. Marullus—Barry David. 1st Citizen—William Godden. 2nd Citizen—Bill Gray. He refolded the paper, replaced it. Then die, Caesar. In the distance a train clashed away, its diesel horn sounding a melancholy third. Mary was unmoving deep in the bed. Words he had learnt at school tumbled to his head, signalled, cautioned, strengthened.

> 'Then burst his mighty heart;
> And in his mantle muffling up his face
> Even at the base of Pompey's statue
> Which all the while ran blood, great Caesar fell.'

He put his thumb into his mouth, stood stock-still in the half-light. No move. No. He yawned his way out, to bed.

18

SUNDAY BEGAN slowly for the Allsops.
   They did not eat a formal breakfast, and soon after ten, often before Bernard was up, Mary cleared off to her Sunday School. The two men cooked the dinner, talked, read the *Observer*, tidied the house in a desultory way. While Mrs. Allsop was well, this had been a highly organised morning. Breakfast was cleared by eight-thirty, dinner prepared, beds made, instructions issued so that at half past ten exactly the mother, in her best, bustled out to chapel. She'd be back at twelve-fifteen and they would begin eating exactly on the one o'clock pips.
   Now the men were slipshod, missing the tension, the air

of purpose. As long as Father was away by two to catch a bus to the hospital, no one panicked. Bernard might find himself at three o'clock alone at the sink scratching at the whole range of saucepans they had fouled between them, but as he did no serious work on Sunday this did not matter.

Today, without intention, they finished the meal in good time and Bernard pretended to get himself ready for a visit to Jacqueline's, where he was to spend the rest of the day. He and his father walked down the road together, plodding, silent. Allsop was a difficult man to accompany; his steps were short, and he veered. Besides this, he rarely spoke and seemed utterly intent on his progress, incapable of hearing, so that any remark had to be repeated. This had always annoyed the forthright Mrs. Allsop. 'Once your dad's in the street, he's just like an idiot,' she'd say. 'It must run in the family. Jessica's the same. She will not hear anything unless it's repeated three times.'

'You offer her a five-pound note.' Allsop.

'What do you think of that's so absorbing?'

'It's . . . Well . . . You, dear.'

'Well, whatever Jessica's got on her mind, it's not me,' Mrs. Allsop had said, laughing.

Today, cold again, murk still about, the two men went down the hill, past the terraced houses, together. Half-way along they rounded three drinkers, talking broad, in salt-and-pepper caps, propping themselves on a Ford Popular. Chimneys wound smoke straight up into the still air, but no fires blazed in parlours. A married couple, carrying ragged greenhouse chrysanthemums, picked their way in new black towards the cemetery. Children shrieked in one entry. A scented miss minced past, clicking, swinging a shining, flat handbag. A smell of roast meat, apple pudding oozed about the houses.

'Are you bussing it today?' Allsop said, when they reached the main road at the bottom.

'No, I'll walk.'

'It's going to be foggy tonight.'

'Give my love to my mother.'

Allsop's grey face was pinched and his ungloved hand holding the bag white. He stood at the bus-stop, alone, one man in a dun, empty, urban world. From a hundred and fifty yards on, Bernard looked back. The road was deserted, but thick with trolley standards, traffic directions, bus-stops, bollards, garage signs, swinging lamps, wires. Newspaper blew about the grey, greasy surface. The Sunday sky dropped low, leaden; mist loitered. There were lights behind the opened windows of the bars in the Oxford, though the doors were locked now. And at his request stop then, upright, shopping-bag dangling, stood Ernest Allsop, human being.

Bernard tried to think himself into his father's mind. He could not. He hoped the old man was anaesthetised against his life. Turning right round, he waved vigorously with both hands, a big motion, to express what he wouldn't put into words. His father did not see him. By the time the bus caught him Bernard had almost reached the level-crossing. From the nearby empty trolley, Allsop raised a finger.

In the street, outside Jacqueline's back gate, two dogs leapt in a copulative dance. He hissed at them, and one turned mild, brown eyes in his direction. The garden was damp, with earthy, open spaces, neat, ravaged. It walled its own pocket of mist; its own dingy afternoon. When he tried the back door he found it locked, and moved round to the porch. That door was shut. He pulled faces of surprise, touched his lips before he went to look for the key.

It was dark in the hall, and warm.

He slung his coat on a hook and called, unexpectant, to Jacqueline. Again baulked, he waited, then paraded about in mock indecision, taking his time. In the study, on the writing-desk, she had propped an envelope with his name written, 'Bernard'.

A pang thrust into his belly. He stopped, felt the edges, corners of the envelope, carried it to the window. 'Bernard', in her writing. This was his dismissal. She had considered last night, judged him, thrown him out, impersonally, like this, with a note. The ache spread in his shoulders, his loins froze, a shudder creased him, dragged him forward, slightly nauseated. Very slowly he took the thistle-headed paper-knife from its tartan case and slit the envelope.

Daddy has been taken ill. The doctor think it's a stroke. He's still at home, can't be moved. I've gone up there. Don't stay, because I might not be back.

Love,
Jacqueline.

Love. That was better. He went through the motions of sympathy. Poor old Butler. With his wavy hair. They say he drank too much, so this might be the end of him. Bernard did not claim even now to like the man, but this was Jacqueline's father, a cause of sorrow. He wondered when she'd written. Again he prised it from the envelope, re-read it, examined the handwriting. In biro. Letters as well formed as usual, rather big and dashing for a slight woman. He imagined the phone call this morning, unprepared, early. A shudder prodded his back. But she'd remembered to write this note, seal it up, lock the house, see that the key was out. She'd be well dressed, stockings unladdered, before she went to see her father die. That was like her. But his mind switched. How had she acted when the news of Ike Ridell's death was broken to her? In this room? Somewhere in this house? She knew then that her husband, whatever he was, would never be back, to storm, bully, beat, charm, straddle her. She knew it in this place, here where the world was changed. Odd so little of Ridell remained. No photograph, pipe-rack, ash-tray. That strong man had vanished. She had obliterated him, in her small efficient way.

The telephone rang.

He gulped in fright, looked about him. When he answered, Jacqueline spoke.

'You're still there?'

'I've not been here long.'

'I thought I'd catch you before you left.'

She sounded primly cheerful.

'How's your father?' he asked.

'Oh, it's good news. He's not nearly as bad as they thought he might be. He's ill, of course, but the doctor says it's quite likely that there won't be any permanent paralysis.'

'Can he speak?'

'Yes. Not very clearly, but he can.'

'When did it happen?' he asked.

'Early this morning. He got out of bed to go to the lavatory and when he came into the room again, he collapsed.'

'Yes. Anything I can do?'

'No. I don't think so. You might just look round the place to see if everything's all right. I had to leave in a rush this morning. Are you well?'

'Yes.'

'Your mother?'

'No difference. Dad's gone this afternoon.'

'Yes. I shan't be back tonight. I'll stay with Mummy. She's all worked up. Daddy's been a handful for some time now, and then this. She's a bit weepy.'

'I see.'

'I've got her upstairs in bed too. I'm going up with tea in a minute.' Light laugh at nothing. In the pause he could hear her breathing. Science.

'I love you,' he said, not easily. It jerked into the mouthpiece. She perhaps thought he was shouting at her.

'Yes,' she said. 'I love you.' In, out, in, out, in. ' 'Bye then, Bernard. See everything's safe. I might come back tomorrow or Tuesday. I'll see. Give me a ring.'

'Sure I can't do anything?'

'No.'

That was it. He walked into every room in the house, moved curtains, opened drawers, went home.

There, Mary was sitting by the fire reading.

'Hello,' he said, 'back from the Sabbath to the secular.' He tapped her book, lurid green S.F.

'Hello,' she said. 'Just going out?'

'I've just come in.'

'Oh.'

They grinned at each other.

'How was it last night?' he asked.

'Great.' She closed the book. 'They really were good. I was interested all the way through.'

'And does he still love you?'

'Don't be daft.' She blushed, but was pleased. The evening had been a success. Pleased. Pleased.

'He's not a bad lad, our Mr. Parkes,' he said, Co-op manager, city councillor. 'Are you serious?' He dropped it, pebble into pool, but turning away from her. She didn't answer immediately, even opened her book again and glanced absentmindedly at it.

'How could we be?' Mary smiled still. 'Not at our age.' Our.

He was delighted at her answer, drew up a chair, talked, explained about Mr. Butler's illness, listened to her acting grown-up. She was blind-happy, love-struck, but under control. She could read a book, speak about Eric, offer correct precocious remarks on Jacqueline's father, whom she'd never met, and his chances of recovery. Bernard did not often understand happiness, but this seemed perfect. He was exactly sure that he was not projecting his own relief into Mary's actions, for she did so little. And yet every word, slither in the chair, twist of foot from slipper, sketched intense, private, universal satisfaction. For this afternoon, in this room, as far as he could make out, this child was supreme in joy. He watched. She spluttered on about Eric's father, who'd nearly won a fortune on the Pools on Saturday and who'd given a circumstantial account over dinner, hours long, Eric claimed, of how he'd spend every penny of fifty thousand, a hundred, two, a quarter of a million. They must have walked back together then. Bernard looked. No, he was not sure. The kingdom of heaven is within you.

'You're happy,' he said, interrupting, almost roughly.

'I can't grumble.' She was amused, adult.

On Thursday, Mrs. Allsop died.

She had been unconscious most of the week, and on that morning the authorities rang Allsop at work. He, considerate even then, phoned a message to Jessica, arranged to meet her in the ward. They sat, brother and sister, watching, listening. Once Ivy stirred, opened her eyes, and he leaned over her, offering himself. It was nothing. About two, while a nurse stood behind them, Mrs. Allsop moved her head to one side, and it was over. They kissed her. A doctor, a young podgy Indian, came, touched, fussed, nodded, and the two were ushered out of the ward. About everybody a gentle, beautiful politeness settled.

Allsop had been preparing himself for what he had to do, and he did it. Calmly he made the necessary calls to undertaker, parson, sat down to write letters. Jessica bustled about the house nearly all the time, crying now and then, a nuisance. He did not send for the children, waited until they returned home, and then undemonstratively reported the death. He showed no emotion, but kissed them, a movement unusual, serious, perfect, memorable.

At tea, he and Jessica described the last moments. Visitors came, said nothing, prayed, fidgeted, bit knuckles. The house was never empty; tea was always on the brew. The three went down together with Jessica and her husband to see the corpse. Mrs. Allsop looked tidy, but not beautiful, sallow, unpretentious, weak, muddy-faced near the new wood and the finery. They bent and kissed the cold mouth; felt the tip of the nose on their cheeks. Horace and Jessie both cried, a few tears. Allsop walked out slowly, did not look back, nodded, quietly thanked the attendant. The black tie and grey suit made him drab.

Jacqueline came over, drove the car about for them, appeared at the cremation in black, with a new hat and half-veil. Her father was getting better, sent his condolences, said he hoped to visit Allsop soon.

Bernard felt grief, wept in private. He had thought that he would be glad of his mother's death, once it was pronounced inevitable, but found this untrue. He'd been clinging to a hope, undefined, that this had smashed. The little turn of the head, the stoppage of breath which he'd expected so long, cut him deep. Mary said nothing, seemed unaffected except that she kept out of the way more than ever, and was less noisy. He had no idea what she thought, and did not ask. They affected joviality towards each other, but shortly, skipping off as if some secret would be divulged, some confidence, self-confidence breached.

Jacqueline mentioned the marriage on the evening of the funeral. She had fixed the date, and it was put to Allsop. Solemnly, still in his Sunday trousers, his mourning tie, shirt-sleeves, he agreed, approved.

'That's what your mother would have wanted,' he said.

They nodded.

Mary looked up, inquiringly, frowned. At that moment she seemed to represent life, the spark of reality, in a solemn entertainment of wax, lugubrious figures, but she said nothing, hurt nobody. Bernard wondered how his own marriage would end, what sons or daughters would walk out on him, parade their future, their pleasure, in his despair. That was wrong. His father had looked after himself now long enough, had taken his own decisions, had no more slogs up Hospital Hill, could please himself. Bernard's eye moved from Allsop, legs crossed, stiff, important, to Jacqueline still but marvellous, cooping herself up, energetic, elsewhere to Mary, who clearly wanted the television on, to Jessica who saw herself as ring-mistress, marshal, major-domo, to himself, a bit of a nobody about to be allied, like his father, to a woman stronger, livelier, wilder than himself. And the join would break. For him. For them all. He grew sorry for himself.

'Can I put the telly on, Dad?' Mary said. Jessica tutted, stood outraged. Allsop nodded, vigorously for him, made his face smile.

'You do,' he said.

'If you don't want it . . .' Mary began.

'You put it on, girl,' he said. Mary looked scared, and Jessica, trundling up, tolerant, moved round to switch on.

'It's generally pretty good, this is. We watch it at home, usually, me and our Horace. It's a good programme, we think. Not daft like.'

They adjusted their positions, all but the father, who sat unmoving with his back to the set. A picture appeared.

'Is that what you want?' Jessica asked.

'Yes, thanks.'

STANLEY MIDDLETON

Holiday

The Booker Prize-winning Novel

On holiday at an English seaside resort, Edwin Fisher is trying to come to terms with the breakdown of his marriage to Meg after the death of their baby son. But Meg's parents are also staying in the same town and are keen to help them patch up their relationship. As Edwin seeks to understand what went wrong, he must confront the past and decide upon his future.

'*We need Stanley Middleton to remind us what the novel is about. Holiday is vintage Middleton . . . One has to look at nineteenth-century writing for comparable storytelling.*'
SUNDAY TIMES

'*At first glance, or even at second, Stanley Middleton's world is easily recognisable . . . The excellence of art, for Middleton, is an exact vision of real things as they are. And because he is himself so exact an observer, his world at third glance can seem strange and disturbing or newly and brilliantly lit with colour.*'
A.S. BYATT